VICTORY OR DEATH

JOE KASSABIAN

aethonbooks.com

1

"You're supposed to be getting ready for your Wedding, Consul Solaris." Scowled a voice from the door of his office. Vincent Solaris looked up from his desk to see who was talking. His right eye, the real one he still had, burned with exertion. He had been reading over reports for so long he had lost track of time. The glowing white backgrounds of the countless data displays had seared his brain.

His left eye felt nothing, however. Ever since it had been replaced with an augmetic it never felt anything. Sometimes he wondered to himself if the Black Coats, the death cult that had formed around the Chairman of the Central Committee, had done him a favor by blowing him up on Mars. He could read and study the various reports that were fed into the Consul's office endlessly, assuming he closed his right eye and did not eventually fall asleep at his desk.

Standing in front of him was Captain Felicity Haagen, his long-suffering aide. She was dressed in a sharply pressed khaki uniform. Its creases looked sharper than the blade on the Officer's sword that dangled from her hip. Her black boots were polished to a high shine and her frizzy hair was pulled back into a tight bun.

Though the drab khaki had become the standard uniform for the newly christened Volunteer Army of Elysian, she had always made sure hers looked better than anyone else's. He assumed it was a leftover from her time as a student at the Grand Titan Officer's Academy.

The truth was she had become so much more than just an aide ever since he had deserted the Titanian Army and joined him. Most aides Vincent saw brought people cups of Kaff or delivered mail. While she did do that, she also did much more. She had become one of his best friends and closest, most trusted advisor. She was also planning his wedding.

"I know." Vincent sighed. "But I always feel like I am forgetting something."

"That's because you are always forgetting something." She rolled her eyes. "That is why you have the Marshals and I to help you."

"But they are all getting ready for the wedding."

"*Your* wedding, Vincent. They are getting ready for your wedding." The venom she added to his name forced him to yield. He put his hands up in mock surrender.

"Okay, okay." She approached his desk and moved aside the cluttered pile of data displays and set down a crisp black bag, half the size of a man, in the open space. "What is that?" He asked.

"Your uniform." She unzipped the center zip down the length of the bag, revealing a khaki uniform of his own. For the upcoming nuptials nobody was entirely sure as to what traditions he and his bride to be should adhere to.

On Earth the married couple would both wear the same uniforms they wore on the day they became Citizens. It was supposed to show that while they were devoted to each other, they were also equally devoted to the Chairman, having bestowed upon them Citizenship when they graduated Ethics School and all.

That wouldn't work in this situation for several reasons. Vincent had been declared The Great Traitor by the Central Committee over a year before, thus having his Citizenship stripped. Ever since he had been waging a war spanning all of Human and Alien Space attempting to destroy their government with the help of a confederation of alien races known as the Fidayi Clan. A show of loyal citizenship to an enemy government just didn't seem right.

Then there was his fiancé, Fiona Olympus. Fiona hadn't had her citizenship revoked as he had. She had never received it in the first place. Born on the streets of Mars she was doomed to spend her entire life in servitude to the Earth Defense Forces. Instead, she joined Vincent on his misguided crusade through the galaxy. She had never been entirely clear on the marriage traditions of Mars, though if Vincent's brief time on the planet had taught him anything it was probably something deeply horrifying and violent.

It had dawned on them that they had told the now several million humans that had flocked to what had been dubbed Free Human Space on the planet of Elysian that they were breaking the chains of the Committee and forging their own way. So, it made sense for them to develop their own traditions. Hence, the military uniform.

Though, in truth, the khaki uniform of the Volunteer Army was more than just a military uniform. Ever since the free humans joined the Fidayi Clan they had been locked in a two way fight to the death against the Central Committee and the Alliance, their entire society had rapidly become militarized. It was the only choice they had if they wanted to survive.

Belonging to one of the Army's Regiments had become something of a status symbol. While there had been hundreds, or maybe even thousands of children born on the planet by the masses of Humans that had come to call Elysian home, they were still babies. The adults that made up the population of Elysian had fled the war on Mars or survived the destruction of Earth. Others migrated from Titan or Lunar City wanting to start a new life or running from their old one.

The first humans on Elysian had to scrape and struggle to make their way. They fought against both distrust from the rest of the Clan due to the actions from the Committee, as well as a Civil War against the Black Coats who thought them traitors. They had then been bonded together on the battlefields of Mars and the killing fields of Victoria. After that, humans and aliens on Elysian saw no more backstabbing or strife. It became clear to everyone that they could not survive unless they worked together.

The khaki uniform began to be seen as the symbol that tied them all together. Therefore, Felicity and several others opined, it only made sense that Fiona and Vincent both wear their uniforms as they said their vows. Their relationship had somehow, through the whirlwind of countless battlefields, been the foundation for the entirety of Elysian society. It only made sense that they made it official while wearing the symbol of it.

"Will it fit?" Vincent asked.

"Of course."

"How do you know?"

"Because I'm the one that handles all of your clothes." She sighed. "Just put it on and get outside." He had to admit, her additional duties had piled up so much in the last few months he wasn't entirely sure what parts of his life Felicity didn't control.

She left the room to give him some privacy and Vincent pulled his uniform from the bag. It was pressed as neatly as Felicity's but had rows of medals and ribbons along the left side of the chest. On the right was the Riten and Dagger badge that recognized him as the leader of Humanity on Elysian. He shuddered to think of the fact that after the defeat of the Earth Defense Forces on Mars, he was the commander of the strongest force of Humans left in the universe.

He changed out of the clothes he was wearing and slipped on the new uniform. Felicity was right, it fit perfectly. She had painstakingly spit shined the new boots at the bottom of the bag, even the eyelets seemed to be shining. He reached across his desk and fit his gun belt around his hips. Dangling heavy from the right side was his Riten.

The Riten was a large six chambered pistol that had been awarded to him by the Warlord of the Fidayi Clan herself, Arai. They were the ultimate symbol of a Mawr Warrior, considered to be the most fearsome fighters in the entire galaxy. So feared that the Anarchs had attempted to simply wipe them out completely rather than try to conquer them. A Warrior would rather die than part with his Riten. For reasons that Vincent had never been entirely sure of, she had deemed Fiona and him worthy of that title.

He laced up his boots and found the mirror that Felicity had placed by the door of his office. She insisted that all military leaders gave themselves a once over before going out and seeing their troops. Vincent had never been one for pomp and circumstance, neither had the Clan for that matter, but he understood the soldiers and Council members might begin to become concerned should their leader start to look like an unkept street rat.

The mirror was dusty, because despite all of Felicity's insistence, he had largely ignored it. He cleaned it off with the sleeve of his jacket and took in his own reflection. His dead, black augmetic eye stared back at him. Around it was a spattering of small scars from where the truck bomb with his name on it had sent shrapnel and glass into his face. His dark brown beard covered most of the worst ones, but it could only do so much.

Ever since the surgery to replace his eye, he had kept his hair short. An army regulation buzzcut allowed the augmetic engineers easier access to port behind his left ear, should any adjustments need to be done to the implanted computer chips in his brain. Vincent never pretended to understand how any of it worked, but he was happy to accommodate the engineers that allowed his eye to function correctly.

He did not like the face that he was looking at. Vincent had never been a vain man. He was never thought of as attractive and most of his Ethics School love life was thanks to his place as the star of the District track team. Something about having his face flayed open and stitched back together, his eye blown out, and his nose broken had made him incredibly self-conscious.

He pulled himself away from his reflection and went out into the hallway. An impatient Felicity was waiting for him. She hurried over and began to fuss over his uniform, ensuring the ribbons and medals were straight. She produced a small cloth from her pocket and rubbed it against the brass Clan insignia, bringing it to a shine.

"Would you knock it off?" He waved her off.

"There is going to be thousands of people in attendance, Consul. Tens of thousands even. If they aren't there in person, the rest of the Quarter will be watching it on their displays at home."

"They know who I am. They know I'm not about this kind of thing." Felicity huffed.

"But they also know I'm your aide and if you look bad, I look bad. Got it?"

"If you're here, who is helping Fiona?" He asked. Felicity dropped to a knee and quickly buffed out a scuff from his left boot.

"Marshal Erin is her Maid of Honor, so I assume she is." The tone of Felicity's voice made it clear she was not jealous of the person who had to handle Fiona Olympus on her wedding day. She was standing again, squinting at his ribbon rack one for time.

"Am I presentable yet?" She frowned at him.

"It'll have to do." She turned on her heel and began to march down the hallway.

The Office of the Human Consul was a new building, though constructed in haste. His staff had quickly outgrown the spare office that had been afforded to him to share with the Consul of the Rhai. As his staff swelled and he brought in elected officials from the newly established Union Council, the Rhai Consul complained to the Warlord. Arai finally relented and authorized his own office.

A few Human and Mawr work crews labored together to construct the building in the classic Mawr style. That is to say they constructed it badly. It was a squat and unremarkable building that began to show settling cracks within a week of completion. Vincent didn't care. Not only had the Humans staked their claim in the Clan, they had their own Consul office, built with their own hands, in the center of the Government Quarter. The red phoenix flag flew above it with pride.

As the double doors creaked open Vincent was greeted with the hot, dusty air of Elysian. Two soldiers in full dress uniform on either side snapped to attention and rendered a salute.

"Good morning, Consul!" They both barked. On their left sleeve they both wore an old battered patch that showed a red phoenix. Though new patches had long since been created, the veterans of the Martian Campaign continued to wear their ruined ones as a badge of honor. He made sure to wear his own worn patch on his jacket too as a show of solidarity with the old guard.

Standing at the foot of the stairs was someone Vincent couldn't escape if he wanted to. The short, muscled form of the Warlord's brother, Zinvor, waited for him. He was dressed in the closest thing resembling a khaki uniform that could be made for the strange, body type of the Mawr. Unlike Vincent, Zinvor did not wear a Riten on his side.

Zinvor had been grievously wounded on Mars while smothering a machine gun with his own body. An action that preserved the entire mission and saved Vincent's life in the process. As he had previously been made a Tsarra, a Warrior sentenced to die in combat as a form of penitence, it was what he wanted. But the Human in Vincent wouldn't allow him to watch his friend bleed out on the battlefield.

Zinvor had been evacuated from Mars and treated aboard the Titanian hospital ship *TNS Mercy*. Through hours of surgery he died on the operating table but had been brought back to life multiple times. Zinvor was not happy with Vincent when he found himself alive in the recovery bay a few weeks later. Arai could not publicly thank Vincent and the Doctors for their work, tradition forbade it, but she did in private.

That left Zinvor in something of a limbo. He had technically died on the operating table and death was death as far as the Mawr were concerned. The Warlord decreed his mission as a Tsarra had been dutifully carried out on Mars, releasing him from his sentence. The problem was, as he was stripped of his status as a Warrior by being made a Tsarra, he was legally dead in the eyes of the Fidayi Clan, and only a Warrior could wear a Riten.

Since then, he had retaken his position as Vincent's unofficial bodyguard, though unarmed. Not that it mattered. Vincent had seen with his own eyes what a pissed off Mawr could do to their enemies with their bare hands. Not to mention just the presence of the fearsome Zinvor, known throughout the entire Fidayi Clan for being the Undead Tsarra, was enough to protect Vincent from anyone who was foolish enough to wish him harm.

Vincent slowed his stride so as not to tax Zinvor's body. His short, thick legs made keeping up with Vincent's long stride, nearly double his size, a chore. A chore only made worse by his wounds. He wheezed and struggled when he was forced to walk too fast and his knees ached when he walked for too long.

"Everything okay?" Vincent asked over his shoulder. He knew

it was considered dishonorable for a Mawr to show weakness Warrior, Tsarra, or otherwise, but try as he might, the pain was as clear as day on Zinvor's face. He grunted a response.

"There are many people in the Quarter for the.." Zinvor coughed, catching his breath.

"Wedding." Felicity added helpfully. Zinvor nodded.

"For the wedding." He finished.

"So, I've been told." Vincent sighed.

"Were weddings not a big event on Earth?" Felicity asked.

"Not really." He said. "They were more of a bureaucratic thing I think." He had never been to a wedding, but his late Father always made it seem like he just went to the District Office of Family Planning to apply for a license and sign some paperwork. In Ethics School he learned if two people applied for a license, they would be investigated by the State Ethics Police to make sure they were Citizens in good standing. If they were it would be approved and be issued a family home and a license to rear three children. His parents had managed two. Vincent was the only one still alive. "What about on Titan?"

"Oh yeah." Felicity said. "When my sister got married our entire extended family went. There was music, dancing, food. It was like a giant party that went on all night." He always forgot that though he and Felicity had grown up under the rule of the Central Committee, their worlds could not have been more different. The iron fist of The Chairman was reserved for Earth, the Moon, and Mars. Titan would be allowed to do things their own way as long as they supplied soldiers and fuel for the Committee's wars.

"Sounds nice." He said.

"It was great." She smiled. "And before you say anything, I already planned the reception." He raised an eyebrow.

"Do we have the supplies to be throwing a giant party?"

"Oh relax." She waved him off. "The Union of Grocers voted

to allow it. It is good for everyone to blow off steam every once and awhile."

Two Rhai in white robes were standing at either side of the entrance to the Human Quarter. What had once been a badly constructed tunnel, cracked and falling apart, had been revitalized into a transit hub. Ramps and skyways that arched towards the Rhai constructed elevated walkways and tramways stood where before there was nothing but trash and burnt out hulks of tanks or trucks.

The elevated tramways snaked and spiraled into the air in every direction. They cast odd shadows down onto the ground below them as they twisted around each other and made their way towards their destinations. Every major building, road, and marketplace on Elysian was now interconnected, bringing all of the races of the Clan together. Humans and Rhai had become fond of the tramways, the Mawr hated them and many outright refused to go near them. They preferred to have their own two feet planted firmly on the ground.

The once crumbling edifice of the Quarter entrance was left standing as a memorial of the struggle against the Black Coats in the early stages of Human history of Elysian. The names of the soldiers who died fighting in what had become known as The Black Coat Rebellion were etched all over it by the hands of those who mourned them.

The Rhai in white robes used to be members of what was called the *Gummi,* or Mawr for Peacekeeper. They acted as Clan police and interspecies mediators should any problems arise. Their ranks quickly became dominated by the Rhai and Human membership was banned for the first year of their history on the planet.

After months of arguing Vincent finally successfully lobbied for the dissolution of the Gummi and the establishment of the Public Order Cohort. An interspecies police force divided equally between the races and commanded by a triumvirate of one representative per race. He was happy to give the people he represented more opportunities but deep down inside he was even happier to get one over on his Rhai Consul counterpart.

The two Rhai bowed slightly at the waist and chirped in their high-pitched way of speaking in broken Earth Standard.

"Congratulations on your Union with Woman Olympus, Consul Solaris." He didn't bother correcting them, he knew they meant well. The Clan races had taken to learning the human language very quickly and many were already fluent. The humans haven't fared as well.

"Thank you." He smiled.

Vincent knew he should have been feeling nervous on the day of his wedding. He had heard that people would be paralyzed with nerves, their legs would get weak, and overcome with emotion. He thought after waiting out an Anarch plasma artillery bombardment or assaulting Victoria his wires were crossed in his brain. That maybe he just didn't feel things like normal people anymore. War had just kind of burned away the edges and made him numb.

Then he stepped into the Human Quarter.

Thousands of tan uniformed soldiers stood pressed shoulder to shoulder. The entire area of what had become something of an unofficial town square was packed with life. Streamers and balloons hung from lampposts and buildings. It seemed like the entire Mawr, Rhai, and Human population of Elysian had all shoved themselves in the Quarter to watch them get married.

Slowly the crowd noticed him and the thousands of side conversations died away. The crowd began to part in half, forming a path for Vincent to make his way towards the Eagle and Bar.

The bar had been the birthplace of the Volunteer Army of Elysian and had stood as a defense against the Black Coats during the rebellion. It had also acted as Vincent's headquarters, a supply depot, and field hospital at various points of its short life. Since then, it had taken on something of an aura amongst the humans of Elysian as being the closest thing anyone had to a place of reverence. It was also still the best bar in town.

At the end of the path stood Fiona Olympus. She was wearing a tailored tan uniform, like his own, resplendent with medals and ribbons. It was still dark enough for her pale skin to shine. It was tracked with dozens of small black tattoos covering her hands, neck, and several newer ones on the left side of her face. She had grown her white blonde hair out for the first time since Vincent had known her and had it pulled back into a ponytail. Her ice blue eyes locked with his and his heart leapt in his chest.

That was the feeling. No matter how long they had been together and how many times her eyes met his, she never failed to fill him with butterflies. Though there were thousands of people crowded into the Quarter's square, they melted away as broad smile spread across her face. It was the only thing he could focus on.

Felicity snapped him out of his trance by tugging on his sleeve and goading him forward. They walked through the path the crowd had created for them. Many of the soldiers removed their caps or saluted as the group passed them, most of them were already visibly drunk, swaying back and forth with the slight breeze.

Next to Fiona stood the imposing bulk of the Warlord Arai. She was the same height as Fiona, a full head shorter than him. Like most Mawr, she was built as if thick slabs of muscle had been carved out of stone and then brought to life. She was wearing her ceremonial burnt yellow armor. A tapestry of scrolls flapped from each of her pauldrons, accolades from battles that Vincent only knew from the legends spoken by Mawr Warriors.

To her right was Vincent's Second, Ezra Vorbeck. Ezra leaned heavily on a cane with a toothy smile plastered across his dark, wrinkled face. His pilot's cap sat crooked on his head and thick black and silver hair poked out from one side. Always the one in touch with his emotions, he was barely holding back tears as they turned his brown eyes watery.

The concept of a Second was something that had been unfamiliar to him. Fiona had explained in Olympus when two people got married the man had his best friend watch over the woman to make sure his enemies did not come and try to snatch her away before the ceremony. Vincent assumed it was more of a ceremonial role, but Fiona insisted it was rather practical in her experience. If someone had attempted to kidnap Fiona, he felt sorrier for the pain she would inflict on her assailants rather than anything Ezra could do.

Ezra had never cut an intimidating figure. He always reminded Vincent of more of a concerned father figure than one of the top pilots to ever come out of the Titanian Navy. This image was only strengthened after he was wounded in Victoria and was now forced to hold himself up with a cane, aging him beyond his years.

Behind Fiona stood her Maid of Honor, Erin Olympus. The stern look on Erin's face made her look as if she was sitting through another staff briefing rather than a wedding. Her white blonde hair was shorn to a fine fuzz and her pale blue eyes were ringed with small black tattoos. The tapestry of tattoos continued down the left side of her face and neck before disappearing under her khaki jacket. Her stone-faced expression cracked when she afforded Vincent a small smile as he approached.

Vincent stood next to Fiona and took her hands in his.

"You look beautiful." He smiled. She perched herself on her toes and kissed him on the lips.

"I know." She smirked. Vincent glanced down at her boots. He could see his reflection in them.

"Erin's doing, I assume?"

"Obviously." Fiona rolled her eyes. Arai cleared her throat, pulling their attention away from one another.

"I think we should be starting, Solaris." Grumbled her deep voice. Never one for ceremony or circumstance, the Warlord had been confused when Vincent and Fiona had gone to her and asked her to join them together in marriage. She only relented when they explained it would be a perfect image of union between the Clan, Earthians, and Martians all at once.

Arai looked out into the hooting and cheering crowd and held up a single hand. Slowly the crowd fell into silence. Conversations ended and thousands of pairs of eyes fell upon the group that stood in front of the Eagle and Bar.

"We have come here on this day, at this place of importance, to join these two Humans together in the bonds of marriage in the custom of their people and ours." Arai began. "If anyone wishes to stop these proceedings for any reason, step forward now."

"I fucking dare you!" Fiona screamed and the crowd broke out into laughter and more cheering. Vincent couldn't help himself but join in. Arai glared at the gathering, waiting for it to die down again before moving on.

"Consul Vincent Solaris." She continued. "Warrior Fiona Olympus." Vincent held back a snicker at the title chosen for Fiona. She had been listed as killed in action by the Central Committee and had never been officially enlisted back into the Volunteers once they had been formed. Nor had she been given an actual job within the Consul's Office. Vincent thought giving a job to his girlfriend would have probably looked bad and knew she wouldn't suffer office work. Instead, she was recognized as a Warrior within the Clan at large, which is something she probably preferred anyway.

"Do you hold each other as equal amongst equals?"

"Yes." They answered in unison.

"Do you promise to protect and love each other?"

"Yes." They said again.

"Do you promise to honor and care for one another for as long as you both shall live?"

"Yes." They answered again. Fiona's eyes began to well up with tears and caused Vincent to let go of what he was holding back. His good eye burned and a single line of tears cut down his face.

"Then with the power given to me by the Cohorts of the Fidayi, I now name you Broodmates for life eternal. This bond shall join you two for as long as the sun remains in the sky and stars hang in the night." Fiona leapt up and wrapped her arms and legs around him, nearly pulling him over. She kissed him deeply and heard the crowd rise into a roaring cheer once again.

From the front row of the crowd came a man in a dark red uniform. There were no ribbons or awards hanging from his chest and just a single star wrapped in a wreath sat on either of his shoulder boards. Tattoos covered both of his hands and most of his face. He carried a small box in his hand and his pale face was creased with a smile.

"Erik?" Vincent asked. Erik Olympus was the Commander of Mars. He had been appointed the de facto Dictator of the newly liberated planet by the People's Congress, a strange form of direct democracy that sometimes looked as if it was more of a bar fight than a form of government. Mars had largely been reduced to rubble in the effort to free it from the Central Committee. Ever since, the Clan and the Union of Titan had poured untold amounts of money and supplies into the planet in a massive rebuilding effort. Vincent assumed the leader of Mars had more important things to do than travel to the edges of space to attend his wedding. "Did you think I would miss your wedding?" Erik beamed.

"Well, yeah actually. I assumed the leader of an entire planet had something better to do."

"It is all about delegation of authority, Vincent." Erik winked. "You'll learn that one day. And besides, I was invited here by the Warlord. It would be rather uncouth for someone in my position to turn that down for diplomatic purposes." Vincent wanted to tell him that the Mawr really didn't understand the concepts of Human diplomacy, but he stopped himself.

"What is in the box?" he asked. Erik's eyes lit up.

"Well, we are at a Martian wedding, we have to do things the right way don't we?"

"I'm not following." Vincent raised an eyebrow. Fiona smirked.

"We have to get our blood mark."

"Why does everything you do sound so terrifying?" He sighed. Erik opened the box, showing its contents. A small needle and a bottle of red ink.

"It is Martian tradition that when two people become Partners-" Fiona cut him off.

"I think we are technically *Broodmates* here."

"Whichever." Erik rolled his eyes. "They both receive a tattoo in red, signifying a blood pact between them."

"On Earth we just got each other rings, can't we do that?"

"Don't you want to show unification with the Martians?" Fiona asked, her voice thick with sarcasm. She knew Vincent hated needles and would go out of his way to avoid them whenever he could. "And you would look hot with a mark under your eye."

"Wait, I have to get this on my damned *Face?*"

"Something wrong with that?" Fiona narrowed her eyes. Her face was covered in tattoos. As was most other parts of her. Vincent sighed, defeated.

"No. Let's get this over with." Erik handled the small needle to Fiona who dipped the spike of it into the red ink. She jabbed it into Vincent's face, just below his augmetic eye, a few times in quick succession. He winced in pain and gritted his teeth.

"*That* is what that feels like?" He dabbed away some blood with his uniform sleeve and heard Felicity groan behind him. He took the needle from Fiona and returned the favor, stabbing a small, misshaped dot under her right eye. Unlike him, she didn't flinch.

Erik and Erin began to clap, and Erik turned to the crowd.

"The Consul is a regular Son of Mars, isn't he?" He joked and again, the crowd began to cheer, this time the Martian contingent went wild. Several tan hats were sent up into the air. People ducked reflexively when a sudden burst of celebratory gunfire broke out and sidearms were discharged into the sky in the traditional Martian way.

"Everyone!" Felicity called out, struggling to be heard over the crowd. "Drinks and food are on the Office of the Consul!"

2

The Eagle and Bar had turned into the biggest party Vincent had ever seen. Soldiers and civilians from various different races and planets danced amongst one another, the various different human unforms swirled together into a kaleidoscope of color. The aliens, unsure of the human activities, watched from the outside with curiosity.

Soldiers shook their beer up and sprayed it into the air when Vincent and Fiona entered. Music thumped from the overhead speakers and seemingly every inch of the small bar had been taken up by people. Erik waved them over from a corner booth. A small sign sat at the center of the table that said 'Reserved.' Seated across from him was Ezra, who already had a drink in his hands. Erin sat next to him, her hands were empty.

They squeezed into the seats alongside them and Erik passed them a drink. It was an unknown mixture that was clear, but smelled of pure chemistry.

"I never thought I would catch a Martian wedding so far from Mars." Erik Beamed.

"Stick around." Vincent said. "With all of the Martians moving in there will be one every few days soon enough."

"Might even fix Erin up with someone." Fiona said. Erin didn't take the bait, she simply glared at her.

"How about some of this fine Titanian stock." Erik reached across the table and slapped Ezra on the shoulder. Ezra's eyes went wide and he quickly took a drink.

"Sorry." Erin said. "Vorbeck isn't my type."

"Too old?" Felicity asked. Ezra frowned.

"Watch it."

"No, he's a guy." Erin shrugged. The table burst out into laughter as Ezra's dark features turned red. "So, be honest, Erik." Erin eyed the Martian Commander. "You didn't come here for the wedding and Arai wouldn't exactly send out invitations for something she didn't know was important. What gives?"

"You're good." Erik nodded. Vincent had long ago understood his shortcomings as a leader. He also knew in order to make up for those shortcomings he would have to surround himself with people who knew what they were doing. Erin had started off as his volunteer bodyguard during the Black Coat Rebellion and quickly ascended up the ranks of their fledgling military.

Erin excelled at many things, but the most important was her ability to question people and read them like an open book. He had never seen anyone lie to her and get away with it. If people wanted to stay a closed book, well Erin had tools for that too. Horrifying, nightmarish tools.

"So, what is it?" Vincent asked.

"A planning meeting. Tomorrow. I thought I would come in early for the ceremony." Erik said. "The office of the Warlord requested mine and Field Marshal Denta's presence."

"A planning meeting." Vincent rubbed his beard. "You mean for the Lunar City operation." Erik lifted up his glass in toast and downed it in a single gulp. "So, it is finally happening." He sighed. Vincent grabbed his glass and took a drink. Its contents burned his mouth and it immediately reminded him of the swill they had drunk while on Mars. "Did you bring this with you?"

"It isn't a Martian wedding without a Martian drink." He winked.

"Getting married and finding out I get to invade Lunar City on the same day?" Fiona smirked. "This really is the best day of my life." She downed her drink and smacked her lips. "But that's enough about work, this is a damn party." The bartender brought over another tray of drinks and once again they all indulged.

Vincent stared up at the ceiling above him. The brown bricks had hundreds of cracks in them and he was sure he had counted them all just as many times. The only sounds that broke the silence of the night was the dull breathing of Fiona, sleeping away the long night of heavy wedding drinking and the quiet hum of the environmental control unit.

This had become a routine night for him. No matter how much he drank or how many days he stayed up without break, he would always end up staring up at the ceiling. Fiona would and could sleep through anything. He had once watched her sleep through an artillery bombardment.

In the few moments he did doze off his mind immediately brought him back to Victoria. He smelled the smoke of the burning buildings, tasted the ash on his tongue. He saw the vaporized human shapes that had been burnt into the concrete. Staining the ruins of the city with evidence of his crime forever.

He would wake up in a cold sweat and the scenes would run through his head until he finally gave up on trying to sleep for the night. Vincent had tried to keep all of this from Fiona and the others. But he could only coast through the day as a husk of exhaustion and nerves for so long before someone noticed. They always told him that he had nothing to feel guilty about, Victoria was a city that needed to be destroyed. They would tell him they would have done the same thing.

None of them cast the deciding vote on the mass murder of tens or hundreds of thousands of people. Nobody would ever be sure of the body count, because even the bodies had been atomized. He could understand why Erik didn't feel the way he did. The collective Martian hatred for Earthians went back so far he wasn't sure if he had ever met a Martian who would have passed by the opportunity to obliterate a Central Committee held city. He knew for Field Marshal Denta, the commander of the Titanian military, wouldn't bat an eye at it. He was a cold, calculated military man. After spending a few weeks with him, Vincent was sure the man would kill a loved one if it meant winning him personal glory.

None of that ever helped him. He hated the Black Coats. But the people they had in the city with them were just regular people, trying to live their lives. He had no doubt that every person he ordered destroyed in that city would have personally killed him or Fiona if they had a chance, but he didn't hate them for it. If he was in their position, still under the influence of the Chairman, he would have done the same thing. Who was he to condemn them?

He cursed himself and sat up in bed. He was done trying to sleep. Vincent rolled over and pulled on his pants. There was some mysterious dark stain on his leg from the night at the bar, but he chose to ignore it. Fiona grunted and rolled over at the disturbance, but didn't wake up.

He found his shirt and tossed it on and washed out his stale mouth with a tin cup of water. His mouth tasted like an ashtray and felt as if he hadn't drank water an a year. He grabbed his Riten and strapped it around his waist before silently leaving the apartment, Fiona still fast asleep in their bed.

Zinvor was waiting outside as always. Vincent still wasn't

sure when he slept, but he hadn't seen him do it since before he had become a Tsarra. He had grown accustomed to Vincent's nightly routine by then. When it had begun, he used to be concerned for his health, but had long ago stopped insisting that he sleep and just escorted Vincent wherever he wanted to go.

The early morning of Elysian was Vincent's favorite time of day. He could see both the rising sun and the faint outline of the stars in the grey sky. The air was cool, but not enough to chill him. A nice reprieve of the heat that would greet the city in just a few hours. The market workers were just beginning to set up their stalls for the morning rush. Shopkeepers busied themselves, not looking up when he and Zinvor walked by them.

He stopped by a small cart, its glowing orange lights telling him they were already open. Vincent had grown accustomed to stopping there every morning around the same time. The cart sat on four fat tires that had clearly been salvaged and had seen better days. The walls had been made from repurposed tin siding that looked like it wouldn't have been out of place in one of the early huts that had been built in the human quarter.

The cart was run by an older looking Titanian man and what looked to be his young daughter. They had hung a sign out that read in handwritten script 'Kaff and Go!' The daughter was holding a scorched black pan over an open flame. Dark liquid sloshed around inside of it.

"The same, Sir?" The man asked.

"Please." He nodded. The daughter picked the pan up and poured a measure of its contents into a strainer she held above a small metal cup. After a moment she handed him the cup, the familiar scent warming his face.

Formations of soldiers undergoing basic training wearing khaki pants and white short sleeve shirts jogged by, their black boots clapping off of the street in unison. At the head of each passing formation a soldier held a flag that designated whichever one of the Volunteer regiments they were part of. Each flag was decorated by the soldiers of the Regiment and showed things like Dragons, swords, and variations of the Elysian phoenix flag. Underneath of the flag were streamers that denoted which battles they had taken part in. A red streamer showed a unit of Mars veterans, a tan one veterans of the Black Coat Rebellion.

Next to the flag bearer was their training Sergeant. Each regiment was in charge of training and recruiting its own soldiers, most of them coming from the same neighborhoods, jobs, and Unions. From his understanding the meanest person in every Regiment would be appointed the training Sergeant to give new recruits a proper welcome. Though, unlike Vincent's days in training, beating recruits and physical punishment was now strictly banned.

"What?" Called out the training Sergeant. She was a short woman of Titanian descent with a bald head. "You don't say good morning to the Consul?"

"Good morning, Consul!" Came the ragged voices of the trainees. Vincent smiled and raised his cup at them as they trudged by. At nearby stations soldiers who were done with training waited for the morning trams to take them to their place of duty for the day. They exchanged idle chatter, smoked, and laughed at the hazing of the recruits. They turned and gave lazy salutes to Vincent as he walked by.

"I do not understand why so much Human military training consists of running." Zinvor said.

"The Warlord doesn't want us burning up all of our ammunition supplies shooting at targets. And it turns out when you give a bunch of Officers an order to train the soldiers without ammo all they do is run in circles."

"I do not get it."

"Me either."

"Why are you going to the office so early?"

"Well, Zinvor. Like most respectable government employees I put off a lot of work until the last minute and there is a Union meeting in a few hours I haven't spent a single minute getting ready for."

As the human population of Elysian skyrocketed after the fall of Mars it quickly had become apparent that Vincent could no longer continue trying to run the local government on his own. Unfortunately, humans really had no experience in anything that looked like a functioning government. They had been conditioned to just listen to the Chairman and his functionaries. If they didn't then the people they loved would vanish. Vincent chalked that attitude up to how he had managed to hold onto control of the population, they were told he was in charge so they simply listened.

The idea that he had waged an interplanetary war against the Chairman just to become a new one, repulsed him. But he had to still work within the confines of the Fidayi Clan system. Thankfully, Arai didn't really have a set of rules to work with as the Mawr government was more of a system of suggestions interspersed with random political violence.

Every race within the Clan ran itself in its own way with their Consul acting as the bridge to the unified Clan government. The Warlord didn't much care what each race did as long as it did not destabilize the others. The Mawr functioned as something akin to a military dictatorship. Though, every couple of decades the Cohort Leaders, the closest thing the Mawr had to military officers, would vote on who would become the next Warlord.

The Rhai were more confusing and Vincent still wasn't sure if he totally understood it. They functioned as something close to a rigid technocracy. They held no elections of any kind and their lives were decided based on tests they took when they were done attending school. They would then be filtered into whatever job their testing algorithm says they would be best at, including their internal governing body and the Office of the Consul. Individual Rhai would be replaced periodically as the algorithm decided someone else would be better at their jobs.

Vincent took inspiration from the Martian People's Congress. Every single person on Mars would be able to vote or voice their opinion on every matter of government. Though unlike the massive congressional halls that Mars had in every city to make this possible, the Human Quarter of Elysian had only a single extra warehouse that could be repurposed into a meeting hall. So, he just had to figure out how to get people to vote where they already were.

So, every citizen of the quarter belonged to a Union. These Unions covered everything from Soldiers to day laborers. Union members would elect their representatives from amongst themselves to argue in their favor to Vincent as Consul as well as vote on whatever matters were at hand. As the Unions already existed, he could just turn them into local government. Each Union representative would poll their workplace and bring the results back to everyone else, passing things into law.

They could, and did, pass things totally independently of his control. Some of the best things they passed he hadn't even been there for like the tram system and guaranteed housing for everyone in the Quarter. His office only existed to represent his race at Clan meetings. This generally meant interspecies rivalries, cooperation, and military actions. It wasn't his job to actually run the Quarter itself, but to act as an intermediary between the local government and the Warlord.

"You have to go to this meeting?" Zinvor asked. "You normally skip them."

"Yeah." He nodded. "If Erik is right and the next Clan meeting is about Lunar City, she is going to want to know if the Volunteers are ready to go or not."

"And are they?"

"I don't think we have much of a choice but to be ready by this point." He sighed. "How much time do I have until the meeting?"

"One hour." Zinvor answered. How he had managed to memorize Vincent's schedule no matter the day, was a mystery to him.

"That is not nearly enough time." He groaned. "I'll have to leave now just to get there on time."

"You would have more time if you had simply done your work when you were supposed to." Zinvor stated matter of factly.

"Yes, thank you, Zinvor. I know that."

"Then why did you not do it?" Vincent bit his lip. How he ended up losing an argument to an alien that did not understand things like human context or nuance let him know he had really dropped the ball. He changed directions towards the Union Hall. Zinvor chuckled to himself and Vincent tried not to bring up how much faster he could have gotten to his office if his bodyguard had not been afraid of the tram system.

He passed by crowds of construction workers who were just starting their day as the sun was coming up. They walked down the street with their tools towards one of the countless building sites that were under construction in the quarter. Ever since the Union Council had voted on infrastructure projects the construction had not slowed. So much construction was going on at all hours of the day and night at one point the Council had to vote on a different measure banning it after sundown so people could sleep undisturbed.

Vincent could tell he was getting closer to the Council Hall. It had once been a transportation hub for the Clan, how many decades ago that was he couldn't be sure. In the years since the Clan had built a proper hub that could land and launch modern spacecraft and this one, like the rest of the quarter that they had moved into, had fallen into disrepair.

The Hall was one of many abandoned warehouses in the area. They lined each side of the road and stretched several stories into the air. A lot of work had been done to convert them into institutions that the quarter desperately needed like a few schools, a hospital, and a couple greenhouses. The few that still remained and were being converted into housing. The Hall had not been the recipient of the same amount of attention as the others.

Taking an idea from the Mawr, nobody thought a government building needed the same treatment as a hospital or greenhouse. The floor was cracked and missing in some places, more than one section of the wall had been replaced with bits or tin or a length of plastic tarp. The hall was drafty and leaked when it rained, though that was rare on Elysian.

Security around the area was light. A single Public Order Officer strolled around by the entrance of the hall. The security wasn't in case of some kind of imaginary attack on the Council, but rather because the Council had a tendency to devolve into a swirling intra government fistfight and the Officer would have to break it up before someone got seriously injured. The Officer was Martian and their pale skin blended into the off white of their uniform jacket.

"You're late, Sir."

"I know." He sighed. The Officer laughed. He had always found himself posted outside of the Council which meant he was all too familiar with Vincent running late due to the overland trek Zinvor forced him to take. He glared at the tram station that sat at the center of the warehouse district. He could have made it there in minutes.

They walked through the door and were greeted by a heated discussion. The union representatives did not stop their argument on his account, though seated against the far wall were the Marshals of the Clan who rose to their feet. Ezra and Erin sat alongside Aron Victoria and Vadim Presan. After the bloodbath on Mars, it quickly became apparent that he would need to relinquish his control over the Volunteers over to people who knew what they were doing.

So, he submitted the idea to the Council who voted to approve the promotion of several leaders to the new rank of Marshal. Each one would control a specific part of the Volunteers. Vincent assumed that the Council unanimously voted in favor of his idea because most of them had survived the Battle of Victoria by the skin of their teeth and recognized as well as he did that maybe he wasn't the best man for the job.

Ezra became Marshal of the Fleet, a job that had caused him endless stress ever since. Aron became the Marshal of the Army, a job he initially refused to take. For someone like him who had spent his entire life as an enlisted man the idea that he would suddenly become the highest ranking officer in the Volunteers repulsed him. It was only after the urging of Presan did he grudgingly accept his promotion. Though, in a small sign of defiance he never adopted the Marshal's rank, on his shoulders still sat the chevrons and star of a Sergeant Major.

Presan had been grievously wounded outside of Victoria. How he survived losing both of his legs and a rampant infection that devastated the rest of his body nobody was entirely sure. He was left badly crippled and as his body rejected his augmetic legs, he was forced to use a wheelchair. As Vadim knew he could no longer travel with the Volunteers he accepted the position of Marshal of the Quarter. Instead of commanding hundreds of thousands of men into battle he would be the human representative at the Public Order Triumvirate. Everyone knew it was a demotion of sorts, but Vadim never showed that it bothered him. He took to his new job with the same passion and dedication as his old one.

Erin had become the Marshal of Special Activities. It was her job to do her best to become the human equivalent of Pharos, the FIdayi Clan spy master. She commanded intelligence assets, special forces, and an unknown number of spies. There was some contention within the Council that Erin's position needed to exist at all. They eventually came to the conclusion that as friendly Pharos had been to their faces, they could hardly trust them. It was in their best interest to have some clandestine abilities of their own.

The Marshals all rendered salutes and waited for Vincent to return the gesture, which he did. At that point the Council stopped yelling at one another, noticing he was there.

"He showed up!" Called out a mocking voice. It was Anit Vorsajan, the Soldier's Union representative. She was a First Sergeant of a company of scouts in a Regiment that Vincent couldn't remember.

"Yeah, yeah." He waved her off. "Sounds like I missed a good fight?"

"The Soldier's Union and the Agriculture Union are yelling at each other again." Aron sighed.

"About what?"

"Representative Vorsajan wants to suspend military training so soldiers have more time to spend with their families before our campaign on the Moon." Aron said.

"Wait, how did they hear about that?" Vincent raised an eyebrow. "I just heard about that."

"Commander Erik brought a large number of soldiers with him and soldiers talk." Anit shrugged. Vincent sighed, knowing better than to question it. The soldier rumor mill and grapevine was more effective than most of their intelligence services by that point.

"So, how does that effect the Agriculture workers?" Vincent asked.

"Well." Began the Agriculture Representative, he was a short, fat man that looked like he was old enough to be Vincent's dad. The Agriculture Union frequently fought amongst themselves and elected different representatives every few weeks. He wasn't even sure what this one's name was. The Representative seemed to notice that. "Representative Corbin, Consul." He nodded, motioning for him to continue. "The Soldiers want to take all of this time off but we have a manpower shortage in the greenhouses because of everyone enlisting in the Volunteers."

"And the Laborer's union?" Vincent asked.

"Already seconded to the Construction Workers to help with the infrastructure projects." Came the voice of the Labor Representative from the back of the room.

"And how many hours a day are soldiers training right now?"

"Currently Marshal Victoria has them slated for eight hours of training, five days a week." Anit answered.

"Marshal Victoria, do you think they could go without the training you have for them for a few weeks?" Vincent asked.

"Training." Aron scoffed. "The Warlord won't let us do any real training." Aron grunted. "But having hundreds of thousands of soldiers sitting around with nothing to do is a recipe for disaster. I am just keeping them busy."

"What if they spent half that time working in the greenhouses a few days a week? It would give them more time to spend with their families and make up for the manpower shortage."

"The labor would keep them in fighting shape at least." Aron scratched his chin. "I don't see why not."

"I don't see the problem with that." Anit nodded.

"Agreed." Corbin smiled.

"Glad we could get that figured out." Vincent sighed. "Since everyone seems to know more about the Warlord's plans than I do, I suppose we should get to it. She is going to want to know if we are ready to go back on campaign. I need to know if we are." For reasons that he was unaware, the eyes of the room landed on Ezra who scowled at them.

"Our fleet has problems." He said.

"Problems?" Vincent raised an eyebrow. "What kind of problems?"

"The fleet is badly understaffed. We haven't gotten a single graduate from the Titanian program as of yet." Ezra said. It was a shortage that was bound to happen. Pilots, like Ezra, take years to train. In order to combat it, the flight academy on Titan had developed an abridged program. In the year since it started thousands of Elysian humans had been enrolled in it. Unfortunately, it was a program that still took a year to complete, assuming the half trained pilot candidate didn't kill themselves in the process.

"We have a solution to that, but Marshal Vorbeck refuses to implement it." Anit said.

"Your solution is suicidal!" Ezra shot back.

"What is the solution?" Vincent asked.

"We cut the program short another six months and graduate any pilot that can pass flight exams immediately. According to the numbers we have that would immediately give us five hundred new pilots tomorrow."

"Have you talked to the Titanians about this?" Vincent asked.

"Yes." Ezra said. "They claim it will work, but how do they know? We would be their test dummies!"

"Do we even have enough ships for all of these pilots?" Vincent asked.

"Sort of, Sir." Answered an older gentleman with a pair of augmetic hands and glasses perched at the end of a crooked nose. Vincent recognized him as the Representative of the Machinist Union.

"That is not an answer I like to hear when we are talking about spaceships."

"Well, the factories on Mars are doing their best-" The Representative began, but Ezra didn't let him finish.

"Their work is half assed at best!"

"How so?" Vincent asked.

"They managed to scavenge some old Reaper blueprints from one of their mothballed factories and are pumping out copies as fast as they can. I've even heard of them slapping repairs together for grounded battleships that are a hundred years old. None of it is quality controlled or tested. It is all a crapshoot." Vincent remembered fighting alongside several homemade Martian tanks inside Olympus. Many of them simply burst into flames at the slightest blow or fell apart. The idea of riding something like that into space terrified him. It didn't seem like they would have much of a choice, however.

"The Union has put forward a proposal that we also begin manufacturing parts for these ships. The Martian shipwrights have forwarded us their blueprints to work with. It would help lighten the load on their factories and ensure we have the ability to repair ships our uh less than expert pilots may wreck." The Machinist Representative said.

"You've got to be kidding me!" Ezra screamed. "You're machinists not shipwrights!"

"Our forces fought on Mars without body armor, some without uniforms, some with weapons that didn't work. We fought anyway. If I remember correctly, we even had Sergeants commanding entire Squadrons. We fought anyway." Aron said, smirking at Erin. "We knew about all of these problems before we landed on Mars and we fought anyway. We should discard the idea that we are functioning within the confines of the traditional military and accept this is what we have to work with. For better or for worse. And I personally refuse to accept that this will slow us down unless we allow it to."

"I agree, Marshal Victoria." Vincent nodded. "I support these measures if the Council has voted on them."

"We have, Consul." Anit nodded.

"Good. Marshal Vorbeck, I trust you are prepared to welcome your new pilots home." Ezra gave a curt nod, Vincent had no doubt that he would be entertaining an incredibly pissed off Ezra in his office for several hours later than evening. Vincent made to get out of his seat to leave.

"Not staying, Consul?" Anit asked.

"As much as I enjoy our meetings together, the Warlord has requested my presence. And unlike you, she doesn't take it so well when I am late."

"To be fair, Consul." Corbin raised a hand. "We don't like it either but your wife threatened to kill several people last time we brought it up."

"If it makes you feel any better, those are mostly empty threats." Vincent shrugged.

3

Vincent led the group of Marshals out of the Hall and into the street. Felicity was standing outside of the hall and greeted them with a salute.

"I'd rather you didn't make us go to these meetings with you." Aron frowned.

"All of the other Consuls have their military staff with them." Vincent said. "I need you there to make me look good."

"You mean in case the Warlord asks a question you don't know the answer too." Erin snickered.

"Like I said, to make me look good." Vincent repeated.

"It is bad enough we have to go to the Union meetings. We don't even have a union." Aron said.

"Technically you're all soldiers, so you do." Vincent laughed.

"You mean that uppity Sergeant Anit?" Groaned Ezra. "If I would have known that I would have voted against her."

"You should really be more involved in your local politics, Ezra." Felicity said. "I voted for her. The fact that you hate her means she is doing her job."

"You would." He sighed. Felicity smirked. "And how come

nobody told me politics would require so many meetings and I would have to be part of them?"

"Government is nothing but meetings." Vincent said. "Meetings with different people for different reasons and then more meetings after that because you probably pissed off the wrong person at one of the previous meetings. Then you wake up and do the same thing every day until you finally piss someone off enough to kill you on the way to a different meeting."

"You sounded happier talking about possible political assassination than you did anything else today."

"Having thousands of people all come together to vote so we can listen to the results only to argue with one another all seems.." Erin thought for a moment. "Very inefficient."

"The Chairman thought that too." Vincent nodded. "So, he got rid of all the voting and arguments and shot people instead."

"Fair enough." Erin said.

"Tyrants take the easy way out."

"And we go to meetings." Erin said.

"That's right."

The government quarter was abuzz with activity. Whenever the Warlord called for a Hamagumar, or Gathering, the thousands of far flung Cohorts that make up the Mawr and Rhai militaries return to Elysian. Even though the Clan had been doing this since the destruction of the Mawr home world and long before the inclusion of the Rhai, they had never expanded the city of Elysian to include housing for all of its temporary inhabitants. During the times of a Gathering the entire Government Quarter would be transformed into an open air camp ground with tens of thousands of Warriors pitching tents and starting cook fires. They could end up staying there for months and the Public Order Officers would be stretched to their limits attempting to stop countless fistfights, stabbings, and revenge killings.

Some of this had to do with the Mawr not being great builders but most of it had to do with the Mawr dedication to tradition. The Hamagumar was, in practice, a sign of fealty from the rest of the Clan to the elected Warlord. The Gathering had no set date or time, it was not annual or bi annual. The Warlord simply called for a Gathering and the Consuls and their various military leaders obeyed and showed up.

A Warlord would call for a Gathering for a number of reasons. They could be calling for elections to choose the next Warlord if they were stepping down, to demote a Cohort Leader they were unhappy with, or to solve inner clan tensions. It could also be a time where a Cohort Leader could openly oppose an unpopular Warlord by refusing to appear after a Gathering has been called. From what Vincent heard, that is how Arai's father became Warlord, bringing other Cohort Leaders under his banner to depose a Warlord that he had heard called mad, insane, or psychotic depending on who he was talking to. The Warlord was killed and then elections were held which to the surprise of nobody, ended with Arai's father winning the election.

The one other reason that the Warlord would call a Gathering is to announce a coming war. Vincent knew that was the reason for this meeting, but he wondered how many of the Cohort Leaders knew. He had learned from the various pipelines of soldier gossip, but he was curious if the Mawr or Rhai had something similar and if they did, how far it extended into the depth of space.

They carefully found their way through the large slum that had formed at the foot of the government quarter staircase. Crowds of Mawr were gathered around fires making lunch, reading their religious texts, or wrestling. In the construction of their tent village no room was afforded for the thousands of people who lived and worked in the quarter so they were made to squeeze through awkward gaps in their construction. Annoyed looking Public Order Officers who were attempting to keep lanes for foot traffic open saluted Vincent as he walked by.

The stairway that led towards the Gathering hall was lined by yellow armored Warriors of Arai's personal Cohort. Their uniforms were battle scarred and adorned with ribbons from campaigns Vincent had never heard of. They stomped their hooved feet into the cement of the stairs as he approached and their waists snapped down in deep bow. At the top of the stairs the hall's double doors were flanked by two yellow armored Warriors. Their armor had more ribbons on it than any of the others Vincent had seen. He knew the Warriors, they were Arai's personal guard, the *Pahapan*. They were considered the most elite Warriors in the entire Clan and chosen from throughout all of the Clan Cohorts by the Warlord herself. They bowed deeply.

"Greetings Consul Solaris. The Warlord awaits." The Warrior to the left grunted in the Mawr's guttural language. "In accordance with Hamagumar tradition the only weapons allowed inside are those of Warriors of the Clan."

Vincent glanced down and realized that he was carrying his Riten on his hip and the staff he had brought with him also carried sidearms. Though, in the Pahapan's eyes he was the only one allowed to be armed. He was a Warrior, so named by the Warlord herself and gifted a Riten. His Marshals might as well have been random people from the street.

"Leave your weapons with them." Vincent told him over his shoulder.

"You're kidding." Erin frowned. "I'm a Marshal of this Clan."

"And they don't care." He said. The gathered humans rolled their eyes, unholstered their pistols and handed them over to the Pahapan. They stored them in a box next to the door that was already overflowing with weaponry.

"You may proceed." The lead Pahapan Warrior nodded. Vincent bowed in thanks and the double doors swung open.

Hundreds of bodies had packed into the Gathering chambers. The vast majority of them were in auditorium style seating that ringed the center of the room. Cohort Leaders in an array of different armor colors sat shoulder to shoulder, busy in thousands of different side conversations. Their collective voices rising to a deafening roar.

"Who are they?" Aron asked, leaning in close to Vincent's ear so he could be heard.

"Cohort Leaders." He said.

"But why show up? Is this like our council?"

"They don't get to vote on anything, they are only here as a sign of respect to their Consul."

"Who is also the Warlord. Who, I assume appointed herself?"

"Yeah. Their system has its flaws."

"It sounds like the Central Committee with extra steps."

"If that was the case she would have already shot me." Vincent laughed.

"She would but she probably has to have a meeting first."

At the center of the chambers was a low table that rose to about knee height for a normal human. Ringed around it were a series of cushions upon which were already dozens of government representatives and Consuls. He could see the Martian delegation, headed by Erik, sitting at the far end of the table. Vincent picked a spot next to Pharos, the Special Activities Cohort Leader, the widely feared and respected so-called Spy Master.

It had taken Vincent a while to get used to sitting on the floor with his legs crossed for hours at a time. The Marshals had not developed such a tolerance. Aron groaned as he lowered himself down to his seat, Vincent could hear his knees popping and snapping in protest of such an effort. Ezra, leaning on his cane, had to be helped down by Felicity. He sighed.

"One regular chair is all I ask for."

"They'll have a meeting on it and get back to you." Aron joked. Vincent rolled his eyes.

"Felicity, can you make sure Ezra gets a chair next time?" Felicity made a note on her display.

"Thank you." Ezra shifted uncomfortably, eventually leaning heavily on the table in front of him.

"Greetings, Consul." Rasped Pharos. Most Rhai spoke in a high pitched squawk. A noise that Vincent had never heard any other living thing make. Their language was nearly impossible for anyone else to pick up, forcing pretty much every Rhai to become multilingual. Pharos was the only Rhai he had never heard speak in the manner they did. Vincent assumed that the Spy Master had done one too many backroom deals and someone had shot them, but that may have been wishful thinking. Instead, their voice just became another part of the mystique that surrounded them.

"Greetings, Pharos. How are you?"

"I am well." They nodded. "I did not congratulate you on your wedding, for that I apologize. I could not pull myself away from my work."

"Thank you." Vincent nodded. He didn't want to tell Pharos that he was so busy with work he had almost missed his own wedding, so he could hardly blame them for running out early.

"How is yours.." They thought for a moment, looking for a word. "Spouse?"

"She isn't stuck in a meeting all day, so better than either of us." He laughed and Pharos hissed, the closest thing they had to laughter. The countless conversations died away when the door to Arai's office opened and she stepped out into the chamber. Like her Pahapan, she wore her dark yellow armor decorated with a rainbow of ribbons and medals.

Humans disregarded the Warlord's version of politics for being uncouth or barbaric, but they never noticed the nuances that made her an incredibly flexible and surprisingly empathetic leader. She was wearing the Cohort ribbons of every formation in her Clan. A small nod of respect to a group that meant everything to, even if she probably didn't know most of their names. Another was the Phoenix flag, the symbol of Elysian humanity, on the breastplate of her armor.

The Pahapan of the inner chamber also showed strategic inclusion, representative of the Clan's strange intergalactic demographics and power dynamics. Marching out to the table were three armored members of the Pahapan. One Mawr, one human, and one Rhai, each of them carried the standard of the race they represented. The group stopped near the table, stomped their feet against the ground, and loudly announced in all three languages.

"All rise for Warlord Arai of the Fidayi Clan!" And they did so. Felicity scrambled to pull Ezra to his feet. He grunted in pain before finally getting his cane under him and taking the pressure off of his wounds.

"I hereby declare this Hamagumar of the Fidayi Clan has begun." Arai said curtly. She lowered herself down to her seat slowly. Vincent wasn't sure if it was the countless wounds she had received from her hundreds of campaigns that slowed her movements or the overly decorated armor that looked to have taken several aids to put on correctly. The rest of the table followed suit, the Cohort Leaders in attendance in the gallery remained standing.

"Many of you have been able to surmise why I have called this Gathering." She began. "It was too long ago we were able to stamp out the Human traitors on Mars and chase them off to their final hiding spot on their blasted moon." Vincent fought back laughter at the idea of someone calling the Central Committee the traitors, rather than him. "I say it is about time we brought that chapter of our struggle to an end."

"Forget the Humans! What of the demons?" Called a Cohort Leader from the gallery. "They must be destroyed!" A chorus of rough cheers went up in agreement. Vincent saw a few quick exchanges from those at the table before Arai cut them off by pounding her fist against the table. The table shook and felt as if it cracked under her strength.

"The Alliance will be dealt with." Arai nodded. "But these Committee whelps have shown they will wait until our backs are turned before plunging a knife into our ribs. Or do you not remember what they did to us on Grawluck?" This time a chorus of cheers went up in agreement with the Warlord, the dissenting Leader sat down in shame. "They do not pose a threat to us like they once did, but once we step off to stare down the final battle with the Anarchs, we cannot have any possible distractions."

"My Warlord." Spoke Pharos. "I agree in our need to snuff out this bastion of resistance, but I wonder if planning such a campaign will in itself, distract us from our main mission."

"I hear your concern, Cohort Leader Pharos." She nodded. "I am sure you're not the only one to have such concerns about any operation we launch against the Human Moon. We are not the military juggernaut of the Alliance and we have finite resources. We thank our allies of Mars for helping us on that matter." She motioned to a seat at the far end of the table where Erik was sitting. He bowed slightly.

"It is the least the gracious people of Mars can do to thank those who helped us liberate our home."

"That being said, our military forces have rapidly developed since our Martian Campaign. The Human Cohort-" Vincent cut her off, clearing his throat. "-The Volunteer Army-" She corrected, he could sense the tone of displeasure in her voice. "Is four times the size it was since its planet fall on Mars. Its fighting capabilities continue to expand and with the help of our allies on Mars and Titan it will soon field a mighty fleet."

Felicity leaned in close to Vincent.

"Why is she singing our praises? Nobody ever notices we exist."

"I don't know." He whispered. He had felt his pride begin to swell within his chest as the Warlord lavished attention onto the Volunteers. He had to admit it felt good to have their progress be noticed in front of all of the hardened Cohort Leaders that still didn't think Human soldiering was anything close to what a Mawr was capable of.

"From my experience." Cut in Aron. "When a Commander is puffing up someone like this they are about to drop a stupid mission into their lap." Vincent groaned.

"This is why I am putting forward a plan to use the Volunteers as the vanguard force to prosecute our offensive against the Human Moon." The table erupted into various arguments between leaders, the audience followed suit. The humans at the table exchanged confused glances.

"Wait, does she mean we are going to invade Lunar City on our own?" Vincent sputtered.

"Damn, I hate being right." Aron sighed and rubbed his temples. Arai pounded her fists against the table again and the arguing died down.

"Again, I hear your concerns!" Her voice boomed. It was clear she was sick of the arguing. "But the Mawr and Rhai formations bore the brunt of the fighting on Mars and are still resting and recovering." Vincent could see a few faces in the crowd rising to argue with the Warlord but she headed them off. "The first Leader who rises to lie to my face about the state of their Cohort I will have shot where they stand!" She snapped. "Consul Solaris, this Clan asks you if your Volunteer Army can conduct war in its name. What do you say?"

Vincent suddenly felt countless eyes upon him. The weight of the entire room fell onto him and he swallowed hard. He glanced at Aron who nodded. Aron rose to his feet and rendered a salute to the Warlord.

"My Warlord." Arai looked unfamiliar with who exactly Aron was. He continued. "I am Marshal Aron Victoria, commander of the Volunteer Army." Arai nodded for him to continue. "The soldiers of the Volunteer Army have been waiting for this opportunity and will fight harder than any Cohort in this room." Arai flashed a toothy smile, it was an irregular expression for her and she looked as if she was in pain.

"Of course, no Cohort in this Clan fights alone." Arai said. "We will hold our forces in reserve, should they be needed."

"Warlord, if I may." Erik raised his hand. She nodded. "The idea of assaulting the final bastions of the Central Committee is something every Martian boy and girl grows up dreaming about. Allow us to throw our full support behind the Volunteers so your formations can have the rest time they need."

"I see nothing wrong with this idea." Arai nodded.

"Commander Erik." Aron said. "As a Martian myself, I understand where you are coming from. But how do you think the people of Lunar City would react if tens of thousands of Martian soldiers streamed into their city?"

"Probably about as well as the Martians reacted when tens of thousands of Earthians streamed into theirs." Erik shrugged. Aron was about to respond when Vincent cut in.

"Commander Erik, last I remembered that just sparked another war."

"Another *several* wars." Aron added.

"So, Consul Solaris, what is it you suggest we do?" Erik asked.

"We hold the Martian People's Army in reserve. If the Central Committee decides they want to turn Lunar City into another Victoria, we deploy your forces against them and give them exactly what they want." Erik pinched his chin and leaned against the table. It was obvious he wanted his forces to be the ones who destroyed the Central Committee once and for all but he gave in.

"This could work."

"This is a good idea." Pharos said. "Our intelligence on the Central Committee is not great, for reasons you would expect, my spies have had a hard time infiltrating Lunar City."

"And they aren't letting Martians anywhere near their center of power anymore." Erik added. "I tried sending moles in acting as Committee loyalists fleeing our government on Mars. I haven't heard from any of them since."

"But, we have reason to believe the Central Committee and the EDF is on its last leg." Pharos presented a display that had a long list of EDF units, some with their names crossed out, others colored red. "Their most experienced units and most talented commanders were destroyed on Mars. By any measure of a military campaign, this was an unrecoverable defeat for them. Along with their best formations went a large portion of their fleet, now under the control of Mars, as well as most of their military supplies. Even if they enact the Committee Emergency Conscription Law they could only field an understrength army group full of hardy trained, badly equipped, and terrified humans they had probably previously excused from military service."

Vincent was about to ask Pharos how they had such in-depth knowledge of Committee regulations and laws relating to military conscription and policy but the Spy Master continued. "I believe that there is a good chance that we can win this war without fighting it."

"Wait, what?" He asked.

"Being around you humans for so long now has taught me much about how you think and feel." Vincent groaned. Pharos was about to give their 'Humans are fear driven animals' speech again. "Humans aren't like Mawr or Rhai. A rational human only fights when they see no other way out, and while we think of them as enemies the only irrational humans are now out of the equation." They were speaking about the Black Coats, fighting to the death or blowing themselves up in suicide attacks to defend Victoria. All while normal soldiers tried to run for their lives or surrender. "Consul Solaris, you detest this war but only fight it because you think it is the only way to secure a future for your people. Commander Erik you believe as long as the Chairman exists, the people of Mars will never be safe."

Vincent and Erik exchanged glances. They had to admit, Pharos really had figured them out.

"So, we simply give the Committee an out. Demand they surrender." Erik shot to his feet, his fists balled.

"You say you already know why we fight this war, and this is your solution?" He spat. The normally cool, calm, and collected man was red faced in rage. "Would you ask the Warlord to come to terms with the Anarchs? You're asking us to make peace with the people who enslaved us for generations!"

Erik's aid pulled him back down to his seat by his arm. The two exchanged a heated conversation between themselves.

"I understand your concerns, Commander Erik. But the times have changed." Pharos said in the most soothing voice they could manage. "The Committee no longer has the power to subjugate you. Earth is destroyed, Mars is liberated and has powerful allies. The Committee stands alone on their desolate moon. They know this as well as we do."

"So, you want Consul Solaris to demand their surrender and hang the threat of Martian vengeance over their head to scare them into accepting it?" Erik's voice had softened a bit but he was still unhappy with the turn of events. "And then what?"

"We can't just trust them to stay out of the war. Especially after embarrassing them with a surrender." Vincent spoke up. "The Committee wouldn't take that lying down."

"We could occupy them." Aron said. "Until the war is over and then leave."

"Seems like a drain on resources, does it not?" Arai asked.

"It would drain less than continuing to fight a two front war as we have been." Pharos countered. "And head off anything they might plan while our backs are turned."

"Peace terms I can support." Erik said. "however, I cannot agree to any plan that ends with the Committee being in power anywhere in this galaxy regardless of how weakened they have become. My people will not stand for it." Arai frowned. It was clear to Vincent she was not used to meeting other people's demands.

"If this is what it takes for your cooperation, so be it. I do not care what you do with the Central Committee so long as it does not hamper our collective ability to deal with the Anarch threat." She said. "Would your people stand for this, Commander Erik?"

"I believe they would, Warlord."

"Good." She nodded. "I know many of you came to hear about our plans for our final campaign against the Anarchs, but myself and Leader Pharos are still finalizing our ideas on this matter. Furthermore, our timeframes will also now be directly impacted by the success or failure of the allied Human campaign against Lunar City."

"So, uh no pressure." Felicity laughed sarcastically.

4

Vincent stepped out of the Gathering hall and took in a lung full of fresh air. Or as fresh as Elysian had to offer. He was still trying to wrap his head around how he went from being the commander of the weakest part of the Fidayi Clan to suddenly being in charge of the invasion of Lunar City.

Aron stepped out after him, lighting a cigarette and adding to the pollution around him with a cloud of smoke.

"Why did you tell her we could do this?" Vincent began to panic.

"You weren't understanding, Consul." He smiled, gently. "She wasn't really asking us anything. She was telling us to be ready. Alien or not, she is still a commander and those are the same throughout the universe."

"How can you tell?"

"Seriously?" Aron laughed. "You've never been asked to do anything before that you were sure they weren't actually asking, but rather, they were just being nice?"

"Shit." He sighed. "I still suck at this."

"That's alright, that is why you have us." Aron smiled. "Speaking of which, why didn't Titan send a delegation?"

"They sent their regards." Vincent made quotation marks with his fingers. "But they won't be taking an active part in our campaign against the Committee anymore."

"Because they see they can't threaten them anymore?" Aron asked.

"No." Vincent shook his head. "Our dear Field Marshal Denta got embarrassed and word got back to Titan he nearly got his entire army wiped out. Last I heard they were doing some 'military reorganization.'"

"That sounds like Denta and his inner circle are fucked." Erin laughed.

"It does look that way. Unfortunately, that also means a lot of the decisions they made are being reevaluated. They did reassure us that they committed to supporting our efforts as well as our war against the Anarchs though."

"Speaking of which." Erin said. "Shouldn't we be involved in the Warlord's planning in regards to the Anarchs? We will be fighting them after all."

"One thing at a time." Vincent said. "Let's worry about taking over the entire moon before we worry about invading the Anarch home world, okay?"

The Hall door opened again and the Martian delegation exited out onto the stairs. Erik still looked to be in a foul mood but quickly plastered on his usual smile. Vincent wasn't sure if it was the politician in him coming out or if Erik really did always try to be as pleasant as possible. Being the Consul had crossed the wires in his brain and made him think of people as naturally suspicious even when they were being genuine.

Erik clapped him on the shoulder.

"I suppose since we will be in this together, it is a good time to give you your wedding present."

"A wedding present?" He asked.

"It might help us on the Moon too. Well, it certainly won't

hurt." Erik grinned. "Follow me." He began to walk before pausing. "For the life of me I can't seem to figure out your tram lines. Which one takes us to the Spaceport?"

"The green line." Ezra pointed out. The tram station was crowded with all forms of Clan membership from Humans going to work to curious Mawr, unsure of how the new system worked. Because of the lack of space on Elysian the trams came into the stations vertically. Riders only had a few minutes to push their way in and have a seat on one of the bench seats.

"I will meet you at the spaceport." Grunted Zinvor. He frowned at the tram car that sat parked in front of him and eyed each person with disdain as they bumped into him, squeezing by him to find a seat. "I feel like a walk."

"Of course you do." Vincent smiled. "I'll see you there." Zinvor turned and quickly pushed through the crowd and vanished. Erik led them aboard the tram car and had a seat. Vincent remained standing, grabbing onto an overhead handle.

"Is he afraid of the tram?" Erik asked.

"Something like that. I think it is heights in general." The tram shook and the track hummed as energy coursed through it. After a few moments the car soundlessly left the station and zipped down the track. The city around them went by so fast the buildings all blurred together.

"I've seen him charge into machine gun nests and trench lines, but using the tram is just too much to ask." Felicity laughed.

"So, why are we going to the spaceport anyway?" Vincent asked. Erik folded his arms and smiled at him knowingly.

"Like I said, a gift." The tram began to rattle as it slowed down to pull into the station. Ezra glanced out of the window and his eyes went wide.

"Wait." He said. "What is that?" Vincent moved over next to him. Every few seconds their vision was obscured by passing buildings, creating something of a strobe effect as they tried to look at the spaceport. From what he could see, he was looking at the biggest ship he had ever seen parked on a planet.

"Every fleet needs a flagship doesn't it?" Erik asked. The tram pulled into the station and the people inside disgorged onto the spaceport. Ezra began walking as fast as he could, his cane struggling to keep up as he rushed by the rest of the group.

Vincent caught up with him and laid his eyes upon Erik's flagship. It was massive. He was no expert of the navy but it looked to be some kind of destroyer. He could see weapons pods the size of entire Reapers mounted every few dozen feet. Along its two weapons mounts that jutted out from its raw, gunmetal grey body like stubby wings, long, slender cannons were mounted. Each was as large as a Rhai skyscraper.

Ground crews and workers milled about the base of the ship like worker bees. Crew people driving forklifts loaded and unloaded crates onto the tarmac. So many were coming and going that it created something of a traffic jam of bodies, each in a different colored jumpsuit.

"Behold, the newly christened *ESS Olympus*!" Erik said, his hands outstretched in front of him. "A ship with a name that celebrates our friendship." The gathered Marshals seemed impressed, with the exception of Ezra. He stood, arms folded, squinting at the ship.

"You renamed it." He eyed the craft.. "What was it originally called?"

"The.." Erik turned to speak to his aid who whispered something in his ear. "The *ESS Claymore*." Ezra's suspicious face turned beat red.

"I thought I remembered this piece of shit!" He spat.

"Wait, what?" Vincent asked.

"When you graduate from the academy they make you rack up some hours in space before they let you start flying on your own. I got stuck on the damn Claymore. Even back then it was the oldest ship in the entire damn fleet!"

"Old doesn't mean bad always." Aron shrugged. "It means it's reliable."

"Oh no." Ezra shook his head. "The Claymore broke down so often that it got stranded so many times in orbit that the Navy just permanently attached a repair tug to it just to be safe."

"That does not sound so reliable." Aron frowned.

"Where did you even find this piece of shit?" Ezra asked. "I thought they decommissioned it a decade ago."

"They uh did." Erik nodded. "We found it in the Naval scrapyard outside of Tharsis."

"You gave us a destroyer you found in a dump?" Vincent laughed. "Did we do something to piss you off or something?"

"I don't know if you've noticed, Consul, but while our factories are still coming online we aren't exactly cranking out any new destroyers. We can manage barges and Reapers-"

"Of dubious quality." Ezra added.

"-But" Erik glared at Ezra. "We won't be able to manufacture anything like that until far past the time we will need them. In the meantime we have started retrofitting things that maybe the EDF thought were outdated or scrap."

"Beggars can't be choosers." Vincent said. "It is one more destroyer than we had before."

"We still don't have a destroyer!" Ezra cursed. "We have a flying bucket of trash!"

"That flying bucket of trash is your flagship, Marshal." Vincent smiled and Ezra rolled his eyes.

"Okay, fine. What kind of retrofitting did you do?"

"Well, as you know, the power plant of most spaceships burns out before the structure itself is no longer orbit worthy." Ezra nodded knowingly. "Generally the EDF would scrap a ship rather than replace the power plant due to costs and labor concerns.

Every once and a while they might slap a cheap replacement in it and it might be used to teach new crewmen. That was probably why you ended up on it. Unfortunately, we can't exactly just build a new destroyer power plant, but we did have some blueprints for some old barge power plants."

"You put a barge power plant in a destroyer?" Ezra asked, incredulously. "How does that even work?"

"Not great, but it is what we have." Erik began walking further into the Spaceport. Crews of Martian workers greeted him with a quick salute before going back to work. "The *Olympus* isn't going to outrun anyone. So, we had to think of a new defensive tactic."

"All of the weapons." Vincent said. "I don't think I've ever seen so many on a ship of its size."

"That's right." Erik nodded. "The *Olympus* will protect itself by hiding behind enough firepower to lay waste to an entire sector of space on its own."

"Wait, hold on." Ezra said. He was eyeing down his new flagship, skepticism plastered across his face. "I'm not an engineer, but I'm pretty sure the power plant does a lot more than just affect acceleration." Erik bit his lip and sighed.

"From what I was told it also impacted the ship's ability to regulate heat and power for the crew cabins."

"From what you were told?" Vincent asked. "Didn't you ride here on it?" Erik laughed.

"I'm the Commander of Mars, do you think I am flying to Elysian on *that?* Congress would never allow it."

"You said something about heat." Ezra said. "That seems important as we fly through the cold vacuum of space. What can we do to offset that?"

"I suggest you pack a jacket, Marshal." Erik smiled.

5

Dozens of barges had landed at the spaceport. Each time one landed thousands of Martian ground crew would rush out from their rest areas and begin unloading them at a frantic pace. Each barge unloaded different things. One was a dozen Reaper clones packed into the barge so tightly it left room for little else. Another was the particular Martian invention of homemade armored vehicles.

While the Martians had found the EDF blueprints to manufacture their fearsome standard issue tank, they lacked the resources to do so. Titan had the resources, but were wary of supplying the newly churning Martian war machine with resources and weapons that would have quickly turned them into the premier human power in the galaxy. The Titanians for their part, made the excuse that due to their current wartime manufacturing output, they had nothing to spare. Everyone knew they were lying.

Instead the Martians put their efforts into working on what had been called War Wagons during the war on Mars. Slapdash armored fighting vehicles made out of anything they could get their hands on. Vincent remembered the brave Martian rebels riding into battle on what looked like repurposed farm tractors, braving EDF tanks and machine gun fire on something that was already hundreds of years old. The vehicles looked ridiculous, but their effectiveness couldn't be denied. Without them the attack on the Mons would have failed spectacularly.

Now, rather than bolting weapons onto anything with an engine and riding it into battle, the Martians had streamlined the process. They had produced a vehicle with tracks, armor, and a small dome shaped turret which housed a cannon. The armor was bolted together and the quality of either one varied. They shot plumes of black smoke into the air whenever they accelerated and seemed to only go a fraction of the speed any tank should. Their only real strength was the factories could clearly pump out the vehicles at a breathtaking pace.

In the short amount of time Vincent had watched the barges come in the Martians had offloaded enough of their new tanks to furnish the Volunteers with enough of them to outfit an entirely new armored regiment, something he never thought possible. Within a few short hours Erik had supplied the Volunteers with more weapons, ships, and tanks than they could make for themselves in years.

They could not, however, render the same miracle for the pilots. Ezra watched with concern as the newly minted pilots of the Volunteer Fleet took to the skies for the first time, fully graduated from their abridged training program. He stomped around and cursed at each one of their faults as they clumsily attempted to hold a formation in the crowded skies above them. They bumped into one another and more than one of them dropped back to the spaceport like a meteor to a planet's surface.

Medical crews rushed out in teams to pull the pilots from their burning wrecks, of which there were several over the course of the day.

"I told you this was a terrible idea!" Ezra cursed. "How many ships did we lose because these idiots can't fly yet?"

"A few." Vincent said. "But all of them survived, and thanks to the Martians we have more ships than we know what to do with. Consider it extra training."

"And besides." Felicity said. "A few times the engines just caught on fire, that can hardly be blamed on the pilots."

"So, either my pilots suck or the engines are time bombs. Your version of optimism is horrible." Ezra fumed. The ground rattled with an explosion, it was not the first one of the day. Ezra rolled his eyes. "And what was that?" He moaned.

"Hard to tell." Vincent said. "Erik said they are training your ground crews for service aboard the *Olympus*. Loading and unloading weapons, stuff like that. Maybe they dropped something." A plume of black smoke rose in a wisp above a nearby hanger. "Which hanger is that?" Felicity quickly scrolled through her display.

"Looks like the power plant repair hanger." She said.

"Great." Ezra sighed. "Times like these make me jealous of Aron."

"I wouldn't go that far." Felicity said. "Last time I saw him he was screaming at a group of soldiers for drag racing their new tanks down the middle of the street."

"Was everyone okay?" Vincent asked.

"Physically, yeah." Felicity nodded. "But I think a few people got demoted. Also, I think your wife was running a gambling circle based on the results."

"That does sound like her." Vincent laughed. "speaking of Aron, I should probably check in on how the training is going over there. Good luck on your end, Ezra." He leaned heavily on his cane and gave a lazy salute.

"With the fleet you have bestowed upon me, I will surely need every bit of luck I can get."

When Vincent arrived at one of the Volunteer's training depots, he was not greeted by smiling faces as he had come to expect. The soldiers, who had only hours before been granted extra time off in exchange for limited labor in the greenhouses, had had all of their passes revoked and been pressed into training full time once again.

As the Martians had flooded the Elysian stores with surplus gear and supplies, there was no longer a worry for conserving what they had for the coming war. Few people doubted the Volunteer's fighting abilities after their actions on Mars, though one who did was their own commander, Aron. The ranks of the Volunteers were staffed with a mix of hardened veterans of their Mars campaign, gangers from the Martian streets who were well used to violence, or new recruits who had not yet seen combat, but had received some kind of training in their previous life with the EDF.

However, their command structure had gone through radical change. Many of the leaders within the Volunteers had no formal education and had simply risen to the top to meet a desperate need in the middle of a war. As the Volunteers expanded, more leaders were needed. So a more standardized system of testing and school was put into place. Soldiers who were recommended to become officers would pass a test and be sent to either Mars or Titan for education, returning to Elysian a newly minted Junior Lieutenant after a few months.

The problem was, the supply problems and Arai's reluctance to conduct normal training meant these new officers, of which there were now thousands of, had never put their education to the test. More importantly, the Marshal of the Army had little clue as to what his own army's capabilities really were. In order to test them, while under strict orders to not expend ammunition, he had ordered them to convert a warehouse into a full training center.

Soldiers had labored for weeks to do their best to turn the old, dilapidated warehouse into something that reminded Vincent of the simulation bay that he had used aboard the *ESS Victory*. The warehouse, which seemed big enough to fully house the newly acquired *Olympus*, had been transformed into a battlefield. Cement bunkers had been built, framing long reinforced trench lines of razor wire and dirt. The entire scene looked as if Aron and purposefully recreated the battlefield of Victoria.

To make sure he and other high-ranking commanders could watch the soldiers train, a walkway had been built several stories into the air, crossing from one side of the warehouse to the other. It was a rickety work of metal mesh that Vincent could look straight through. Its construction did not inspire confidence and Zinvor took one look at the contraption and refused to go near it.

Vincent rode the elevator up into the air for a few minutes. Once he reached the top a soldier opened the door for him and welcomed him to the walkway with a salute. The soldier walked him over to Aron. Aron was surrounded by several people who Vincent didn't recognize. His General Staff had quickly grown to the size where Vincent could no longer keep track of all of their names or faces. The Generals around him quickly spun around and saluted Vincent, Aron hardly looked up from his display.

"Nice of you to join us, Consul." He said. "I assume that means Marshal Vorbeck's boys out on the spaceport are doing well."

"Not even remotely." Vincent scratched his beard. "But I wanted to get away from there before I watched him have a heart attack. How is everything here?"

"You're just in time actually. We are about to find out." Aron said. Vincent walked across the walkway and to where Aron was standing and looked down. The trench line was teeming with soldiers, each wearing a grey jacket to simulate EDF personnel.

"Looks like you are reenacting Victoria." Vincent said.

"Something like that." Aron nodded. "Some of my staff thought I should give the new kids baby steps to prove themselves. Then it dawned on me: You, Marshal Olympus, and Captain Haagen didn't have that luxury did you?" Vincent thought for a moment, he supposed Aron was right. "Captain Haagen." Aron glanced at Felicity. "Had you ever commanded a unit before you took to the field at Victoria?"

"No, Marshal." Felicity answered.

"Exactly." Aron said. "They already got babied when they went off to fancy military school on Titan. The kid gloves are off, because the next time we will have to figure out what they are made of they could get my soldiers killed. And Consul, that is not something I will do."

"So what is the plan?" He asked.

"We throw them into the biggest cluster fuck the Volunteers have ever been in and see what happens."

"What happens if they fail?" Vincent asked.

"Consul, you don't understand. They will fail." He said. "The plan is to put them in over their head and see what they do. Do they make good choices and give orders that make sense? We can work with that. Do they freeze? Lose control of their soldiers? Then they have no place commanding soldiers in this army."

"What about all of the time we wasted educating them?" Vincent asked. "That is months lost that we don't have time to send someone else in their place."

"In all due respect, Consul I only went along with your joint officers training because I thought it would help bring us, Mars, and Titan closer together. On that front it is still a success. If you thought so highly of their education I would assume you would have appointed someone who went to officer's academy to command your army and instead you picked me."

"Fair enough."

"We already have a roster of high performing Sergeants that will be promoted in their place should they fail." A General said. He was an older Titanian man with a chest full of medals Vincent assumed were from his prior service.

"Who is playing the EDF?" Vincent asked.

"That would be Marshal Olympus' Special Activity Commandos." Aron smiled. Erin's Commandos were easily the highest trained and most capable soldiers in the entire Volunteers. They shot better, moved faster, and fought harder than anyone else. Erin ran her own selection program and training regimen for soldiers who wanted to join her unit. Vincent had never witnessed the training but he always saw the hospital wards fill up after a fresh group of soldiers had failed out of it. Vincent broke out into laughter.

"You really did create a cluster fuck didn't you?" Aron grinned.

"General Xosa." He looked at the Titanian General. "Give the signal." Xosa motioned for a soldier to come over to the group. The soldier was wearing a radio set on his back. Xosa grabbed the radio's hand mic and spoke into it.

"You have a greenlight to begin your attack."

Vincent felt the steel walls of the warehouse rumble and below him a line of tanks came into view. Machine guns under their barrels began to rattle as they fired a storm of bullets at the trench line in front of them. Behind the tanks groups of dozens of soldiers marched, each trying to stay behind the vehicle in front of them, using them as a shield. Vincent noticed that the soldiers were wearing the simulator harnesses that he had once worn aboard the *Victory*. The ones that would send a crippling blast of electricity through your body if you happened to be shot with a training round.

"They are advancing in good order." Xosa noted.

"So far." Aron said.

The soldiers ducked behind the trench line were holding their fire. They knew shooting at the tanks would be pointless. That was when he saw the slender tubes of rocket launchers appear over the top.

"This is going to get interesting." Vincent said.

Smoke popped from the end of the rocket launchers. The fire was disciplined, timed to fire all at once like a broadside. Each targeted a different tank and the training projectiles thumped off of the front of the tanks and after a few seconds, each ground to a halt. Soldiers behind the dead tanks stopped as well. To their left and right tanks that were still mobile crept forward, exposing the flanks of the other soldiers. The Tanks that were still moving opened fire on the rocket launchers but it was too late. Another salvo of rockets stopped them dead.

Only then did the soldiers in the trench open fire with small arms. Dozens of machine guns and rifles opened fire. Soldiers stuck out in the open twitched and fell as electricity ripped through their body. One of the surviving tanks swept the top of the trench with machine gun and cannon fire, sending several of the Commandos to the ground, wracked with pain.

One by one it seemed the soldiers realized their plan of hiding behind the tanks and advancing was now dead in the water. Slowly they began to put a base of fire onto the trench so another group could try to advance under cover. The advancing soldiers were cut down as they ran. After a few dozen feet the survivors broke and ran back towards the tanks, getting shot in the back as they did so.

"Captain Haagen." Aron said. "What would you do in this situation?" Felicity thought for a moment.

"I would withdraw, Marshal."

"You would give up the fight?"

"Giving up the fight is not the same as surviving to fight another day. After all, a key to winning any fight is bringing as many of your friends as possible with you and not fighting fair."

"And what would you bring?"

"Now that we know the disposition of their forces and their defenses I would hold my attack until it can be softened with artillery or airstrikes. An unsupported frontal assault is a plan made by a man who should no longer have the ability to command soldiers." She saw the entire staff turn and glare at her. She cleared her throat. "In my opinion, Marshal."

"Consul Solaris, her talent is wasted in her current position." Aron said. "She should be commanding a Regiment."

"I told her the same thing." Vincent shrugged.

"I am the Consul's aid by my own choosing, Marshal."

"And why is that?"

"Because he needs all the help he can get." Felicity smiled and Aron laughed.

"You got that right."

The stricken soldiers were now split into two groups. One group remained hiding behind a cluster of broken down tanks not even trying to return fire and another across the battlefield that had taken cover behind a slight dip in the terrain. Though, the second group of soldiers were firing back and it seemed like someone in the middle of them was taking charge. The person who Vincent assumed was their commander was yelling over to the other group, attempting to get them to do something, but they refused to budge.

The second group tossed a few smoke grenades towards the trench. After a few seconds the area became obscured with thick white smoke. They then jumped up from their cover and charged towards the trench. They didn't fire, not wanting to give up their element of surprise. Seeing them act forced the first group from behind their dead tanks and into the open as well. They lacked the drive of the second group and instead of a disciplined charge it was more like a slow trickle of soldiers, some remained behind the tank, declining to join the attack.

The mass of men vanished into the smoke. Sporadic gunfire erupted from the trench line broken up by the shouting and screaming of soldiers fighting. The smoke dissipated and revealed a roiling fist fight between the two sides. Grey and tan uniforms intermingled, swinging wildly with their weapons like clubs or shooting one another at point blank range. Elements from the first group broke from the fight and began to run back towards their comrades who were still hiding behind the tanks. The second group, now cornered on the far side of the trench, did not retreat. Instead they dug their heels in and fought tooth and nail. Unfortunately, they didn't stand a chance. After the other group abandoned them they were outnumbered, outgunned, and facing the best soldiers in the Army.

To their credit none of them tried to surrender. Several of them crumpled from blows from rifles while others were shot, dropped bonelessly by searing blasts of electricity.

"Well." Aron sighed. "They didn't make the best choice, but they at least made a choice. Who was in charge of that other group?"

"Looks like a Junior Lieutenant named Baskerville." Said Xosa.

"Fire them." Aron ordered. "And send in the next groups of soldiers." A few more gunshots came from the trench. "Once Marshal Olympus' boys are done having fun, anyway."

"Yes, Marshal." Xosa nodded and walked off.

"What is your verdict?" Vincent asked.

"To be honest, I expected nothing from this newest crop of graduates." Aron said. "So to get one that could get their shit together long enough to lead an assault is at least gives us something to work with."

"How many more groups are you running through this?"

"Hundreds." Aron said. "They won't be getting any sleep until we step off from this rock."

"Will they be ready, Aron?" Vincent asked.

"Of course." He nodded. "We don't have any other choice."

6

Vincent awoke to his apartment door being nearly knocked off of its hinges. He sat bolt upright in his bed and grabbed his Riten from his bedside desk. Fiona remained asleep. For all of her stories that told of her miraculous survival on the streets of Olympus that required her to be ready to fight for her life at any moment, what she could sleep through never ceased to amaze him. The door rattled again and with that she stirred. She sat up and looked at him.

"Everything alright?"

"Do you not hear the door?" He exclaimed.

"Oh. I thought you were going to handle that." She groaned. She rolled out of bed and grabbed her Riten as well. She thumbed the hammer back and walked and marched with a purpose towards the door wearing nothing but tattered tan underwear and a white tank top. She flung the door open and brought the Riten up to about face level as she did so.

"Holy shit, Fiona!" Screamed the voice of Felicity. "Put that thing away!" She cried.

"Damnit Zinvor!" Swore Fiona. "I thought your job was to keep people away from our house!" He heard Zinvor call back.

"Am I not to allow the Consul's aid to call on him for official business?"

"Let her in Fiona, damn." Vincent groaned. Arai hardly ever slept so sending Felicity to his door at all hours of the day or night was hardly new. "What's going on Felicity?" She stepped into their apartment and eyed Fiona.

"Uh, aren't you going to put clothes on?"

"Do I barge into your house and tell you how to dress?" Fiona frowned. "I didn't think so." Felicity rolled her eyes and handed Vincent her data display. He looked down at the display, an old cracked model that looked like the same one she had brought with her from Titan. Glowing white words rose above the damaged screen.

The Human Cohort of Elysian in conjunction with the People's Army of Mars and supported by the coalition Cohorts of the Fidayi Clan is hereby ordered to conduct military action against the Earth Defense Forces garrisoned within Lunar City, formerly Central Committee of Earth held space. You are hereby ordered to bring about their defeat through any means necessary as soon as possible.
May Exalted Paternazm guide you,
-Warlord Arai I, Supreme Commander, Coalition of the Fidayi Clan.

He looked up from the display and his throat went dry. He knew this was coming. They had just talked about it. He had just seen the fleet and the army training for this. But he had never held orders that would send his soldiers into war before. Arai didn't order them. She gave the orders to him to pass down and he would have to tell them to board the ships that would take them to war.

"What is it?" Fiona's words snapped him back to the display he was holding. He swallowed hard.

"Marching orders." He said. "We are going to war." He rose to his feet, his legs unsteady. "Felicity, alert the Marshals. We leave as soon as possible." Felicity smiled.

"I already did." She said. "I thought they could use the extra time."

"Thank you." He nodded. "Can you head out and help them?" She saluted, and marched back out of the room. Vincent stumbled around, still not entirely awake, looking for the rest of his clothes. He found his pair of worn out boots and put them on without tying them.

"So, is this real?" Fiona asked, a smirk spreading across her face. He handed her the display. She read it slowly and handed it back. Vincent found his uniform jacket that Fiona had thrown into the corner of the room the night before. Most of the awards were still attached and he slipped it on. She walked over to the desk and found a flask, popped it open and took a drink.

"It is a little early for that, isn't it?" He asked.

"It is a toast." She smiled. "Every Martian girl wants to storm Earth, but since the Anarchs took that away from me, Lunar City is just as good." She handed him the flask and he took it.

"I'll celebrate when-" He began to say but she cut him off.

"Let me guess, you'll celebrate when all of this is over and we aren't dead?" He laughed and took a sip from the flask. It was the homemade Martian stuff that Erik had brought them. He coughed and handed it back.

"Yeah, something like that."

"Well excuse me if I celebrate without you." She said, taking another drink. Gunfire erupted outside the windows followed by cheers and joyful hooting. The word had spread as the Marshals passed on their mobilization orders to the hundreds of thousands of soldiers around the quarter.

"Sounds like you won't be the only one." She leaned forward and grabbed him by his beltline, pulling him in. She perched herself up on her toes and kissed him.

"I love you." Vincent said

"I know." She smirked. "Now go win me the Moon."

7

Despite the late hour, the Quarter was fully alive. Soldiers crowded the street in various states of dress and sobriety. Every few feet someone would fire a burst of celebratory gunfire and the crowd would hoot and holler. Public Order Officers ran around trying to get people to stop, but as they had no guns of their own they didn't want to press the issue too much.

Sergeants and officers stood on street corners and shouted out names as soldiers gathered around them. Vincent felt bad for them. The Marshals had developed a detailed plan for a muster system that included designated rally areas and communication systems but it was just a plan still on paper. Nothing had ever been done to actually implement it, so they resorted to standing on a street corner and screaming out the names of their soldiers over random spurts of drunken shooting and yelling.

The tram system was packed with bodies as people attempted to make their way towards the spaceport. Entire units stood in line waiting for the next tram to pull into the station. The line stretched hundreds of people back. Zinvor refused to wait in line and instead took the lead, pushing through the crowds like a living bulldozer.

They followed the flood of soldiers as they made their way to the spaceport. Soldiers walked, ran, and jumped aboard passing utility trucks. Zinvor stuck to the side of the road.

Unlike before, the spaceport was now under heavy guard. Groups of Elysian and Martian soldiers milled about at the entrance. They eyed people as they walked by and turned anyone who wasn't in uniform away. Huge crowds of civilians gathered at the entrance to see off their loved ones. Men and women carrying children hugged their spouses, not wanting to let go. Every once and a while one of them would make an argument as to why they should be able to walk their loved ones onto the spaceport itself. The guards were kind, but each request was rejected.

A woman in uniform pants and a tan shirt argued her case that she had never been issued a full uniform and therefore couldn't put it on, but the guards weren't hearing it. They saw Vincent approaching and stopped arguing with her, they saluted and one of them, an older Martian with a beard and a dark red jacket stepped forward to open the gate for him.

It was as if the entire population of the Quarter had moved into the spaceport. A sea of khaki and red covered the area where the giant *Olympus* had once been parked. Vincent had no idea how many soldiers were gathered there but it had to be the most he had ever seen. They sat in small groups, or lounged on their gear catching up on their sleep. Some took the chance to get in a game of cards, while others chatted with each other nervously.

Zinvor found the Marshals gathered in the port control building. Thankfully the Mawr had allowed the Rhai to build the short alloy spire that controlled everything entering or leaving the port. It meant it wouldn't collapse, but Vincent was mostly just happy because it meant it was climate controlled. He mopped the sweat and dust off of his face with his sleeve and breathed a sigh of relief.

"Nice of her to give us a warning." Aron said, speaking of the Warlord.

"You knew before I did, if it makes you feel any better." He said.

"It doesn't, but thanks." Vincent looked around and noticed both Erin and Ezra were both missing.

"Do Erin and Ezra plan on making the flight?"

"They are already up in the *Olympus.*" Aron said. "Ezra was paranoid that the ship wouldn't be ready for all of the soldiers to come aboard so they went into orbit a few hours ago."

"And is it?"

"Not even close." Aron laughed. "But we don't have much of a choice, do we?"

"I suppose not." Vincent sighed.

"We have too many soldiers and still not enough transport ships so we are going to have to ferry them up to the ship little by little. It could take hours."

"And how are we planning on assaulting Lunar City if it comes to that?"

"Well, if our great and glorious Warlord could have waited another few months the Martians could have given us enough ships to make a proper landing possible."

"Well, she didn't." Vincent said curtly. "Bitching about what we don't have won't get us anywhere."

"I've been talking with Erik." Vincent watched as a transport barge swooped down and landed. Its belly opened and soldiers began to load themselves into it by the hundreds. "We have an idea. But do you think Pharos' idea will work?"

"What?" Vincent raised an eyebrow. "Scare them into surrendering? I doubt it."

"I know if I was the commander of that garrison and I knew what was coming for me and the Committee told me to defend the city until the last man, I'd just shoot them."

"Probably the reason why Erik said no Martian soldiers ever got stationed there, huh?"

"A valid point." Aron nodded.

"You think we are looking at a Black Coat situation again?"

"Most likely. Normal people just want this to end. But the Committee was never propped up by the strength of normal people. We should make sure we are prepared for the worst."

"We've been preparing for the worst ever since we met each other, Aron. Why would we stop now?"

"Sir." Came the voice of one of Aron's staff, an older woman with gray, curly hair. "The *Olympus* has just informed me that the Consul's personal ship is on its way to pick him up."

"I have a personal ship?" Vincent asked. Prior to this campaign and his promotion to Marshal, Ezra had been his de facto personal pilot. It wasn't for any reason other than he had managed to keep the Black Coats from stealing his ship. The fact they wanted Ezra dead too only made it easier.

"Ezra must have forgotten to tell you." Aron motioned for him to look out the window. The strange form of the *Shanna II* peaked through the clouds. The ship was a Rhai creation from the remnants of various human crafts they had salvaged during the migration to Elysian. It had been gifted to Ezra after he wrecked his first ship fighting the Black Coats.

"I thought we destroyed that thing on Mars?" Vincent asked. The last time he saw the *Shanna II* it was little more than twisted wreckage on the outside of Victoria. Another casualty on their drive to kill that bastard Brusilov. The ship had served them well, but he assumed nobody would bother scraping it up from the rocks and slapping it back together.

"Oh, you did make no mistake." Aron laughed. "But as you can see the Martians never saw any military equipment as truly wrecked, just temporarily sidelined. Erik saw the ship about to be scrapped for parts and realized it was the ship that killed Brusilov.

He said it was a gift." Vincent thought that last bit was a stretch. Brusilov's ship had shot them out of the air and then they managed to return the favor through either luck or the expert piloting of Ezra, he still wasn't sure which.

"So, who is flying it?" The ship touched down in one of the few open spaces in front of the building. A few soldiers frantically dragged their belongings out of the way so they didn't get crushed. The cockpit depressurized and the gull wing doors slowly opened to reveal the rail thin form of Tyr. The Rhai Cadet had been loaned to Ezra has a part of his flight crew for their mission to Mars and had stuck with them all the way to the bitter end.

"Tyr?" Vincent asked. "I assumed Ezra would want to keep them for the *Olympus* crew."

"He wanted to." Aron confirmed. "It turns out, however, if you have a Rhai follow you with your promotions they don't consider it a sign of friendship or loyalty. They assumed they had failed Ezra's evaluation and would not be getting their own ship so Tyr requested to go back to the Rhai Cohort."

"Ezra was supposed to be evaluating them?" Vincent asked.

"Ezra asked the same thing." Aron shrugged. "Nobody ever told him. You know how the Rhai are obsessed with that sort of thing. Anyway, Ezra quickly backpedaled and offered Tyr the highest promotion he was authorized to give them and any position they wanted." Aron saw the look of confusion on Vincent's face. His unfamiliarity with his own military's rules and regulations never seemed to bother the former Sergeant Major. "Captain." Aron added helpfully. "Anything higher would have to be approved by the Union."

"And I assume Tyr wanted this position because my last pilot became Marshal of the entire fleet?"

"I would assume so."

"How pragmatic of them."

Tyr clambered out of the cockpit, as talented as a pilot as they were the were still about half the size of the species that the ship had been built for. They jumped down to the ground, a feat for a human that would have only required a simple step.

"I supposed I should go." Vincent said.

"Good luck, Sir." Aron smiled. "I'll see you up there."

Vincent and Zinvor exited back out onto the spaceport and were greeted by heat and dust, blown about in thick clouds by countless engines. Tyr straightened themselves and bowed slightly, the traditional Rhai show of respect. Though Tyr had been inducted into the Volunteers by accepting the rank of Captain they made no attempt to adopt human gestures or military traditions. It wasn't something that was expected of anyone and Vincent had seen a few humans render a bow rather than a salute to the hundreds of Rhai who had joined the Volunteers ever since the liberation of the Rhai home world.

That aside, the tailors clearly had a problem sewing such a small flight suit. The tan suit hung off Tyr's slight frame and looked about three times bigger than it should have been. He assumed the Volunteers were not used to sewing uniforms for someone who was the size of a human preteen.

Vincent returned the bow.

"Marshal Vorbeck is expecting you, Consul." Tyr said. Vincent nodded.

"After you, Captain Tyr." Tyr's faced screwed up onto itself for a moment, unsure of what he had just said.

"No, Consul. It must be after you as I am piloting the ship." Vincent rolled his eyes, forgetting for a moment that while many of the Rhai could become fluent in multiple languages, they could never quite pick up the correct nuances of speech.

"Sure, fine, whatever." Vincent sighed.

8

The usual empty, inky blackness of space above Elysian had transformed into a traffic jam that spanned as far as Vincent could see. Thousands of ships of various makes, sizes, and origins jockeyed around one another for space as they attempted to get into position. The *Shanna II* glided through it all. Ships quickly parted and made way for the Consul's ship. Others dipped their wings to the left and right in in a show of respect.

In front of them was the massive bulk of the *Olympus*. Smaller ships buzzed around it like a cloud of insects around food. Tyr brought the suddenly much smaller feeling *Shanna II* in line with the belly of the much larger destroyer. Hundreds of rows of berthing's were laid out in front of them, each with a segmented folding door emblazoned with yellow paint denoting the door's number.

"*Shanna II*" Came a voice over the radio. "You are authorized to proceed to berthing five eight four."

"Received." Tyr answered. The ship swung to the right and Tyr brought them to their corresponding berthing number. White clouds vented from the door as it purged the oxygen and it began to roll up. The *Shanna II* swung deftly through the door and before Tyr brought the ship down to land the door quickly rolled back down behind them. The ship touched down and rocked gently as it settled.

In front of them on the wall was a red light. It blinked slowly as air rushed back into the berthing, hissing so loudly Vincent could hear it inside of the ship. After a few moments the light switched to a solid green.

"It is now safe to disembark." Tyr said. Zinvor eyed the door with suspicion, sure that they would be sucked out into the vacuum of space if they left the ship. It still amazed Vincent that someone who had spent so many years of his life in space was still terrified of every step of the journey. Maybe it was this healthy fear that had kept him alive for so long and Vincent was just being irresponsible. Thankfully, that suspicion was relieved when a door below slid open and Felicity and Ezra entered the berthing. They were dressed in bulky overcoats and knitted caps pulled down just above their eyes. It looked like they had just come in from some kind of winter expedition.

Tyr opened the sliding troop compartment door with the flip of a switch and the air of the *Olympus* rushed in. The blast of air was frigid, colder than anything he had ever felt in his life. The cold cut straight through his uniform and down into his bones. His nose and fingers began to tingle before he exited the ship.

"You look cold." Ezra laughed. Vincent noticed ice had formed on the ceiling of the berthing and icicles crept down from the corner of the room. Ezra motioned for a soldier who was standing by the door. The soldier, dressed the same way as Ezra and Felicity, walked forward and presented Vincent with a red overcoat and cap of his own. Vincent quickly put them on. They smelled old and musty, like they had been left in a locker for way too long and then forgotten about until a few minutes ago. One shoulder of the jacket had the outline of a Martian flag that had been hastily cut off and replaced by an Elysian one by an inexperienced hand.

"Erik wasn't kidding about the cold was he?" Vincent said, his voice shaking.

"There is a good reason why he isn't here."

"How is everyone handling it?"

"The cold?" Ezra raised an eyebrow. "Terribly. Erik did his best to supply us with these jackets but there isn't enough to go around." The group exited the berthing into one of the hallways of the ship. Ice clung to the walls and small bits of gravel had been poured on the ground in order to give foot traffic some kind of traction on the iced over walkways. Human ships were always grimy and unadorned. They were never built for comfort because in space any little extra thing added extra stress to something so precise that if even the smallest of those millions of systems failed they were all likely to die a horrible death out in the vacuum of space. Even the Titanian flagship the *TSS Denta* was a cold, grey, and unadorned piece of engineering. Even so, the *Olympus* was by far the ugliest ship Vincent had ever laid eyes on.

Rather than dull and gunmetal grey like the inside of most ships, the *Olympus* was a patch work of browns, blacks, and greys. Rust had eaten away at every corner and every door. The patches of corrosion had been hastily repaired with a silicon paste which had been smeared all over with reckless abandon. In some places large sections of decking had obviously been cut away and then been replaced with other scavenged pieces of metal. They too had been slathered with the paste, sealing it all together. The cutting and sealing of the scrap metal had been done haphazardly and things did not always fit into place. This left jagged edges of metal at various places perfect for snagging stray uniforms or skin. Vincent suddenly thought about how much more likely he was to get tetanus from rounding a corner too fast than he was anything else.

"Oh." Ezra said. "Make sure you don't touch anything metal with your bare skin or a medic will have to come and rip them off. We already got an infirmary full of people who are missing chunks of their hands." Vincent stuffed his hands into his pockets as a precaution.

"Are we doing anything to fix this?"

"What can we do?" Ezra shrugged. "I already sent word to the Unions that we need more jackets, more hats, more everything. They are doing their best but by my estimates there is no way we will have enough to go around by the time we leave."

"What about extra uniforms?" He asked. "They have to have a stockpile of them laying around somewhere. People can at least put on a few layers."

"I already did that." Felicity said. "It helped, but not as much as we hoped." Ezra glanced sideways at her.

"I wasn't aware that was something a Captain could do."

"It isn't." Felicity admitted. "Wasn't the first time I forged the Consul's name on an order. Won't be the last."

"People forging my name on things is something of an unofficial policy by this point." As they rounded the corner of the hallway Vincent noticed an acrid scent in the air and the walls and ceiling of the ship had been stained with a black coating of something. "Was there some kind of fire?"

"You could say that." Felicity said.

"The soldiers have been tearing up everything that isn't nailed down and burning it to stay warm. It has been playing havoc with the air filtration system. I'm assuming the Martians replaced the old system with something that was already substandard so thousands of people burning wood pallets they looted from the storage bays is overtaxing it a bit to say the least."

"I can hardly blame them." Vincent sighed. "We locked them in a giant refrigerator."

"I understand their plight, Consul." Ezra coughed waving away some of the smoke with his hand. "But our military operation against the Committee will be much harder if we all choke to death on smoke or carbon dioxide before we even get there. I've ordered the Public Order Officers to arrest them and throw them in the brig. But now the brig is full and I don't know what else to do."

"At least their body heat will keep each other warm in there." Felicity said. Ezra ignored her.

"How is the Volunteer's supply system so busted?" Vincent groaned, not asking anyone in particular. Ezra had led them further into the ship. Soldiers wrapped in various bits of cloth and layers of uniforms walked by them alongside ship crew who were swaddled in the same thick red coats that he had been given. They walked into the bridge. Soldiers of various race and species shot to their feet.

"Marshal on deck!" Announced a voice. Ezra motioned for them to go back to work with a wave of his hand.

"I might have an idea about that." Felicity said.

"An idea about what?" Vincent asked.

"The supply problem."

"Oh right." He said. "Shoot."

"Look around here, what do you see?" Vincent glanced around the bridge. The fleet crew were wearing several layers of clothing but each also wore a thick coat, much like his own that Ezra had given him along with the hat. He noticed none of the black smoke that had stained the hallways had made it into the bridge, despite it being as cold as everywhere else. They had to have been as cold as everyone else but it wasn't unbearable enough for them to start setting fires to stay warm like the others had.

The soldiers in the hallway that they had seen were wearing everything they could get their hands on and even with the extra uniforms given to them it wasn't enough. It was clear to him that the fleet was much better supplied than the army was.

"How did the fleet get so much more stuff than the army?"

"That is just the way the supply systems work." Felicity said. "The Marshals all have control over their own supply systems. Marshal Vorbeck's fleet crew had access to the Martian supplies that they had brought with them before anyone else so they stocked up. Marshal Victoria had no such luck, so the soldiers are suffering. Though, in Victoria's defense he is doing his best with what he has, but what he has isn't a lot."

"How the hell did each branch end up fending for itself?" Vincent asked. "Why didn't anyone point this out?"

"We never saw the problem." Ezra shrugged. "We're doing fine all things considered." Felicity rolled her eyes at him.

"And Aron?"

"He is an old Sergeant Major, when was the last time he ever heard of someone of that rank admitting they needed help?" Felicity frowned.

"Okay, fine." Vincent sighed. "We need to centralize this so people stop setting the goddamn ship on fire trying not to freeze to death." He rubbed his face, his exposed cheeks burned from the cold.

"Well, Sir." Ezra said, handing him a display. "Before you magically fix all of our supply woes, the Warlord sent a dispatch, she wants to speak to you."

"What?" He asked. "We haven't even left yet."

"We will be soon, but it does say to contact her immediately from a secure location. You can use my office." Ezra led him through the bridge to a back room. He pressed his hand to the door lock and after a moment something clicked and the door opened. Inside was a cramped office with a tattered green cot laid out next to a metal desk. Like most furniture aboard it was bolted to the floor.

"You're sleeping in here?" Vincent asked.

"I left the Captain's Quarters to you and Fiona." He said. Vincent opened his mouth to object but Ezra put a hand up. "Before you say anything I prefer to be near the bridge while we are under way. And I don't think I am going to be entertaining any women during our trip, you'll need the bed more than I will."

"Thanks, I guess." Ezra nodded and handed him the display.

"This is an encrypted line, I'll be right outside if you need me." He said and exited the room. The display pinged and a small green light flashed at the corner of it. Vincent clicked the light and after a moment the screen flashed, revealing the face of Arai. She was sitting with Pharos behind her desk, back on the planet's surface.

"Consul." Arai said. Their connection was garbled, but he could understand her well enough. "I am sure you have many questions."

"A few." He answered flatly

"Rushing your invasion force off of the planet was a tactical decision." Pharos said, their voice a dull hiss.

"So much so that I couldn't have been given a heads up?"

"Yes." They nodded. "It is regarding the Anarchs."

"What do the Anarchs have to do with Lunar City?"

"Nothing." Pharos shook their head.

"I am not following you."

"We are currently in our final planning stages to bring about the end of our war with the Anarchs. However, those plans were in danger of being discovered as long as the Martians remained on the planet. As you can imagine telling the Commander of Mars to leave Elysian with no good excuse would be something of a diplomatic mess. So, we pushed our invasion plans forward in order to send all of you off world as soon as possible."

"Why do you think the Martians are spying on us?"

"The same reason we are spying on them. Alliances are not forever, Consul. It is nothing personal, just the way things are. Always will be."

"and you think Erik would tell the Anarchs your plan?"

"No, not on purpose." Pharos said. "Should the Martians discover our plan it could leak to the Anarchs and all would be lost. Need I remind you that the Anarchs have already shown themselves capable of cracking EDF encryption. We are operating under the assumption they have already done so with the Martians, their technology is not far off after all. All it would take is one Martian spy transmitting even partial intelligence and the Anarchs could become suspicious."

"And what plan would that be anyway? Or is that too secret for me to know now too?"

"I must ask Consul, you have fought the Anarchs have you not?"

"Of course. You know I have."

"Have you ever seen them act, independently? As a human, Rhai, or Mawr would?"

"Pharos, in all due respect we have long established I am not as smart as you and can't keep up with most of the conversations we have together. So, can you save us all some time and can you just tell me what you're thinking?" Pharos snorted.

"We have been fighting the Anarchs for years, Consul. Maybe longer than you have been alive." Arai said. "During that time, I or any other Warrior has never seen an Anarch act with independent thought. They move in groups, fight in groups, and die in groups."

"Do you remember the Anarch known as the Red King?" Pharos asked. Vincent shuttered at the thought of the giant armored monster that he had fought on two occasions. For many of his friends the Anarch leader was one of the last things they would ever see. "Anarchs such as those we have dubbed Cluster Leaders. We have discovered that these Cluster Leaders control hundreds of not thousands of soldiers directly."

"Directly?"

"They have direct control over all of their minds, simultaneously. Hence when the Red King was killed, their forces fell into disarray. The entire Anarch society is structured the same way, but on a larger scale. Cluster Leaders to larger Cluster Leaders, all the way back to the Anarch home world itself. We believe that at the very end of all of this is a single Anarch hive mind that controls everything."

"You have got to be kidding me." Vincent said. "Then who did the Rhai and other Mawr Clans surrender to? Why did they form the Alliance?"

"The same reason anyone forms an Alliance, Consul. Self-preservation. As for the surrenders, we cannot be sure as none of us were alive when they took place. Our research show is that not a single representative of the Anarchs was present during these surrenders. It was simply a message: join us or be destroyed, followed by the terms of their subjugation." Pharos said.

"So what are they?"

"Are you alone right now?" Pharos asked, their voice dropping to a hush.

"Yes, of course."

"Not even your bodyguard is in the room with you?"

"No." He said, becoming impatient.

"We know this because as you know we recently liberated the Rhai home world. This gave us a treasure trove of information that has been lost to us for generations. Information that told of us of the origins of the Anarchs."

"Their origins?"

"They aren't like us." Pharos said. For the first time Vincent had ever remembered, they looked deeply uncomfortable. "They are a false specie. Built as a weapon of war by the Rhai."

"What?" Vincent yelled. "What the hell do you mean they are a weapon? Why would you make a living weapon?"

"Much like we do not hold you accountable for the crimes of the Committee I ask you not to hold me accountable for the crimes of my forebearers." Vincent sighed.

"You're right, I'm sorry. But why would they have done that?"

"It was not long ago that Rhai and Mawr were not friends." Arai said. "Rather than the Anarchs it was my ancestors who were expanding across the stars. The Rhai were desperate for an answer to the Clan's armies. Knowing they couldn't do it with their own formations they built new soldiers who could."

"But they lost control?"

"Well, they made a perfect weapon." Pharos said. "One that doesn't require maintenance, training, or organization. It was built to do all of that itself with limited oversight. At least that is what we have learned so far. Our research still continues and will for some time. We have years of data to scour before we will find the data we are looking for. Though, with as large a team as my Cohort working on it, it shouldn't take that long."

"Shouldn't Erik know this? This doesn't seem like something we should leave him in the dark on."

"Matters of ancient Rhai biological weapon development are not what we are keeping from the Commander, Consul. It is what we plan on doing next." Arai said, folding her hands on her desk. Pharos touched a display on the desk and the glowing outline of an unintelligible engineering schematic appeared on the screen.

"Over the last several months my and several other Cohorts have been working in secret. We plan on harnessing Elysian's dark energy power grid to fuel a particle beam weapon that should be able to destroy the Anarch home world and thus killing the hivemind and destroying all abilities of the Anarch to reproduce themselves."

"Isn't that exactly what they did to you?" Vincent gasped an Arai. "We fought an entire campaign on Grawluck to make sure those weapons wouldn't fall into the wrong hands!"

"We are not the wrong hands, Consul." Arai grumbled.

"I bet the Chairman thought the same thing." Vincent shot back. Pharos cut in, trying to play the always respectful mediator.

"We can hardly make peace with a hivemind, Consul. And unless you want to invade the Anarch home world and fight every single last one of them to the death and then tear out their manufacturing systems by hand, there is no other way to end this war."

"This war only ends with one of us being wiped from the universe." Arai said, her voice calming. "And I have no intention on that being my Clan." Vincent wanted to say something, but stopped himself.

"How sure are you about this?" He asked.

"As sure as we can be. After their setback on Grawluck it has taken them some time to rebuild their old capabilities. I am afraid if we do not beat them to it, Mars and Elysian will meet the same fate as Earth." Pharos said confidently. Vincent sighed, he had hardly known Pharos to ever be wrong about anything. He had no room to argue about their plan. He wasn't actually sure if it was within his power to argue with them even if there was.

"Erik and the others are going to ask questions. What should I tell them?"

"Speak of this only to the Marshals, and no one else. As for the Commander we have fed him a cover story about planning for an invasion. They are making the plans for it as we speak."

"So, you lied to them?"

"That is an unkind thing to say. The concept of a lie is a dishonorable thing to humans, we intend no dishonor." Pharos balked. "Consider it a contingency plan. A contingency plan that keeps them busy enough to not figure out what we are doing."

"That sounds like a lie with extra steps."

"Call it whatever you like then, Consul." Pharos snapped. "But, even knowing all of this, your plans have not changed. So, do not worry yourself about it too much." Vincent bit his lip. Yeah, he thought let me just not worry about the fact that you just informed me that the entire Anarch Army was built by the goddamn Rhai and oh yeah, is one giant hivemind like a bad sci fi film. Also you're wiring our entire planet into a doomsday weapon and lying to everyone about it. And by the way, good luck invading the goddamned Moon.

He sighed.

"Got it. Zero worrying going on here."

"Good." Pharos said, totally missing Vincent's sarcasm. "That is all for now Consul, good luck on your mission."

9

Vincent was seated in one of the *Olympus'* cramped mess halls. The ship was originally designed for only one such hall, but the Martian expansion of the ship brought three more. Unfortunately, that did not leave them with much space to work. The tables were so close to one another that as he ate he could feel the person to his left, right, and rear moving. When one person came in or went an entire row of diners had to stand up to make room for them to squeeze by.

The close quarters dinning allowed Vincent to feel like a normal person for a few seconds. He had tried to rejected every sign of respect the Union or the people had given him, but it never did any good. People bowed or saluted whenever he talked by, people gave him things for free, and he heard one couple even named their child after him. Felicity insisted it was because people actually respected him, a concept that was still just too weird for him.

Now, everyone was so cramped together none of that matter. People were still shy about starting a conversation with him but he was at least able to sit in and absorb one of the finest things about military living: the rumor mill. While he ate his thick soup made of mostly a cubed cultivated protein product that reminded him faintly of pork, he just sat and listened taking it all in.

He heard about the possibility that two particular Sergeants had finally hooked up, an idea that everyone seemed to think was hilarious because everyone had thought they hated each other. Someone opined that the hate was all a cover for their hidden liaisons. A soldier wondered loudly if his girlfriend was pregnant and if their Squad Leader found out if she would be sent back to Elysian. Another soldier was worried that his husband was cheating on him while he was deployed.

Vincent would do this three times a day every day as a form of relaxation. During one of those times, that quickly changed. They had been in orbit for three days when a warning sounded throughout the ship. There had once been an actual system of visible warnings lights that would have flashed but those had long since been broken or otherwise stolen. Instead, a woman's voice came over the ship wide intercom.

"Unauthorized ship in berthing number two eighty-eight. Quick reaction force report to berthing area." It then repeated itself over and over again in the same strangely calm voice. All around him soldiers quickly slurped down the last of their meal as reach row of seating carefully stood up to make room for the other so they could run out of the room, rifles in hand.

Vincent helped himself to the remains of a bowl that had been left abandoned and chased off after the soldiers. Public Order Officers had crowded into the hallway to meet with the soldiers. The wave of human movement rushed through the hallways down towards the berthing docks. The soldiers fanned out to secure the hundreds of docks while the Public Order Officers pushed forward to the berthing in question, Vincent followed them.

He pushed his way through the crowds of people until he saw the stenciled numbers *Two eighty-eight* above a door. Outside of it Public Order Officers were gathering. Normally they were unarmed, carrying only a baton and restraints of some kind. These Officers wore soldier's body armor and helmets and held carbines in their hands. On their left shoulders they wore patch that read *Quick Reaction Force*.

A tired looking Sergeant with pale skin and dark hair was screaming for the other soldiers to get back when she saw Vincent approaching.

"Sir?" She asked. "You don't need to be here. We can handle this."

"Sorry, I was curious. What's going on?"

"A ship without a locator beacon docked in the berthing, we have no idea who it is or how they managed to get in. Could be a ship that wasn't equipped with one, we know about the shortages, but it could be something much worse. We can't be too sure." Vincent was going to say something but another one of the Officers, a Titanian man who was looking through the small berthing window called out.

"Someone is getting out of the ship, Sergeant!" The Sergeant bit her lip and went over to the window, screaming.

"This is Sergeant Baskerville of the Elysian Public Order Quick Reaction Force! Identify yourself or we will purge the berthing into void!"

"Hey!" Called the person from inside the berthing. "How about I purge your ass with my foot!" Vincent immediately recognized the voice.

"Sergeant." Vincent sighed. Baskerville turned from the window to look at him.

"Yes, Consul?"

"You can stand down, that's my wife."

10

"Miss me?" Fiona grinned. She was wearing a thick, blue winter jacket with its hood drawn over her head. The pants she had on were so thick with warm padding that her gun belt hardly fit over them. She and another Martian were offloading boxes from a ship that Vincent had never seen before. He noticed its tail registration number had been painted over and it had no running lights. He wasn't very savvy on the ins and outs of legal trade in the universe, but he knew a smuggling ship when he saw one.

"I'd ask where you've been that seems kind of obvious." He said.

"Someone has gotta do your Marshal's jobs eh?" She said, pulling out a pack of cigarettes from her pocket and lighting one. He noticed it was a Titanian brand. He hadn't seen one of those on Elysian in some time. It wasn't a quality thing. Titanian customs agents were the hardest ones to bribe so the various groups of smugglers went with the much easier route to get Martian brands.

"What do you mean?"

"What do you mean, what do I mean?" She scoffed. "Did you think I was just smuggling porn, booze, and smokes in here?"

"To be completely honest, yes."

"Well, some of it is." She shrugged. "But we heard about what was going on and got our hands on some coats and hats for the poor bastards that got put on this flying tub of shit."

"Where the hell did you find those? I thought we had already picked everything clean?"

"Sure, we depleted the official stocks. But you ignored all of the middlemen. Warehouse people, random tailors, and officers that squirreled some of them away. You'd be surprised at what people horde in a pitch. Every level of logistics something moves through a little bit leaks out."

"And these people just gave it to you?" Fiona laughed and the rest of her strange crew joined her. She shot them a look and they quickly got back to work.

"Oh honey, what is it you think I do?"

"Ugh." He sighed. "You didn't kill anyone did you?"

"No. Though some had to be *persuaded*." The emphasis she put on the word persuaded made him not want to pry further. "Hey!" She snapped at one of her crew. "Drop that box and I'll throw you out of the airlock!"

"Uh, Sir?" Came a voice behind him. Vincent had forgotten the Public Order's Quick Reaction Force had stopped from venting the berthing into space only because he had asked them kindly not kill his wife. Baskerville stood there, impatiently. It was obvious she did not enjoy having anyone, even the Consul, step on her toes while she was trying to work.

"They're fine, let them in."

"Are you sure? I'm pretty sure they are smugglers."

"Someone give that one an award." Fiona laughed. "An absolute fucking genius." Baskerville bit her lip, probably thinking it would be bad if she told the Consul's wife to shut up. Vincent would have hardly blamed her if she did.

"No, they're good. They are under my office."

"Even that one?" Baskerville asked, pointing. He glanced over to see one of Fiona's smugglers frantically repacking a box that had been knocked over vomiting pornography magazines all over the ground. Vincent groaned.

"Yeah. Those are for the uh morale of the soldiers."

"Right." Baskerville frowned.

"You're reporting this to the Unions, aren't you?" Vincent asked her.

"Oh, yes." She scowled before turning and marching out of the berthing.

"That is what you get for hiring cops that aren't corrupt." Fiona said. "Those bastards are as hard to bribe as Titanian ones."

"Going to pretend I didn't hear that you're bribing the cops." He said, pinching his forehead.

"I said I *tried*, That is different."

Vincent thought about momentarily letting Baskerville put him in restraints and deliver him to the front of the Union right then and there. and there but the appearance of Felicity in the doorway stopped him. He waited to hear her explode on him for allowing Fiona to openly break the law in front of half of the population of the *Olympus* but the look plastered across her face wasn't scolding or admonishment. It was as if something incredible had just dawned on her.

"Go ahead." He said. "Let me have it."

"No. wait." She held up a finger. "Fiona, where did you get this stuff."

"Nice try, cop." Fiona screwed her face up at Felicity. She held her hands up.

"You're right, fine. Could you do it again? I mean can you keep finding stuff like this?" Fiona looked at her like she had been personally offended.

"I could do this every day. I ain't never seen a blockade, cop, or custom agent that could stop me. Titanian, Earthian, Martian, or Elysian."

"Consul, I have an idea." Felicity said.

"About?"

"Our supply problem." Felicity's eyes began to glow in the way they did when she was working her way through a problem. "The Fleet and the Army aren't working together on the supply issue. Victoria is too proud to say he needs help and Ezra doesn't see the problem because the fleet is doing just fine, right?" He knew she wasn't actually asking him for his input, so he kept his mouth shut. "So, what if we put someone in charge of all of the Volunteers supplies. Someone neutral that wasn't part of any branch. And most importantly someone who didn't take shit from anyone whenever they tried to do their job."

"You mean Fiona." Vincent said.

"You mean me?" Fiona gasped, nearly swallowing her cigarette.

"I know it sounds crazy but hear me out. Nobody would enjoy taking shit away from the good old boys and officers who managed to horde stuff away more than Fiona. She would never cozy up to any of them. I don't even think their bribes would be worth it to her. The feeling of shaking down the bastards would be worth more to her than any actual money."

"I might not like this one, but I can't lie, she knows me." Fiona shrugged.

"You want me to make Fiona the head of all logistics and supplies for the entire military?" Vincent asked, incredulous.

"Why not? You're the one that is always saying she can get her hands on anything. She has more experience doing that than you did as a leader before you became Consul. Give her a shot. What is the worst thing that happens? We get locked inside of a half dead space fridge, freezing to death in the middle of the void?" Vincent held up his hands.

"Okay, okay! So, what do I do, just appoint her?"

"Well, it would have to be a position that would force others to listen to her." Felicity pinched her chin.

"You mean Marshal. You want me to be a fuck'n *Marshal*?" Fiona spat, not holding back laughter. "I hardly graduated basic training and you want me to be a fuck'n Marshal."

"She has a point." Vincent agreed. "Nobody could say no to a Marshal other than me or the Unions.

"She wouldn't be a military commander like Aron or Ezra. Marshal of the Commissary or something, the title is a work in progress. And before you say anything nobody can accuse you of nepotism because a Marshal can only be appointed by a Union vote."

"I can't believe this is happening but go ahead and send them the request." Felicity saluted and walked away. "Are you sure you want to do this?" Fiona cackled.

"You're asking me if I want to steal from uppity officers and rich people for a living? I was born for this. Let me pick my own crew and you got a deal."

"Deal."

"When do I start?"

"You already did." He gestured at all of the boxes in the berthing. "Keep up the good work." Fiona gave a limp wristed, sarcastic salute.

"You got it, Boss."

The Union vote was a swift one. It turned out that Fiona's smuggling skills were already well known throughout the Quarter and Vincent had just been left in the dark the whole time. He wasn't sure if she had dirt or bribes on any of them, but the vote was nearly unanimous. He had heard through the rumor mill that the only union whose votes she did not get was the distillers and brewers. They had not questioned her ability for the job, but instead because she may have been too good at it. Due to her rampant smuggling of alcohol, their bottom line had been impacted for months.

The only outcry came from officers. Vincent had long ago established an open door policy so anyone, military, civilian, or otherwise could walk into his office and talk to him. This was almost always used for complaining about things he had no intention or ability to fix. People generally just felt better after yelling at him for a while, he became the communal blow off valve and he was happy to let people vent. After Fiona's promotion to Marshal of the Commissary, he wished he didn't have the rule at all.

Officer after officer walked into his office and screamed at him about how they deserved the promotion over Fiona. More than once Zinvor simply got tired of their yelling and physically removed them from the room, throwing them out into the hallway outside. After a few days the complaints began to die down.

Not because Fiona's promotion ceremony was attended by nearly every single person on the ship or because the thousands of soldiers in attendance cheered so loud for the woman who had saved them from eventually burning their own uniforms off of their backs for warmth. He had heard a rumor that all of the bad mouthing of Marshal Olympus-Solaris finally ended because a Colonel got stabbed for daring to do so in front of his soldiers. The Colonel lived and the soldier was transferred to Fiona's detachment, without charge.

With the supply system centralized and under Fiona's control the berthings turned into a never-ending traffic jam of incoming ships. They were emblazoned with symbols showing Martian, Elysian, Titanian, and Clan craft each of them offloading huge amounts of supplies. Vincent or anyone else in charge had any idea how she managed to pull it off, but in accordance with her agreement with the Marshals, the Union, and Vincent nobody asked either. Things were going so well that Vincent nearly forgot that they were slowly lurching their way towards an invasion of the Moon. Until the Committee found them.

Vincent was in his office on a call with a Union member when the ship shook.

"Attention, attention. what follows is an address by your Captain." Came the calm, robotic voice over the ship's intercom. The voice switched from the computerized prerecorded voice of the *Olympus* to that of Ezra.

"This is Marshal Vorbeck, we have made contact with the Committee fleet. All crew report to their battle stations. Army personnel shelter in place. This is not a drill." Vincent leapt from his desk and took off running down the passageway. The hallways were deserted, as he lived near the Volunteer Army billets nobody would be going anywhere. Out of each door the curious faces of soldiers peered out watching Vincent and Zinvor sprint by, the Mawr struggling to keep up.

The ship shook again and the overhead lights flickered like they might short out. He lost his footing, tripped over a bulkhead and went headfirst into the floor. His face smacked off the metal and he could have sworn his augmetic eye went fuzzy with the impact. Blood trickled down his face and he was finally pulled back to his feet by Zinvor. The shaking of the ship continued, now without break. Lights swung back and forth and fluid leaks burst out from the pipes that lined the walls and ceiling, raining a thick green slime down onto everything.

Vincent had been locked in the bowels of a Capitol ship during battle while on the *Victory*. He and his fellow soldiers sat, trapped, helpless in their billets as the ship rolled and shook like it was about to be torn into pieces. While all of that was going on, he assumed the crew of the ship were frantically running around in a haze of chaos with a thousand people all trying to do different things at the same time. Like he had experienced during his time fighting wars on the surface with his two feet securely on the ground. That was not what he saw when he entered the bridge.

Ezra was standing at his command position, staring out of the viewing port that took up the entire front of the bridge. Computer reticles in orange, red, and blue danced all over like a laser light show. Long lists of numbers scrolled up each side of the window as the reticles moved. Throughout the bridge the crew was focused on the computer panels in front of them, too engrossed in deciphering the vast quantities of data that was being fed to them via their displays to speak to one another. They all knew exactly what had to be done, no further communication was needed.

A fireball bloomed out in front of them, momentarily flashing brilliant light through the darkness of space. The ship shook violently as they were rocked by the blast wave.

"Scanner!" Ezra called. "Give me a reading on how many enemies we have coming at us!"

"Yes, Sir!" answered a voice.

"Update on the rest of the fleet."

"Sir, Martian Command is reporting minimal losses."

"And us?"

"We have lost contact with Barge *I-657* and *I-876*."

"Damnit." Ezra fumed. "Where are our interceptors?"

"Second and third squadrons are deploying now, Sir. The first squadron is landing to rearm. No reports on losses yet." Vincent watched as hundreds of Martian built Reaper copies zipped past the viewing port.

"Sir, scanners are confirming at least five-hundred enemy fighters and torpedo bombers."

"Where the hell did a force so big come from?" Ezra demanded. The scanner operator fiddled with their display screen for a moment and turned back to him.

"It looks like they were deployed from a carrier destroyer, like us. The location of the enemy destroyer is being forwarded to your command display." Ezra glanced down at the display and grimaced.

"No, it's not like us. If it was like us this wouldn't be such a fucking problem, would it? It is bigger, faster, and stronger than us in every way. We are probably already in their main battery's effective range."

"Y-yes, Sir."

"Move the *Olympus* to intercept. Ready every weapon we have."

"Sir, didn't you just say the ship is stronger than us in every way possible?"

"We can't hope to win a duel at this range with a modern

destroyer and we are way too slow to outrun them. But if we bring them in close to us, maybe all of these guns that Erik slapped on this heap can overwhelm their defenses. Now, do it before they put a missile up our ass!"

"Yes, sir!" Ezra looked over his shoulder and saw Vincent. "Consul, Sir. You might want to have a seat." Vincent was going to object until he saw another Reaper explode out of the void in front of them. The *Olympus* charged forward through the debris field in front of them that grown to cover the entire horizon. "Direct all power from non-defensive and life support systems to the engines. If we can't get this bucket of bolts in front of them, we are as good as dead."

The ever-present hum of the ship's powerplant rapidly shifted to a rumble. The lights flickered and went out, leaving only the illuminated keys of the ship's control displays. The *Olympus* shook as if someone had grabbed it in their hands and throttled it like a child's plaything.

"Engine temperature rising, Sir."

"Ignore it." Ezra ordered. A barge hit by an enemy weapon, limped by. Even though it was still moving, it was clear it was dead as flames could be seen licking out of its cockpit as it drifted out of sight. A dull thump signaled its fuel reserves cooking off.

"Missiles incoming!" called out a voice. In front of them twisting streams of blue fire could be seen cutting through the dogfights and debris. A sharp crack filled the cockpit and in front of them a cloud of shining metal was emitted by the *Olympus,* covering the giant ship like a snowstorm. The incoming missiles spiraled off course into the storm of metal and exploded harmlessly.

"Good job with those countermeasures." Ezra said. Before the crew could congratulate themselves another missile streaked through the metal chaff and exploded somewhere along the bulk of the *Olympus*. The ship shuddered and groaned from the violent impact. The few remaining lights in the bridge flickered and several didn't come back on.

"Shit!" Ezra cursed. "They're hitting us with a rolling attack so they can bracket our countermeasures! Get that chaff reloaded and get me a damage report."

"The water purification system is offline." Said a crewmember.

"And sewage treatment." Added another. "Chaff has been reloaded." Just as the words left the crew person's mouth a missile streaked by the bridge's viewing port, a near miss. Another struck its target. The ship lurched and crew were thrown from their chairs.

"Damnit get back to your stations, we are still in this!" Ezra demanded. Smoke began to fill the bridge. The dull hum of purging fans kicked on and slowly the air began to clear.

"Systems are reporting multiple fires on the berthing deck!"

"We are losing hydraulic pressure, it looks like we are rapidly losing fluid in the starboard reservoir."

"Damage to the main weapons storage bay!" The panic in the crew had quickly begun to set in as their systems displays lit up with various warnings from throughout the ship. Vincent didn't have to understand what the warning lights meant when the sheer number of them was enough to alert him of the seriousness of the situation. Among it all Ezra remained the calm center of the bridge as the madness swirled around him. The only hint of any emotion at all was the almost unceasing tightening of his jaw.

"Sir! I recommend venting the berthings before the fire spreads!" suggested someone.

"No, you damned idiot. They are full of hanger crews for our interceptors. If we lose the ability to rearm them, we are as good as dead. Get fire crews over there and put them to work. And get the emergency repair teams on that fluid leak before it kills us. Which weapons bay was hit?"

"Main weapons storage." A crewman said, checking their display. "It has the ammunition for rearming the *Olympus'* main battery."

"Vent that crap into orbit before it cooks off." He ordered.

"Won't we need that?" Vincent asked.

"Not for what we are doing." Ezra said. "We will only have one chance to get in their face. If that doesn't work, it isn't going to be a lack of ammunition will be our most pressing issue."

"What would be the most of our worries, hypothetically?"

"Trying to breathe as the ship explodes and you're thrown into the vacuum of space I would assume, Consul."

"Noted."

The *Olympus* pressed head through the expanding field of wreckage and the EDF Destroyer came into view. Its massive bulk spanned the entire width of the viewing port. Thousands of bright flashes snapped over and over again along its broadside, like the muzzle flash of a machine gun.

"Incoming enemy missile!" screamed a voice from the crew. "Hundreds of them!"

"Prepare countermeasures!" Ezra shouted. He wasn't yelling out of anger, but instead he was using a booming command voice that let his crew know the seriousness of the situation. Another protective cloud of metal was fired into space. The enemy missiles ruptured and exploded, the rippling fireball quickly expanding across the entirety of the bridge's viewing port.

A hailstorm of debris slammed into the viewing port and dozens of small cracks formed. The *Olympus'* powerplant struggled, moaned, and coughed as it put out every bit of power it could to keep the massive ship going. "We have another close call like that one and our corpses will be adding to the debris field, understand?"

"Yes, Marshal!" The bridge crew responded in shaken voices.

"Gunnery Officer, give me a status on the weapons."

"At our current speed main, secondary, and tertiary batteries will be in range in three minutes." Called out a voice. Vincent tried not to think about how much could happen in three minutes.

"Incoming!" cried a crewmember. Another thump and another cloud of chaff was deployed. A curtain of flame spread across the length of the ship as more missiles exploded against the defenses.

"Marshal, that was the last of the countermeasures! We're all out!"

"Shit, weapon status!" Ezra ordered.

"ninety seconds!"

Vincent tried to focus on the enemy destroyer, trying in vain to see if it was firing on them again. His eyes were instead drawn to the hundreds and thousands of individual dogfights playing out in front of him as Martian and Elysian pilots fought off their EDF counterparts. Every few seconds another one of them would explode, adding to the debris field. From as far away as he was, there was no telling who was who or who was winning.

"Enemy weapons have locked onto us again, Sir!"

"Weapons are within range, Marshal!"

"Firing positions!" Ezra commanded. "We are about to find out if Erik's theory was right." The ship turned, lining it up with the bridge of the enemy ship. "Fire!" the *Olympus* rocked as if it had been hit again. Streaks of fire arced out from dozens of different weapon systems arrayed across the ship. Some exploded early as the enemy deployed their countermeasures. But the destroyer didn't have nearly enough defensive weaponry to stop them all at such a close range.

The enemy ship's bridge exploded, vomiting fire outwards into the void of space. Vincent remembered watching bad war films with his dad growing up and when the good guys landed a direct hit the whole ship always went up like it had been built out of the most combustible substance known to man. This one didn't. It just kind of sputtered and died in orbit. Its running lights flickered and went out and soon all defensive fire from the ship trickled to nothingness. This time lapse probably matched with the amount of time it took for the people who were manning the weapons to either be sucked out into the void or drop whatever they were doing and trying to find a way off of the ship.

The bridge of the *Olympus* was eerily silent as they watched the enemy go dark. Escape pods launched out at random intervals from the ship's underbelly. Soon, the dogfighting ceased and what remained of the Committee fleet began their withdrawal back towards Lunar City. Ezra broke the silence by throwing his hands in the air and screaming.

"We did it!" The rest of the crew likewise erupted with emotion, leaving their stations to hug one another. Vincent pulled himself from his seat, his legs shaking like they were unsure if they were still alive or not. Ezra left his command station and hugged him.

"I didn't think Erik's plan would work, but it did."

"His plan?"

"His overwhelming firepower idea. He knew this tub of shit was never going to win a maneuver battle against an enemy ship, so he outfitted it with so many weapons that it could blow through the normal amount of counter measures a ship would carry. When we scanned the destroyer and I saw it was the *ESS Fate* I knew we could win if we got close enough."

"You knew the ship?"

"It was my second duty ship. A decent little ship." He glanced out the window. "or at least it was. But it wasn't made for this kind of battle, it was an escort model made for fighting off enemy raiding ships or park above a safe planet and deploy bombers to the surface, not slug it out with another destroyer, even one as old as this one. There was no way it had enough countermeasures to stop a full close-range broadside from everything Erik strapped onto this monstrosity. We just had to get close enough for it to work."

"And if they fired on us again?"

"We already expended all of our chaff so we would have eaten the full barrage. We would be doing the escape pod shuffle like we just saw our friends out there doing. In the end it just came down to timing. This time it was on our side." Ezra said, shrugging off the fact that they had very nearly all died only seconds before. "That is why we maneuvered in front of them like we did. They had fewer weapons facing straight ahead, so I took a chance on it. They were probably hoping springing an ambush on us like they did would force us to slow our advance, pull back, and regroup. They didn't expect this giant bucket of rust to charge right at them." Ezra laughed.

"You played chicken with spaceships?" Vincent asked, incredulously. Ezra grinned.

"In war we tend to call that a frontal assault." Vincent watched as Reapers and scout craft flew in formation around the *Olympus*. Making sure the Committee fleet didn't leave behind any stragglers to catch them by surprise.

"You know, I don't think it's fair to keep insulting this old ship. It is about time we gave it some respect. It earned it by now." Vincent said, patting his hand on Ezra's command position. Ezra grinned, he was ecstatic with a mix of relief and joy that only someone who had nearly just died could experience.

"I think you're right."

1 2

The Captain's room was dank and cramped. The stench of a dozen other unwashed bodies filled the already polluted air. That was one of the many side effects of the damage the *Olympus* has taken during the battle. Even though the Volunteers and Martians had come out victorious, there was no time to celebrate.

The *Olympus* had only taken two glancing blows from incoming enemy fire, but it was enough to stagger the giant craft. Shrapnel had blasted its way through several compartments of the ship, killing some people outright and pulling others out into the void in horrific showers of gore. In one case an entire Troop had been wiped out as their billet wall was peppered with shrapnel and exposing them to the vacuum of space, pulling their bodies through holes no longer than a fist.

In other places highly toxic and corrosive fluids exploded from severed lines and sprayed onto soldiers who were cowering in their bays. The infirmary was now full of dozens of chemical burn patients, their screaming could be heard several wings away at all hours of the night and day. And then there was the lack of water. The main waste conversion system, already years behind on maintenance, was another casualty of the battle. The crew was now forced to transport rationed water from the rest of the fleet and vent all of their waste into space.

"Is there anything else going wrong?" Vincent asked. He sipped from a canteen of water that was in front of him and grimaced. The water purification chemicals always made it taste like rotten eggs.

Ezra had spent the better part of the last hour telling the gathered Marshals and aides about everything that had gone wrong since they had fought off the Committee ambush. Life seemed so much simpler when they were all nearly being shot out of space by an enemy destroyer.

"Other than none of us getting a shower in three days now?" Fiona complained.

"Marshal Olympus-Solaris, should I note that you're the one in charge of rationing and the no shower rule was yours?" Aron raised an eyebrow. Fiona rolled her eyes.

"I know, that doesn't mean I can't complain about how much it sucks."

"She is so used to bitching about the people charge she doesn't even stop when it is her." Vincent shrugged. "You have to admire the consistency. Anyway, Ezra how are the repairs coming?"

"Not terrible." He sighed. "We have had repair crews trying to patch all the holes ever since the fighting stopped. We ran out of emergency patching kits and the Martians aren't willing to share so we have been forced to just count a few bays as losses until we get a chance to bring this tub into dock for real repairs. We have no ammo to reload our main weapon systems, so we have whatever left in the guns, hardly enough for even defensive fire."

"How did the attack even happen? How do we get ambushed in the middle of space?" Fiona asked.

"We have been trying to figure that out too." Erin said. "The best thing we can come up with is the Committee has some stealth technology that we were unaware of. Or they knew we would be using the same kind of scanning technology as they use and simply knew how to dodge or jam it."

"So, you have no idea." Vincent frowned.

"We have no idea." Erin confirmed. "But Ezra and I are working together to push out a large screen of scouting ships to make sure they can't surprise us again." It dawned on Vincent that he had no idea that Erin had ships under her command or had trained pilots. She really was trying to become the human equivalent of Pharos.

"Which brings us to the next thing." Ezra turned on a display and handed it to Vincent. "This message was received this morning at the tail end of our night shift's rotation on the bridge." He glanced down at the display. It was an encrypted message sent to the bridge of the ship and then uploaded to the handheld that he was looking at. He read through text slowly and when his heart receded back down from his throat, he read it again.

To the Captain of the Olympus,

I have been instructed to open dialogue between your forces and the Governor General of Lunar City and Interim Chairman of the Central Committee of Earth. If you do not respond to this message within 24 hours I will take that as a rejection of this overture.

Admiral Yakob Merik, Earth Defense Forces Navy, Commander of the Lunar City Sector Fleet.

"They want to negotiate?" He said uncertainly. The words didn't want to leave his mouth and when they did he didn't believe them.

"There is an awful lot of weird going on in that dispatch." Ezra said and Erin nodded in agreement. She added.

"It is certainly strange."

"Since when is the Chairman an *Interim Chairman*? What does that even mean?" Fiona asked.

"Temporary." Said Felicity, rolling her eyes. Fiona scoffed.

"We heard that transmission on Elysian, they made it sound pretty damn permanent when it happened. And now the Governor General is Chairman? The privileged dickhead they give that gig to is certainly high up on the food chain, but the next Chairman?"

"I agree with Fiona." Erin said.

"I bet you never thought you would catch yourself saying that." She cackled. Erin continued as if she didn't hear her.

"Could be a plant. Get us to agree to a meet and then ambush again."

"And this time it would be enough to sink us. Though I doubt they know that" Ezra rubbed his chin. "Or at least slow us down to the point the Warlord calls the whole thing off."

"Could we fight off another ambush?" Vincent asked.

"We could, we still have the Martians with us. We outnumber whatever they have left hiding on the Moon but I wouldn't want to risk it. We already saw how much the last victory cost us." He sighed. "We pay that price again we might as well pack it up and go home, if we could even get that far with what is left of this ship by that point."

"Do you think they would come at us again?" Vincent asked. Ezra and Erin glanced at one another.

"Only a coward accepts defeat." Zinvor growled. "If I was them, I would press the attack." Vincent patted him on the shoulder.

"We know."

"We have been trying to figure out their remaining strength since the battle ended." Ezra said. "Erin's intelligence doesn't exactly show the condition of the Committee Fleet in a good light and our scouts haven't seen a single Committee ship for hundreds of miles in any direction. There is a really good chance they gambled their last destroyer on that battle as well as probably four hundred interceptors judging by the debris field. The way I see it, they tried one last ditch effort to keep us away. If they launch another attack it would be with the dregs that survived our last scrap or whatever they could bolt a missile pod onto. I think even they understand their chances are slim by this point. Not sure how many people they still have ready to run a suicide mission."

"I wouldn't put it passed them." Vincent said, tapping his augmetic eye with a finger. "I don't think any of us saw that one coming last time."

"Wait." Felicity said. "Why would they lure us into an ambush with a letter as off putting as that one is?"

"What do you mean?" Fiona asked.

"I'm unfamiliar with the political machinations of the Central Committee, but we can't rule out that losing Mars or getting their fleet blown out of orbit maybe had a negative impact on whoever is holding power over there. I can't imagine the Consul would be very popular with the Unions or the people in this room if he was in the same position."

"Do me a favor, if you're going to coup me, just shoot me in my sleep." Vincent said, only half joking. It wasn't that long ago that he thought he was almost certain to meet such a fate. Zinvor pounded the table with a fist.

"They could never do such a thing with me there."

"When the time comes, I'm sure I would deserve it."

"Captain Haagen is right." Erin said, bringing the conversation back on track. "We have no spies in the Committee, so we can't be sure of anything that is going on there. But if I was trying to trick us, I would make everything sound as normal as possible. And besides, they sent this message to the *Olympus* because they know they want to talk to the Consul. They know the Martians want to turn Lunar City to ash. They must see the Consul as their only option."

"Only one way to find out." Vincent said. *"Captain of the*

Olympus, set up a meeting." He said, mocking the wording of the letter. Aron smiled.

"I know just the place."

"Are we going to invite them aboard our lovely shit heap?" Fiona said, spreading her arms out wide. Ezra shook his head.

"We can't let them know we are held together by mostly emergency vacuum seals and electrical tape."

"No, though forcing them to come hang out with the unwashed soldiers and chemical toilet smell would be funny." Vincent had to admit, the smells were getting pungent. Using the bathroom aboard a space ship was never a comfortable experience. It was all function over form. Though there was normally a certain amount of water to use to keep the smell down. With thousands of people eating military rations and no water to spare the level of stench had risen rapidly.

"Back when I was a Sergeant, I got stuck on an orbital listening station. Post Vanguard they called it. Obviously, they weren't going to deploy me to fight my own people on Mars, so I spent the entire war there. A cramped, horrible little place they set up to make sure no Martian rebels slipped through their blockade of the planet to try to blow shit up on Earth or the Moon."

"And that is where you want to meet with them?" Vincent asked.

"It is far enough away from the Moon we wouldn't be walking right into the lion's den and small enough that we could blow it to pieces if they did anything funny." Vincent turned to Ezra.

"Can you make that work?" Ezra nodded.

"Of course. I'll send out the transmission at once." Ezra got up and made for the door and Felicity followed him.

"You're going too?" Vincent asked.

"Someone has to put your uniform back together. You're

going to be meeting with the Chairman, I can't let you let us all look as bad as you do right now." Vincent laughed.

"Harsh." Fiona leaned out of her chair and kissed him on his forehead. There was fresh stitches across his left eye up to his hairline from his fall during the attack.

"But true." She said.

Vincent splashed hot water onto his face and he could feel it cutting through the grime and dry sweat that had built up on his skin and hair. Using drinking water for such things was strictly forbidden according to the Marshal of the Commissary's Order Number Three. It was stipulated that resource wastage was punishable by two days in the ship's brig for a first offense. Felicity had to submit a waiver request to his own wife so he could wash his face.

"Hey, let me get in on that." Fiona said, crowding into the cabin's bathroom. The bathroom was hardly big enough for one person. The two of them and the smell of their chemical toilet shared the tight confines.

"You want my used face wash water?"

"It's still warm, scoot over." Fiona quickly pulled her shirt off and spooned water from the bowl with her hand onto her face and chest. "Oh, yeah that's the stuff." She moaned. "Fuck, I miss showers." After they emptied their small bowl of water onto themselves and dried themselves off. They put on the dress uniforms that Felicity had provided for them and quickly put their jackets back on to protect themselves from the cold.

The Central Committee had agreed to the meeting aboard the space station known as Post Vanguard. Their stipulation that was the meeting party could only approach in a single ship and every other element of the fleet must stay out of weapons range. Vincent quickly agreed to the terms against the protests of Zinvor who demanded that they simply blow up the space station and kill the Interim Chairman. Fiona, of course, thought the idea was brilliant.

They made their way to the berthing docks and met Aron, Felicity, Erin, and Zinvor who were all wearing their most impressive dress uniforms, cluttered with various bits of winter clothing to keep out the cold.

"Are you sure you don't want me to go?" Ezra asked. He was pacing nervously with his hands clasped behind his back. It was decided it was for the best if he stay behind on the *Olympus* in case the entire meeting was an ambush the fleet would be needed to rescue them and without Ezra that was a hopeless idea.

"Someone needs to run this whole thing while we're gone." Vincent tried in vain to reassure him. He knew Ezra was a natural worrier and that wouldn't subside until they returned from the meeting at which point he would find something new to worry about. Ezra fiddled with his uniform as he pled his case.

"I know but-"

"Give it a rest, old man." Fiona cut him off, shooing him away with her hands. "Go Command your little ship, we have a war to end." Ezra rolled his eyes. The two of them were nearly always at each other's throats, but not in a vicious way. Their bickering was more like a brother and sister, despite the fact that Ezra was old enough to be her Dad. They looked to be about ready to get in another argument when the berthing door slid open, revealing Tyr.

"Consul, Marshals...Consul's Bodyguard." They said, saluting. Zinvor grumbled in response. "The *Shanna II* ready to depart for Post Vanguard."

"Have necessary precautions been taken?" Ezra asked. Tyr looked as though Ezra had offended them.

"Of course, Marshal. The *Shanna II* has been refitted with a jump jet system to allow it to take off from a landing much quicker than before as well as full offensive and defensive weaponry kits." Ezra smiled at his former co-pilot.

"Thank you, Tyr. I should have known you would have already been on it."

"Yes." Tyr nodded. "you should have." Tyr wasn't making a joke or even coming off as arrogant, that is just how the Rhai were. Ezra should have known better and bit his lip as Tyr eyed him with suspicion.

"I didn't-" He struggled to explain himself. "- uh never mind, just go." He sighed, defeated.

In two weeks since Vincent had last seen Tyr and the *Shanna II* the ship had undergone a full refit. When Tyr originally flew him up to the *Olympus* the ship had just left the Shipwright's shop and it must had taken them quite some time to slap the broken remains of Ezra's old ship back together. Now, an entire other turbine had been fitted above its original dual engines. On two stubby weapons platforms that jutted out like wings on either side of the ship's body dozens of missiles had been mounted. He wasn't sure if that kind of firepower would actually save them should the meeting be a trap, but it was probably enough to take a lot of Committee personnel with them should they try anything.

The ship had also undergone cosmetic changes. The bare, factory default grey metal had been painted tan. The Elysian Phoenix flag had been emblazoned on each side of its cockpit with stenciled letters that read *Shanna II* under its windscreen. Fiona looked at the new paint job and whistled.

"Don't know why they went through all of that trouble. We are just going to crash it again."

"Can we not talk about crashing right now?" Felicity countered.

"If I was superstitious, I would think that is some kind of curse." Aron added.

"If?" Erin raised an eyebrow. Tyr climbed into the cockpit and began to start up the ship. They activated the crew door and it slid open. The interior had also been redone. Rather than the cargo nets that had been bolted to the wall for either storage or seating depending on the mission, there was rows of bench seating. He even saw a thin layer of cushioning over the metal.

"Oh shit!" Fiona exclaimed. "Check out the luxury seating."

"Not sitting on a cargo net is luxury to you?" Felicity asked. "Have you ever taken your wife on a date before?"

"Yes!" He said, but then thought for a moment. "I think?"

"I think our first date was that time we got trashed on moonshine when we were on the *Victory* and I jumped your bones on that bunkbed." Fiona winked.

"Is this normal behavior for a married human couple?" Tyr asked from the cockpit as they went through their preflight checks.

"No." Answered Erin, Felicity, and Aron in unison. Fiona leaned over and put her arm around his shoulder.

"Don't be jealous you pricks." The ship shuddered as the segmented door behind them opened, revealing the blackness of space. The *Shanna II* rumbled as the turbines gently carried them out of the door and away from the *Olympus*.

All around them was the Elysian and Martian fleets as far as he could see. Thousands of ships of every size and shape. In between each ship lines of ships traveled back and forth in an unceasing stream delivering people or supplies. As the *Shanna II* moved upwards through the fleet traffic, he finally saw the full range of damage that had been inflicted on the destroyer.

Starting at the front of the ship and passing right next to the bridge's protruding tower, a gash cut across the length of the ship and through several layers of armor plating. He could see directly into what had once been the quarters for thousands of soldiers that had been blown into orbit. They had all been killed instantly when their walls had been breached. Multiple craft sat above the wound, their repair crews floating out on tethers, attempting to seal the hole with emergency repair kits. It looked as if they were welding large lengths of tin foil into place.

"Whoa." Fiona gasped, pressing her face to the compartment's viewing port. "That was a close call, eh?"

"Looks like we almost ate a broadside head on." Aron agreed.

"Looks like some people did." Vincent said, gesturing at the repair crews.

"There are worse ways one can go." Aron shrugged. "Gut shot and bleeding out on the ground for hours or sucked into space and die in seconds. I know which one I would pick." Fiona nodded.

"That's true. Or getting blown to shit by an artillery shell. Just a bright flash followed by nothing. Going down like a hero seems like it would be painful as hell."

"You are all wrong." Zinvor frowned. "I would simply choose not to die."

"Oh, why hadn't I thought of that?" She rolled her eyes sarcastically.

"So, Aron." Erin cut in. "You said you were stationed at this Post Vanguard, right? What was it like?" Aron laughed.

"Terrible. Damp, cold, cramped, boring. The list goes on. Our entire mission was sitting and waiting for a Martian ship to come near us. They never did of course. The Committee built dozens of the posts over thousands of miles because people were terrified from some rumor about Martian rebels somehow sneaking onto Earth. It was all ridiculous fear mongering. You're all too young to remember when the Chairman made a big speech about the importance of building *a wall as strong as our resolve.*" He mocked in an official sounding voice. "Though I'm sure which-ever Committee members that was connected to the contractor who built them made a killing."

"How long were you there?"

"The entire war." Aron sighed. "They didn't trust Martians to be stationed on Earth or the Moon at the time, thinking we would change sides or something."

"I would have." Fiona shrugged.

"Me too." Erin agreed.

"Well, instead they stuck us in that hellhole. Every Worm or Loonie that got stationed there volunteered to go fight in the war to escape it. They must really mean business if the Chairman himself is hauling his ass up into that thing."

"Consul." Tyr spoke up, leaning back into the crew compart-ment. "Post Vanguard is within sight. It seems they have agreed to keep warships away for the meeting." Tyr looked down at the instrument panel. "Though scanners show at least three intercep-tors docked at the Post."

"That would be normal." Aron said. "They decommissioned most of the Posts after the war was over, they probably staffed them again after we took Mars. That means they have multiple wings of interceptors and several hundred soldiers within fifteen minutes of here. Ten if we are unlucky." Fiona withdrew her Riten from the holster on her hip and checked it.

"I do not like the sound of that." She said. Vincent nodded.

"Me either. Tyr if any interceptors leave the other posts you should treat them as if they are coming to attack us. Shoot them down without a warning."

"Yes, Consul."

"Unidentified ship, this is Earth Defense Forces Post Vanguard, identify yourself or you will be fired upon." Came a voice over the ship's radio. The voice was distorted with static. Tyr toggled the radio.

"This is Captain Tyr, Captain of the Elysian Volunteer Navy's *Shanna II*. Requesting permission to land." A few seconds passed in silence. Vincent was curious if they were wondering what the clearly inhuman voice speaking to them on the other side of the radio was. Finally, the voice responded.

"Request granted." After the voice spoke green landing lights began blinking from one side of the post, guiding them to their designated landing point. A berthing door, just big enough for a Reaper, opened revealing a small landing area. Tyr brought the ship in expertly and landed it so softly Vincent could have sworn they were still gliding through space.

The inside of the Point looked remarkably similar to that of a spaceship, just older. The Point had been built decades before even the *Olympus* and it showed. The pressurization of the berthing was much slower than usual and was so loud it sounded as though they had parked inside of a jet turbine while it was accelerating at full tilt.

There was only one other door in the room, a vault like door with a crank in the middle. The wheel began to spin quickly and the door opened. In neat ranks, soldiers in dress uniform filed in with shiny black rifles held out in front of them as if they were on a parade field. They marched from the door and stopped only a few feet in front of the *Shanna II*. There, they froze in place in rigid formation.

"Is this the part where they shoot us?" asked Fiona. Felicity glanced back from the viewing port to correct her.

"It's an honor guard. Most people don't shine their boots and rifles for a firing squad."

Two more figures appeared from the door. One was a tall, slender woman in the peaked cap of a military officer, a cape billowed behind her as she walked. Her grey hair flowed over her shoulders and she held a cane in her hand but did not use it to walk. The other, a man, looked younger but not by much. He had closely cropped salt and pepper hair and wore the uniform of the Committee government: a plain grey tunic with an Eagle and Star pin over his heart.

"Ready?" Tyr asked. Vincent nodded and Tyr opened the compartment door.

"Let's do this." Zinvor held Vincent back with one meaty paw.

"No." He growled. "I go first." Zinvor didn't wait for anyone to object before stepping off of the ship. He walked out a few paces, turned, facing the ship and bowed deeply. He was followed by Felicity who did the same thing. She then called out in her loudest command voice.

"Consul of the Human Race to the Fidayi Clan and Unions of Elysian, Vincent Solaris!" He swallowed deeply and stepped out. The air inside of Vanguard was refreshingly warm, at least in comparison to the *Olympus*. He could still see his breath in small clouds. The Marshals followed him out, he could hear Fiona's saber bounce off of the side of the ship with a metallic clank.

The two groups eyed each other down for a few moments before finally the woman in the cape stepped forward. The commander of the honor guard stepped forward and announced.

"Grand Marshal Anit Lagos, Commander of the Earth Defense Forces!"

"Grand Marshal?" Felicity asked in a whisper. "I've never heard of a Grand Marshal before."

"Me either." Erin hissed. Aron straightened his uniform and stepped forward to meet his counterpart.

"Marshal of the Elysian Volunteer Army, Aron Victoria!" Felicity announced. Anit eyed Aron, Vincent could register thinly veiled disgust on her face. Aron extended his hand out to her and she looked at it as if it was covered in poison.

"This bitch isn't going to shake his hand because he's a Martian." Fiona spat under her breath. "I'll gut that uppity Worm."

"Keep it down." Vincent hissed at her. The rest of the Martians in Vincent's party began to clench their jaws and fists. He noticed Fiona's hand was resting on the butt of her Riten. Anit looked back at the man who stood, his hands behind his back. He nodded at her. She slowly extended her hand and touched Aron's only as much as she needed to complete the greeting and quickly withdrew it. The two were staring daggers directly into each other's eyes.

The man stepped forward next and the commander of the honor guard again stepped forward to announce his presence. Interim Chairman of the Central Committee of Earth and Governor General of Lunar City, Gideon Han!"

Gideon walked by Anit and Vincent stepped out to meet him. He extended his hand and Gideon took it, shaking in firmly.

"So, you're the so-called Great Traitor." Gideon said. His voice was a friendly, pleasant tone and it was clear he wasn't trying to offend Vincent with the nickname.

"That is what I've heard." Vincent responded. "I never thought I would be standing here, shaking hands with the Chairman." Gideon looked visibly uncomfortable at being addressed by the title.

"Governor General is fine. It is my permanent title after all. Please, come inside. We have a meeting room set aside. Though you will have to excuse the confines, Vanguard is quite austere."

"I've been told." Vincent said. Gideon began to lead the group towards the door. The honor guard fell in behind them as they walked.

"Oh, so you've heard of this place before." His voice sounded slightly surprised. Vincent wasn't sure if the Governor General or Chairman or whoever he said he was, was sizing him up or not. He knew that was exactly what he was doing and expected the man that was supposed to be his peer to be doing the same. Gideon didn't betray any kind of stress or tension. He seemed almost affable, like he was giving a tour to an estranged acquaintance, not a man who had been waging war against him for over a year. Vincent couldn't be more different at that moment. He was a wound up ball of nerves, so tense he was sure his knuckles were white. He just hoped Gideon didn't notice.

"Yes." He nodded, putting on a fake smile. "Marshal Victoria was stationed here during the war. It was his suggestion that we meet here."

"Ah." Gideon said. "I should have known." Gideon led them down a long hallway. The passageways in the space station made the *Olympus* feel roomy in comparison. There was only just enough room for a single human to squeeze down the walkway at a time. If someone approached from the other direction someone would have to hug the wall and let them pass.

Condensation had built up on the pipes that ran overhead, occasionally a drip of chemical tinged water fell onto the people below at random. Rust had eaten away at the deck plates underfoot, badly concealed with several layers of grey paint. The air was stale and smelled of old smoke. He wasn't sure if that was from the old air purification system or because there had recently been a fire, looking around it could have been either or both.

At the end of the hallway two soldiers stood on either side of a door. As Gideon approached one of them quickly turned and spun the crank on the door and swung it open. The room inside was exactly what Gideon had promised them. A simple metal table was in the middle of the room with several mismatched chairs arrayed around it. Someone had gone through the effort of hanging an Eagle and Star flag over the bare metal wall on one side of the room.

Soldiers rushed into the room and pulled out chairs for Anit and Gideon. They thanked them and took their seats.

"If you think I'm pulling out your chair you're out of your mind." Felicity said. Vincent fought back laughter.

"I think I can handle that myself, thanks." He slid out the metal chair and it screeched against the ground. They all took their seats and a soldier closed the door. Zinvor refused to sit, he remained standing behind Vincent, his back against the wall. Gideon eyed Zinvor curiously.

"I assure you, Consul, we mean you no harm. Your bodyguard is it?"

"Kind of."

"Whoever he is, can relax."

"I assure you, no matter what I tell him, he will never relax. So, Governor General, I have to admit I was shocked you asked for this meeting."

"Yes." Gideon nodded. "I must admit, it is not something I saw us ever doing. But, Consul, I don't know how you feel about this war, but I have seen one too many die fighting it. I want it to end."

"It is not a war I wanted, Governor General." Vincent nodded.

"Then why did you invade Mars?" Anit fired back.

"In all due respect, Grand Marshal. I could ask you the same thing." Vincent countered. "We did not conquer Mars. We helped free it from the Central Committee. We didn't fold into the Clan or even occupy it. Mars has been returned to the Martian people, as it should have always been."

"Did you free Victoria when you wiped it off of the planet?" She seethed. Vincent felt Fiona begin to tense next to him and he place a hand on her shoulder. Vincent raised a hand to his face and tapped his augemetic eye.

"Do you know how I got this eye, Grand Marshal?"

"Do you think I care." She frowned.

"I was fighting in the streets of Victoria before the bombardment. A Committee loyalist drove a truck full of explosives into a column of refugees that my soldiers were giving passage to. When the truck exploded it killed hundreds. Wounded thousands more. Men, women, and children. They killed them all just for a chance to get at me. I barely escaped with my life, though I paid my pound of flesh to do so I guess."

"A shame, I'm sure." Anit said, folding her arms across her chest. That was the breaking point for Fiona. Her fist slammed against the table and she stood up.

"Look here, bitch." She seethed. "Vincent might play nice with your ass, but I won't. He is giving you more respect then you deserve and if you keep this shit up I'll make sure you need to use that cane you're carrying!" Anit matched her, jumping to her feet and jabbing a finger out at Fiona.

"Shut your mouth, you worthless Red!" Fiona was nearly over the table before Felicity managed to grab her and force her back into her seat. Anit looked horrified that her words would have invited such a showing of physical rage. The sign of someone who had never been confronted by the people she oppressed. Vincent and Gideon watched the scene with curiosity.

"Governor General." Vincent said, straining to remain calm. "If I hear another racist slur against my staff, our meeting is over. I will return to my fleet and we will replay what happened to Victoria in Lunar City."

"Anit." Gideon said quietly. "Please leave the room."

"What?" She shouted. "You can't be serious!"

"Anit, please." That is when Vincent realized something. He wasn't ordering the Grand Marshal to leave, he was pleading with her. In all of his years in Ethics School nobody ever said that the Chairman had to plead with people to do *anything*. It was humanity's job to simply obey. He glanced over at Erin who was watching the entire scene intently. She had noticed the same thing he did.

"We will talk about this later." Anit cursed and stormed out of the room. Gideon steadied himself and took a breath.

"You'll have to excuse the Grand Marshal. She is quite passionate."

"Passionate is a word." Fiona said.

"Governor General, I suppose we should get to it. I came here to ask for your surrender." Gideon closed his eyes and folded his hands together on the desk.

"Consul, I had a son. A Captain in the Earth Defense Forces. He was stationed on Olympus Mons before the fall of Mars. I know he didn't make it out."

"I am sorry for your loss." Vincent nodded. "I took part in the assault on the Mons. I assure you, he died a hero. The EDF fought like lions." While being sorry for losing his son may not have been a lie, dying a hero may have been. If he had been on the west side of the assault there is a good chance he fell into the hands of the Martian gangers. If he survived long enough to be captured, he would have died long, slow, and bad. Vincent kept that part to himself.

"Thank you." Gideon choked up. "I once believed things like that. And then I saw thousands of parents mourning when it was their turn for a messenger to come to their door and deliver the news that their daughter or son wasn't coming home. It is all such a waste."

"I agree, Governor General. I may not have children, but I buried thousands of my soldiers on Mars. Soldiers who looked up to me to guide them, who followed me into battle." He stared down at the table. "Soldiers." He said solemnly. "They weren't soldiers. They were husbands, wives, daughters, sons. They were people. Now they are all dead." He gathered himself for a moment and swallowed back his feelings. "Many more of us are going to die in this war, but it doesn't have to be fighting one another. Governor General, I may be young, but I'm not naïve. I know you and your Grand Marshal hate us, most people at this table hate you too. But there is no reason for this war to continue.

We should, no, we need to come together to fight against the real enemy."

"You mean the Anarchs."

"Yes. And we are going to need your help to fight them."

"So, you mean to absorb us into your war? To end the Central Committee? "

"No." Vincent shook his head. "Not entirely, anyway."

"You'll have to forgive me, Consul. I don't understand."

"To be honest with you Governor General, I was chosen to represent our coalition because it was thought that I would be the easiest person for you to speak to. The reaction of your Grand Marshal to Marshal Fiona kind of proved that. But I still represent the People's Congress of Mars at this meeting. Commander Erik Olympus, as the elected representative of his people, demands the head of the Chairman as part of his demands to any surrender we might agree on. Otherwise, he believes there will never be peace between Mars and the Central Committee. Hearing about an *Interim Chairman* raised a lot of questions for us. Where is the Chairman, Governor General?"

"I understand your confusion." Gideon sighed. "The Chairman is dead." The Elysian delegation exchanged confused looks. Vincent had long since learned that there had been hundreds of Chairmen throughout the history of the Central Committee. It was a fact they managed to skip over during school. Their deaths were never announced to the public, nor was the elevation of a new one. The idea was to create a single, unbreaking line of stability that spanned through human history. Obviously, their plans went sideways when Earth was destroyed, but it didn't take them long to elevate another Chairman without ever noting the last one was incinerated with everyone else. Vincent had no idea how many Chairmen they had gone through.

"But, how?" Erin finally asked.

"Our late Chairman ordered the strike on your fleet, from

which you clearly emerged victorious. It was something of a last ditch effort by what remained of our fleet. Forgive me, I am not a military man, but from what I have been told by the Grand Marshal, it was an incredibly badly thought out plan with very little chance of success. After ignoring the entire Central Committee and military's objections to the operation and being confronted with failure, the Chairman took his own life."

"And why were you chosen to fill the role?" Erin raised an eyebrow. "Governor General of Lunar City is certainly a high position, but you weren't even a member of the Central Committee. It seems unlikely."

"Hence the *Interim* part of my title, Marshal." Gideon gave a tired smile. "Due to our present conditions, it was decided that going through the full process of choosing a new Chairman would take too much time and I would fill the role until we found ourselves in more agreeable times. Now, it seems I will be the last Chairman."

"Not necessarily." Vincent said. "We have no intention of taking over your city or deposing the Central Committee. Assuming you agree to our terms."

"I am going to go out on a limb and assume these terms are not to be negotiated.

"You would be correct."

"Name your terms." Felicity handed Vincent a display and he clicked it on.

"Lunar City allows for a full occupation to be carried out by members of the Elysian Volunteer Army. Personnel from the Martian People's Army will be held in reserve, off planet. During the occupation the Central Committee, the EDF, and all other civil administration will fall under the command of the Office of the Human Consul. During the occupation, the EDF will be allowed to remain in uniform, but will be disarmed. All EDF military equipment and material is to be forfeited to the Volunteer Army and Fleet for use against the Anarchs. All sentenced soldiers within the EDF are to be immediately released and anyone who wishes to enlist in the Volunteers should be allowed to do so." Gideon pinched his chin in thought.

"And how long does this occupation go on for?"

"Until the day after our victory over the Anarchs."

"And what happens after that? We start trading with one another? We become allies? If anything, having your soldiers patrolling our streets and running our city will only make people hate you more. The Committee will see it as a dishonor to them and everything they stand for."

"To be totally honest Governor General, I don't care what happens between us after the war against the Anarchs is over. We can deal with that when the time comes."

"Those elements." Erin began. "That you named, the Committee, the EDF-"

"The Grand Marshal." Fiona cut in.

"The Grand Marshal" Erin agreed. "Will you be able to control her during the occupation?"

"Of course." Gideon nodded. "Anit might be against these talks, but she is a soldier. She will follow orders."

"She was against speaking with us?" Erin asked.

"Well, you've spoken to her. That is not a kind of act she is putting on. She really does hate you as much as she lets on. If it was up to her, we would be fighting you over every inch of Lunar soil, not speaking to one another from across a table like civilized people. But like I said, she is a soldier and soldier's follow orders."

"See to it that she does. I would hate to see Lunar City turn into a warzone." Erin said. The tone of her voice led Vincent to believe that if she had her choice, she absolutely would have loved to turn Lunar City into a warzone. Gideon furrowed his brow, he had heard the same thing that Vincent did. As agreeable as he had been there was little doubt that he hated being spoken to in such a way by a Martian.

"I will do everything in my power to keep peace in this city. I give you my word."

"Does that mean you agree to our terms?" Vincent asked. Gideon nodded.

"Consul Solaris, I believe the only way I can protect the people of Lunar City and see them through the chaos that is gripping our galaxy is by surrendering it. Neither of us started this war, Consul, but we have the power to end it." Gideon stood up and walked around the table. Zinvor grumbled and placed a hand on his sidearm as the man approached. Gideon extended his hand out towards Vincent. "As Interim Chairman of the Central Committee I hereby surrender the military and government forces under my command." Vincent rose to his feet and gripped Gideon's hand in his.

"As Human Consul to the Fidayi Clan, I accept your surrender."

The occupation of Lunar City came swiftly. Within hours of Interim Chairman Gideon Han officially signing the document of surrender the first barges full of Volunteers were landing on the Moon's surface. It would be the first time in Human history that an enemy army would step foot in the city.

Vincent had never seen Lunar City with his own eyes. The city had been the first human settlement ever built outside of Earth and its age showed. As the first colonists arrived before the advent of terraforming technology they would have to instead dwell within the confines of a dome. As the colony stabilized and expanded more domes would be constructed until dozens of them doted the Moon's surface, each connected to the other by a highway of tunnels.

While the City had been a refuge for the Committee favored elites for generations, it bore the marks of its recent history. A deep scar across around one hundred miles of the lunar surface, leaving behind the ruins of at least three domes. The lasting legacy of the Anarchs' attempted genocide. The destruction was so thorough in some spaces the debris couldn't be distinguished from the ragged topography of the Moon itself. Vincent wasn't sure how much of the Lunar population had been wiped out in the attack, but it had to have been millions.

Aron had insisted to anyone that would listen that the EDF was simply biding their time and would ambush them as they landed. Vincent had attempted to quash the rumors. Not because he didn't fully believe them himself, after seeing the burning hatred that the Grand Marshal had for him, he wasn't sure what to expect, but because he was worried about the effect the rumors would have on the soldiers. Having a tightly wound and trigger happy soldier gun down the first EDF uniform they saw would be bad for business.

Instead of being greeted by the guns of waiting Committee loyalists, they were greeted by nobody. As the first soldiers stepped out from their landing barges, they found the Lunar City Space Dome completely empty. Rows of Reapers had been left on the tarmac fully fueled and loaded but abandoned by their crews. It did not take long for the Volunteer Fleet to claim them as their own.

As the soldiers marched into the city, they found each block void of human life. Not even so much as curious onlookers could be found in the street. Fleeting glances from scared gawkers were all that could be seen peeking out from the windows from the towering grey apartment buildings that lined the streets. If a soldier caught a glimpse of one of them, they would quickly duck away.

The Committee Administration buildings were likewise abandoned. Unlike the Reapers in the space dome however, they were not left untouched. Every computer and display had been wiped clean of any data if they hadn't been taken altogether. The first sign of the Committee government anyone saw was a single secretary hundreds of floors up in the Ministry of Public Ethics and Enforcement building burning what remained of the contents of a filing cabinet.

The Consul's Office of Occupation as it officially became known, set up shop in Central Committee Headquarters. Like every government building it was a giant grey monolith that was largely unadorned outside of various flags and portraits. Above the glass doors on the ground level a large bas relief of an Eagle and Star flag had been etched into the seamless concrete, flanked on either side by a tall flagpoles flying the flag of the same design. The building stretched hundreds of stories into the air, but the Occupation government only requested office space on the first floor. Or, they would have requested it if any representative of the Committee government had met them upon their arrive. So, Aron just ordered the soldiers to occupy it.

"Well shit, is it really an occupation if they don't even take part in it?" Fiona asked. The two of them were standing in the rotunda of the Committee headquarters. The first floor of the building had quickly become populated by hundreds of Volunteer Army and Fleet personnel. The fighting between Staff Officers over particular office spaces had thankfully stopped after only one grievous maiming at the ends of a broken bottle. Vincent was pleased the soldiers were finally learning restraint.

"I don't know." Vincent scratched his beard. "It does make it a little harder to move in. Speaking of which, have you figured out the barracks situation?" The occupation of the Moon had come so quickly nobody had thought of a plan to house the thousands of newly arrived soldiers. They had been left to put up tents wherever they could find space.

"Well, we could house them in the various city barracks, but *someone* promised to let the EDF stay there. Housing here was pretty strictly rationed out, so there was never any surplus. If we could requisition a few of these apartment buildings…"

"We aren't kicking people out of their homes. That is something they would do. What other options do we have?"

"Well, a lot of the domes are used for farming. We could ask the farmers if our soldiers could camp on any extra space they have, but we can't really give them anything. Our money is useless here."

"Our money is useless pretty much everywhere. Hence all the smuggling." Vincent shrugged.

"We could offer them a hand in the fields. An hour or so a day per soldier would probably give them all the help they could use. If they are anything like the farmers on Mars, I'm sure they could use a break from toiling in the dirt all day."

"That is a really good idea." Fiona smirked at him.

"Are you new here? Because all I have are good ideas. Speaking of which, did you want to come with me to talk to the farmers? The Commissary soldiers are delivering a truck of supplies out that way. You could come along." Vincent looked around him at the buzzing foot traffic of the Volunteers. He had no idea what was going on and he wasn't sure he wanted to find out. Arai had made it clear that the occupation of Lunar City was a military operation, meaning it was Aron's job to figure it out, not his.

"Anything is better than in the middle of this cluster fuck. What are you bringing out there?"

"Oh, you didn't see?" Fiona asked, handing him a display. "Published today to pushed out through the Lunar City intranet. Vincent read the message as it scrolled across the small screen.

Occupation Order #2: All Central Committee supply depots- civilian and military – are hereby ordered to submit to a full audit of their stores within 48 hours.

-Marshal of the Commissary Fiona Olympus-Solaris

"An audit?" He asked.

"How do you think I find out who is hording supplies?" She smiled. "On Elysian it is hard because people know they are breaking the law. You have to search their houses and off the book warehouses. But here?" She scoffed. "Resource hording was just another function of the government. They kept track of every bullet, every bean. As much as I wanted to strip every warehouse bare, I didn't. There is still more than enough to go around, more than we ever had on Mars. We haven't even started looking into private stores those uppity fucks keep in their houses or private storage facility."

"You are having way too much fun doing this." Vincent laughed.

"Consider me motivated after seeing the Luna Domes."

"Luna Domes?"

"It is something you should see for yourself. Follow me." Fiona led them out of the Committee Headquarters. In front of the building a convoy of flatbed utility trucks had been parked. Their grey paintjobs and Eagle and Star flag stenciled across the doors showed they had been recently taken from EDF motor pools. The trucks had been stacked high with supplies and groups of Commissary soldiers busied themselves chain smoking and securing the load.

If Vincent was honest with himself, he knew the likes of the EDF and Titanian Army would take one look at a regular Volunteer soldier and look down on them. Despite all of their efforts most soldiers still had mismatched uniforms and equipment. Furthermore, Aron never saw it as overly important to continue to enforce the EDF's old grooming standards. He saw such things as a means of forcing people to conform into an idealized image, which seemed like the antithesis of the entire Elysian experiment.

Even compared to that, the soldiers of Fiona's new Commissary detachment looked especially disheveled. It was clear that she had personally chosen mostly Martians that had only recently joined the army after abandoning their gangs after the liberation of their planet. If they had uniforms, they had discarded them. Instead, they wore a strange mix of street clothing and gear that had taken from one battlefield or another. One of them was wearing cut off red Martian pants paired with a tank top, while another had a carbine slung over their shoulder, a weapon that Vincent had only ever seen issued to Titanian Pathfinders or pilots.

"Hey Boss!" One of them called out to Fiona. The voice came from a small woman with a white blonde mohawk and two pistols shoved into her waistband.

"About ready to head out?" Fiona asked. "We are going to have two extra going with us." She said, thumbing over her shoulder at Vincent and Zinvor. Zinvor had been quiet even for him since landing on the Moon. The entire situation put him so far on edge Vincent was sure he hadn't taken his hand off of his newly acquired rifle since they had arrived.

"Oi!" Called out the woman and the soldiers sitting in the cab of one of the trucks. "Get your stupid asses out of the cabin, the Big Boss and his boy is coming with us!" Vincent assumed he was the Big Boss and Zinvor was *his boy.* He knew Zinvor would hate that if he was bothering to pay attention to what anyone was saying. "Sorry, Big Boss." She said to Vincent. "I'll have some of these idiots sit in the back for you."

"Please, don't worry about it. We will ride in the back. Besides, it'll give me a chance to get a better look at the place." Vincent said, smiling.

"Back of truck is better." Zinvor said. "If we run over a mine, we have a better chance of surviving."

"There is that optimism we all love so much." Vincent groaned. Fiona heaved herself onto the flatbed of a nearby truck and extended a hand to Vincent to help him up. They both had to turn and pull up Zinvor's bulk. The three of them were joined on the flatbed with several soldiers. Other soldiers piled into the back of the remaining trucks and the convoy slowly rolled out.

Vincent and Fiona found seats on top of the boxes of supplies while the soldiers sat down at the edge of the flatbed, their legs dangling off and their weapons held downwards. Zinvor's legs were too short to haul him up on top of the boxes so he found a seat with everyone else. The trucks trundled towards an intersection. The translucent dome came down in front of them to three different tunnel entrances.

One had rail lines running through it, though the train had apparently been shut down since the surrender. Vincent assumed the Volunteers did not bring any tram specialists from Elysian with them. The middle tunnel was labeled with *Pedestrians Only* painted onto its concrete walking surface. A few bored looking Volunteers stood around the pedestrian entrance, guarding it in the off chance someone might actually try to use it.

The lead truck brought the convoy to the tunnel to the far right. It was the largest of the tunnels, labeled *Vehicles Only*. Judging from the size it was main passageway for military vehicles should they need to be moved or deployed around the city. It would have been much easier to use the train to transport any large amount of civilian supplies or people.

"Millions of people living in this city and they only have three roads going into an area?" Vincent asked. "The Committee doesn't exactly have a flare for design but they do know how to make a road system, what happened here?"

"Control." Fiona said. "Every other dome has dozens, hundreds of tunnels going from one place to another. We just left the Committee Headquarters Dome. There are some living quarters there too, but only for the top of the top. The Chairman and the Committee themselves, maybe some of their favorite stoolies. I'm sure that Anit bitch lives somewhere around there too. This entire mother fucker is the beating heart of the government. The Committee knows, or knew at least, that they were in charge. They also knew if you pushed someone far enough, they would rebel against you."

"Like Mars." Vincent said.

"Yep. So, say the Chairman or Governor General finally pissed off enough people to the point that they wanted to overthrow them, the rebels would have to all funnel neatly down these three tunnels."

"Even an unskilled commander could turn such things into a killing field." Zinvor grunted. "A single machine gun at the entrance would cause havoc."

"They don't even have to do that. Look up there." She pointed up at the ceiling of the tunnel. Cutting straight down the middle was a line of small ports, each about the size of a fist. "Vents. Technically they are for fires, but in practice they could vent out the oxygen from all of these tunnels and kill everyone inside in seconds. No fuss, no mess."

"We, uh, control the means to vent the tunnels now, right?" Vincent asked nervously.

"I would assume so or they would probably be waiting for a time like now to use them." Fiona shrugged.

"Reassuring." Vincent sighed. The tunnel was devoid of life. There were few hints that it would have been a heavily trafficked. Rules were painted on the road's surface like *military vehicles have the right of way!* And *No entrance into the Committee Dome from the Outer Domes without a travel permit!*

"Even in Lunar City they limit people's travel?" Vincent asked.

"The Outer Domes is where we are going. You'll see." Fiona said.

The convoy passed by another Volunteer post. Two soldiers sat in folding chairs at the edge of the tunnel. One was clearly asleep until the sound of the incoming truck woke them up. Both shot to their feet and put on their best good soldier act as the trucks drove by them. Vincent laughed.

"This post looks exciting."

"Why would anyone pass by?" Fiona shrugged. "The Outer

Domes are banned from travel outside of their own Domes and nobody is issuing out any travel permits."

"Don't they know we are in charge?" Vincent asked.

"To be honest, probably not. We haven't done anything that impacts them." Fiona patted the supply boxes under her. "Until now, anyway. And remember people were still following Committee Law for months after moving to Elysian, even people who weren't Black Coats. Fear that worms its way into your brain as deeply as that probably requires years to get over. They aren't going to set their Eagle and Star flags on fire just because we've been here a few days."

The Committee Law people of Elysian always confused Vincent. They had deserted the EDF after the battle of Grawluck, a crime that would almost certainly have seen them executed should they have ever gone back, but still devoted themselves to the code that would kill them. They would hold weekly reading circles where they would read from their Ethics Books and engage in endless debates on how to become better Citizens to a government that saw them as traitors.

The Marshals had wanted to consider them criminals or Black Coat sympathizers. Arai had thought them to be a kind of religious cult. Both sides were at least partially right and wanted to dispatch the Public Order Officers to round them up, but Vincent had refused. They had been indoctrinated through a life time of fear and brutal repression, he assumed they would eventually come around once they realized the Ethics Police weren't going to burst through their door and arrest them should they miss a reading circle date. As Elysian society eventually came together, the reading circle attendee numbers began to drop, though some still remained.

Vincent's attention was brought back to the road in front of him when they drove under a sign that read *Outer Dome #1 Ahead. Authorized Personnel Only.* For the first time he saw what had been an EDF position, since abandoned. The road ahead was blocked by a bright orange swinging gate connected to a concrete checkpoint. The checkpoint was decorated with a sign that warned *STOP. Military Checkpoint. Have your papers ready to be inspected. All vehicles subject to search.*

"You said we haven't really done anything for the Outer Domes yet, right?" Vincent asked and Fiona nodded her head. "Well, consider the travel ban over." Vincent leaned over closer to the cab of the truck so the driver could hear him. "Tell the lead truck to blow through that gate." The driver grinned and gave him a thumbs up. The lead truck gunned it and rammed directly into the gate.

The gate bent and then broke under the truck's assault. It snapped off of the checkpoint's swing arm and sent it cartwheeling down the tunnel.

"Feel better?" Fiona laughed.

"A little, yeah."

The smell of the Outer Dome hit Vincent before he saw it. The Committee Dome had looked like any city block he had seen on Earth, abet a bit smaller and built closer together. The buildings were the same, the water that came out of the faucet tasted the same, even the air smelled the same. They had spared no expense in exporting Earthian life onto the Moon.

The Outer Dome was more akin to the Olympus slums. Gone were the immaculately paved and cleaned streets. They had been replaced with dirt tracks, many of them churned to mud by the combination of foot traffic and the overhead intradome rain system, a series of tubes and pipes that spider webbed its way across the dome ceiling and simulated the Earthian rain cycle that brought life to the vast fields of crops that covered the rest of the dome's surface.

The towering blocks of housing and government buildings had been replaced with small, round houses that lined the fields. The looked as if they had been there since the time of the first lunar settlers. They were rough domes made from a kind of plastic paneling whose advanced age required them to have been repaired with whatever could be found multiple times over. Now, they were hardly more than tin and wood shacks insulated from their own rain system by tarps.

"What is that smell?" Vincent coughed. Fiona motioned over to the other side of a field where he could see livestock standing around chewing cud. Vincent had to think back to a biology class he took in school to remember the large white and black animals were called cows.

"We ate synthesized protein while the Committee is out here eating beef and drinking milk." Fiona scoffed.

"We still eat synthesized protein." Vincent frowned. "Do live-stock always smell this bad?"

"The pigpens in Olympus always stank like shit. And they probably use the manure to feed the crops. You don't go over to the hydro warehouses often, do you?" She laughed.

"Do I look like someone who hangs out in a farm on my free time?" That is when Vincent saw them. Confused looking faces peering out from behind thick rows of what looked like corn or from behind cracked doors. "Uh, you said you've been here before, right? Why does everyone look terrified of us?"

"They're afraid of us because we invaded their city, dumbass. Did you think we were going to be welcomed as liberators or something?" Fiona scoffed. "When we came through it was just a scouting mission. We had to make sure the EDF didn't hold up out in the fields or something waiting to ambush us. It was late at night so nobody could see us."

"Well, coming through here like this is one hell of a first impression." Vincent said.

"Oh, we haven't started with the first impressions." She leaned up to the cab of the truck. "Hey, new girl, you ready?"

"Yes, Boss." Responded a scared sounding voice. The trucks ground to a halt and the soldiers jumped off. It was clear they were spreading out for security, but their weapons remained slung across their backs. Vincent was sure their attempts at looking unthreatening were probably lost on the people hiding in their own fields.

"You're up, new girl." Fiona said and the cab's door opened. A small woman jumped out and splashed into the mud. She had large round glasses and wore most of the uniform of the Volunteers, paired with the looted field cap of a common Earth Defense soldier. Her skin was pale, but not in a Martian way and her hair was a thick mop of brown hair, undercut and revealing peach fuzz surrounding a ponytail of hair that stuck straight up. She walked away from the trucks and made her way through the fields. Vincent watched the scene with confusion.

"Who is that?" He asked.

"One of the newer recruits we picked up on Mars, from the Tharsis garrison, I think. Said her name was Akabi. When Erin's agents were debriefing her, she let it slip her dad was the Farm Manager for the Outer Domes of Lunar City."

"Someone was that high up and their kid ended up in the EDF?"

"Being a Dome Manager is about as high as a Luna can go. It turns out it isn't high enough to help your kid if the Ethics Police catch her and her girlfriend making out behind a warehouse."

She appeared again, this time with a small group of older people with him. They didn't wear the normal grey uniforms common to citizens of the Central Committee. They instead wore threadbare and homespun clothes that looked as if they had been repaired over and over again for years. Though, Vincent could still make out the shape of an Eagle and Star badge pinned over their hearts. The badge, unlike everything else about them, was flawless and hand shined.

As they got closer, he could see that the group was some of the thinnest humans he had ever seen. They shouldn't have even been alive, let alone still working on a farm. Their skin looks like it had been stretched over exposed bone. Their cheeks were sunken in and their eyes sat hollow in their skulls. Each of them limped with various ailments and their gait struggled with the exertion of walking the short distance. One man stepped out of the group, he was bent permanently at the waist and he looked so frail that he could have dropped dead on the spot.

"I hear you're the man I have to thank for my daughter returning home to us." His voice sounded as tired as his face looked but he managed a smile.

"From what I hear, she has had one hell of a trip."

"I have heard the same about you. You are The Great Traitor, are you not?"

"I prefer Vincent, but you can call me whatever you like." He smiled. The old man warmed, offering his hand, which trembled as he held it out.

"And you can call me Shay. I am the Manager for the agricultural domes. Though I supposed you know them as the outer domes." Vincent took his hand and was surprised to find Shay's grip strength deceptively strong. "What brings you to our domes, Vincent?" He nodded towards the trucks.

"We came to give you back all of the food the Committee stole from you." Shay looked over Vincent's shoulder, locking his eyes with the hundreds of boxes of supplies that had been stacked up in the trucks. He turned and whispered something with the rest of his group and they began to talk hurriedly amongst themselves. The group approached the trucks and the soldiers watching over them stepped aside. Shay eyed the supplies for a moment before running his hand over the black Eagle and Star flag that had been stamped onto the side of one of the crates. He turned back towards Vincent, his eyes now watery.

"Can we speak in my office?" Vincent nodded and Shay began to lead through them through the Dome. As he shuffled slowly towards his office the people still out in the fields, barns, and warehouses slowly trickled out from hiding in the hundreds and then thousands. Most looked like Shay: Fragile, malnourished, and gaunt wearing little more than rags on their backs. Children with distended stomachs peaked out from behind mothers and fathers, people with homemade prosthetic limbs struggled to keep up as the human parade of misery marched along behind Vincent.

They came to Shay's office. A small, squat cement block of a structure. A small sign was posted next to the door that showed the Eagle and Star insignia above text that read *Manager of Agricultural Operations Shay Daniels*. They stepped into the office and Shay had a seat behind his desk, struggling to catch his breath. Behind him on the wall was a large mural of Lunar City with dozens of domes stretching across the Lunar surface the expanding circular design of habitats was labelled Inner Dome and Outer Dome in flowery script.

"You must understand, I did not want to talk about sensitive subjects out in the open." He said, in between gasps for breath.

"Spies?" Fiona asked and Shay became immediately uncomfortable.

"The Committee have eyes and ears in every dome, even this one. Especially this one. If someone reports that we spoke in my office I can say it was simply pleasantries. Saying hello to the new occupation authorities or something."

"And what is this exactly?" Vincent asked. Shay swallowed hard and steadied himself, leaning forward on his desk.

"Where did you find all of those supplies?" The old man didn't seem mad. He instead looked distraught at what he had seen packed away in their convoy. Vincent wasn't sure what to say. He couldn't have even guessed how Fiona tracked down what seemed like months or years of supplies.

"They were in the Committee warehouses." Fiona said.

"There was more than one warehouse?" Shay asked, his eyes filling with tears again. Fiona was never someone to ever be empathetic towards anyone, even Vincent. So, being confronted by an old Luna she didn't know on the verge of tears clearly unsettled her.

"There were dozens of them. What you saw out there is a small percentage of what we found." At that, Shay broke down entirely. He held his face in his hands and let out full throated, uncontrollable sobs. Fiona looked sideways at Vincent, unsure of what to do.

"You didn't know." Vincent said.

"No!" Shay cried.

"What did they tell you? Where did they say where all the food was going?"

"There was a siege on Mars. Your armies had surrounded Victoria and millions of people who were trapped inside desperately needed food. They said that everyone would be sacrificing for the Chairman's loyal citizens."

"How long has this been going on?" Fiona asked.

"Rationing started after the Alliance attacked. The habitats they destroyed were some of the more abundant agricultural domes in the entire city, so we have been struggling to make do. We have been trying to up our output ever since but.." He shook his head. "It just hasn't been possible with the material shortages. Over the last eight months the rationing has gotten worse and worse. They told us everyone in Lunar City was suffering with us. They said it was a good citizens duty to endure this arduous march for the Chairman."

"And because you're not allowed into the inner domes you could never see how they lived." Fiona frowned.

"Yes, that is right." Shay wiped away his tears with the back of a hand.

"Shay." Vincent looked at the old man. "Mars fell almost a year ago. They have been lying to all of you." The man burst out into tears once again.

"So many of us have lost so much. We have buried so many of our young, our old. For what?" He gasped. "I don't want to believe this. I can't believe this!"

"I know you've probably been told a lot of terrible things about me." Vincent placed a hand on Shay's trembling shoulder. "You have no reason to trust anything I tell you, and I probably wouldn't believe me either if I was you. So, take your people and see how they are living for yourselves."

"We can't. They put all of us under a travel ban. The Lunas can't leave the outer domes."

"The Committee isn't in charge anymore. Consider the ban lifted." Vincent said. Shay stared at Vincent, speechless. Fiona put her hands on the desk and leaned in towards the man.

"Last time I checked your people built all of this. You grew all of these crops. You were the first people to scratch out an existence on this grey hellscape. Then they came in and took if from you. Locked you in this damn dome and enslaved you so they could sit in their dome and live like kings."

"Fiona." Vincent said. "Chill. We just gave him a lot of stuff he needs to process." He had once been in Shay's shoes. Finding out everything you ever believed in and trusted was a manufactured lie is a lot to take in at once. Fiona had the benefit of knowing from the day she was born that the Committee was cold, calculating, and ruthless.

"No, fuck that." She fired back. "Look at you!" She jabbed a finger into Shay's chest who recoiled from the contact. "Look at what they did to your family and your friends! They left you out here to work until you drop dead and you're just going to sit there and take it? Grow a pair of balls and go take your city back."

"Please." Shay sobbed. "Please leave. I need to talk about this with my people. They need to know about all of this."

"Oh, come on!" Fiona seethed. Vincent put a hand on her shoulder.

"We should go."

They had been back in the Committee dome for a few hours when the Lunas decided to test their new found freedom.

Vincent had sequestered himself in Aron's office when Felicity came through the door, a look of fear spread across her face.

"Consul." She said, panting. Her skin was flush and she was sweating through her heavy dress uniform. "The Lunas are here." He shot up from his desk and she led him through the Committee building back out into the street. There he saw the ragged cloaked, emaciated forms of the Outer Dome farmers. They had crossed through the tunnel that had been previously off limits to them and were now staring wide eyed at how the Central Committee had been living.

This was the event that finally brought out the population of the Committee dome. Hundreds of confused men, women, and children had exited their housing units to gawk at the starving people that had appeared. Their looks were not ones of confusion, sadness, or anger like that of the Lunas. They were of outward disgust.

"Go back to your dome!" Screamed an Earthian civilian.

"Loon filth!" Shouted another.

"Shit." Vincent said. "Felicity get the Volunteers out here before something goes bad."

"Yes sir." She nodded and ran off back into the office. A few Volunteers milled about the area, their weapons slung over their shoulder, not sure what to do. Vincent was sure that nowhere in their compressed training had any of the soldiers under his command learned how to stop a riot from happening on a foreign moon.

"Hey!" He yelled at one of the confused looking Volunteers. "Go get your unit and make sure these people don't start killing one another!" The Volunteer saluted clumsily before hurrying back to where their unit was billeted. Unfortunately, Vincent's orders to the Volunteers were too late. Around ten Ethics Police Officers appeared in the growing crowd of displeased Earthians. They wore great coats and peaked caps, their shin high black boots were so polished they shined like glass.

"This area is off limits for Citizens of the outer domes! Return to your domes at once!" Commanded the lead Officer. The Officer was an older man, pushing his forties but with the thick midsection that told of the comforts of a lifetime of service cloistered away on Lunar City.

"We aren't going anywhere!" Screamed one of the Lunas. Vincent noticed it was the partially dressed form of Shay's daughter, Akabi. She still had her issued rifle in her hands. It was the only weapon on the Luna side. "By order of the commander of the occupation, Consul Vincent Solaris, the people of the outer domes can go wherever they want!"

"We don't recognize the authority of the Great Traitor." Growled the lead Officer. Vincent sighed and was about to step forward into the fray when Fiona and her Commissary soldiers appeared from around corner, riding their transport trucks. Their engines spewed black smoke as the convoy of trucks roared across the central dome parade square. The soldiers rode in the backs of the three trucks, weapons held at the ready. The trucks screeched to a halt next to the Lunas and Fiona jumped down from the lead truck. She advanced on the lead officer.

"How about you back the fuck off you jack booted bitch." Her hand was firmly wrapped around the butt of her Riten and she thumbed the hammer back in one fluid motion. Seeing this, the Officers quickly unholstered their weapons, but Fiona was quicker. She leveled her Riten at the face of the lead Officer.

"How dare-"

"I told you to back the fuck off." She interrupted him. "By orders of the Consul the Lunas are free to go wherever the hell they want. Stand in their way and you are violating the treaty and will be dealt with accordingly. And by accordingly, I mean I'll shove all ten pounds of this hand cannon up your fat ass and empty the chamber into your guts."

Vincent ran out to meet her before she murdered a cop in the middle of the square.

"Put your weapon down, Fiona!" She rolled her eyes and slowly lowered it, but kept her Riten clear of its holster. Vincent turned towards the officer. "Is there a problem here?"

"No outer dome citizens are allowed into the inner domes. It was an order from the Chairman himself!"

"Last time I checked the Chairman surrendered." Fiona sneered. The officer's hand slowly began drawing his weapon again before stopping suddenly. His eyes went wide as he looked passed Vincent. Behind him he heard the thundering of boots as dozens of armed Volunteers finally gotten to the scene.

"The Lunas have full authority to go wherever they please as long as Lunar City is under our occupation." Vincent said as calmly as he could. He could feel the overwhelming desire of the gathering of soldiers behind him to gun the Ethics Police down where they stood. For many of them they had been dreaming of doing such a thing since they were kids, Fiona among them. She was literally shaking with anticipation of things turning suddenly violent. The lead officer laughed.

"And you think we will forget about this when you and your army of reds and savages leave our city?" The lead officer pointed at Akabi. "I'll have your entire family strung up in the middle of your dome for everyone to see the second these race traitors leave the city."

"Fuck you!" She screamed at him.

"You have a big mouth for a sexual ethics criminal!" the lead officer countered.

That is when Vincent heard the first gun shot. He went to

unholster his Riten but was shoved to the ground by Zinvor. He landed, sprawled on his back, pinned in place. The crowds of people turned and ran in every direction in a panic. More guns joined the first shots and soon the dome was filled with the staccato rapid fire of a warzone.

After just a few seconds the exchange of fire was over. The air was stained with the copper stench of blood. As the sounds of guns died out, they were replaced by the shouts and screams of the wounded and scared. Zinvor finally stood up, freeing Vincent. When he sat up, he saw the argument that had been going on only a few moments before had been reduced to the twisted forms of the dead and dying.

Dozens of people on both sides of the line were laying on the ground. The Earthians who could still move picked up their friends and family and scampered off back into the city. Their dead were left behind, amongst them was the Ethics Officers, including the lead officer who had been promising retribution against the Lunas only a few seconds before.

Several of the unarmed Lunas had been shot as well. A few laid in crumpled heaps on the ground, not moving. Others writhed in pain as their blood pooled together onto the concrete. They were joined by a few dead and wounded Volunteers.

"Fiona, get these wounded on your trucks and get them to the hospital." Vincent said. Fiona had taken a knee and was quickly reloading the chambers of her Riten. She snapped the ammunition wheel closed and reholstered it. The Volunteers were doing the same thing, fumbling with their ammo pouches and loading fresh magazines into their rifles in case more Ethics Officers or soldiers showed up.

"You heard the Consul!" Fiona shouted at them. "Get these people in the trucks and get to the hospital!" The Volunteers shouldered their weapons and began to help those who had been shot. Together, they helped the Lunas load the wounded into the trucks before the commissary soldiers jumped behind the wheel and sped off. Only the dead were left behind.

With both groups standing in the open as someone opened fire, there was nowhere for anyone to hide. He saw at least twenty dead Earthians, civilians and Ethics Officers. The Volunteers had lined their bodies up and had begun going through their pockets for any weapons or intelligence they might have on them. Any weapons they found were handed over to the surviving Lunas. The emaciated farmers stuffed their new pistols in their waistbands.

Vincent found Akabi standing amongst the dead of her people. There were dozens of them. Her rifle was still in her hands, but its bolt had locked to the rear. She had fired all of the rounds in her magazine during the brief outburst of violence. The cuffs of her uniform jacket were ringed with blood and her glasses were smudged.

"The fuck just happened?" Fiona asked, snapping both of them out of it.

"I…shot him." Akabi said, her voice only a whisper.

"Wait, you shot first?" Vincent asked.

"I think so." She said, her voice trembling. "I don't know… After what he said… What he said he was going to do. I just blacked out." Fiona placed a hand on her shoulder and she flinched.

"It's okay."

"Okay?" Akabi shrieked. "Look at what I just did!"

"That fucker was going to do ten times worse to your people." Fiona countered, pointing at the corpse of the lead officer. "He had it coming." Akabi gestured to the dead civilians that now lined the streets.

"And what about them?"

"We're at war, in case you forgot. War doesn't care who it kills." Akabi bit her lip.

"They weren't at war! We brought war to them!" The few seconds of Fiona's soft touch on her shoulder was gone. Fiona's knuckles turned white as she gripped her.

"Are you kidding me?" Fiona seethed. "Look at how your people were living! Did you see those kids with their bellies hanging out? People having their limbs mauled by farm equipment and the only replacement they get is some junk someone slapped together that hardly works. Your own dad looked like a damned skeleton. How much longer do you think he could survive like that?" Akabi didn't answer. She watched as Lunas loaded their dead onto hand carts and wheeled them back towards their dome.

"First, they took your home from you, then they took your freedom, then relegated you to slopping through pig shit and working the fields until you drop dead all. They've been at war against you since the second they came here, you just never fought back." Fiona said. "The only difference between Martians and Lunas is we just noticed a little sooner than you did."

"What should I do now?" Akabi asked quietly.

"Well." Vincent said. "Whether you meant to or not, you fired the first shots of whatever happens next. Maybe you should go back and talk to your Dad about what the outer domes plan on doing next."

"Is that okay? My Commanding officer will be pissed if I just vanish."

"Don't worry about the Volunteers right now, go take care of your family. We aren't going anywhere for a while."

"You might want to grab some more ammo if you plan on shooting anymore cops along the way, though." Fiona joked.

"I'd prefer if you didn't shoot anyone else today." Vincent added.

"Yes, Sir." Akabi said, saluting. She straightened her uniform and walked off.

"Ugh." Vincent groaned. "Aron is going to have my ass." Fiona lit a cigarette from a Earthian brand packet.

"Why's that?"

"Why do you think?" Vincent exclaimed. "One of our soldiers just started a goddamn shootout in the middle of the Committee Dome and I just let her get away with it." She shrugged.

"Are you going to arrest her? It was self-defense." Vincent rolled his eyes. "What?" She laughed. "That is what the cops always say."

16

Vincent was right. Aron immediately had his ass.

As soon as he walked back into the office that had become the command center for the Occupation, the Marshal was waiting for him and he was about as mad as he had ever seen him. Though, he still had the professionalism to dismiss the rest of the commander center's staff before making the supposed Consul, the one in technically in charge of everyone there, look very stupid.

"What in the fuck were you thinking!" Aron yelled. It wasn't a question and he didn't expect an answer. He had his arms clasped behind his back and was pacing back and forth around his desk. Vincent assumed he had his hands secured behind him so he didn't punch his boss. "This occupation was going to be hard enough with the rest of the Clan and the Martians focused on other things. The Volunteers were hardly ready for all of this responsibility and you had to go out and start a goddamn civil war?" He spat. "Are you actively trying to fuck with me?"

"I didn't start anything, Aron." Vincent said. He hoped by keeping his voice calm, the furious Marshal would bring his down to meet him. That did not happen.

"But one of our soldiers did. One of our soldiers started a

goddamn gunfight in the middle of the city. The most important dome in the city if we ever had a hope of keeping this occupation a peaceful one, may I add. Do you understand how an occupation works?" Vincent sighed.

"Of course I don't."

"Yeah, I could fucking tell. It doesn't matter who did what, why, or when. The only story that is going to get back to the EDF, the cops, the Earthians, and especially that Grand Marshal that hates us so much is that a Volunteer gunned down a bunch of helpless civilians. To make it worse I hear there was direct orders from the Consul that she not be arrested."

"That isn't what happened!" Vincent snapped.

"It doesn't matter! That is what they will hear. And they are going to be pissed."

"So what? You think we should prepare for the EDF to come out of their barracks looking for a fight now?"

"No." Aron shook his head. "The Grand Marshal might be a cold bitch, but she didn't rise to that rank by being incompetent. The Chairman is keeping her close for a reason. We already confiscated what was left of their fleet, tanks, and small arms. Outside of whatever the EDF has managed to squirrel away from Fiona's goons she doesn't have much to bring to a fight. But we can assume that this little incident isn't going to go unanswered. I don't know what she will do, but we should be ready for anything."

"Can't we just put the EDF under watch?" Vincent asked. "Seems pretty straight forward to me."

"You really are trying to start a civil war, I swear." Aron rubbed his face. "You think seeing a bunch of armed soldiers marching towards their barracks isn't going to spark another damn gunfight?" He had to admit he hadn't thought of that.

"How many weapons do you think they could have hidden from Fiona's soldiers?"

"Enough to cause us problems. This is their city and they know the hiding spots. As good as Fiona's lot is, we aren't in Olympus. We just have to hope this Interim Chairman is as rational as he seemed during the meeting and can reign in the Grand Marshal."

"Aron, did you get the feeling he could reign her in during that meeting?"

"To be honest, no. I didn't."

"Me either."

17

The explosion tore through the silence of the Lunar night. The ground shook and it rained broken glass as the fireball rapidly climbed upwards, tearing the façade off of the Committee headquarters. The shattered remnants of the building rained down on the surrounding city like an urban hale.

Vincent and Fiona were thrown from their beds and slammed into the far wall as the blast wave exploded through their window and rushed into their room. Vincent landed upside down as smoke and debris clouded the room. He flopped over, righting himself and coughed as his lungs seized on the suddenly polluted air.

"Holy shit!" Fiona wheezed. "You okay?"

"Yeah." Vincent coughed again. "Are you?" Fiona lifted up her hands and found them bloody, torn by countless of small cuts as she braced herself on broken glass.

"Nothing major." She winced as she pulled some of the larger pieces out. The door to the room burst open and Zinvor rushed in, a look of panic on his face.

"I'm fine!" Vincent called out to him. Zinvor stomped through the glass and debris without worry, hauling them both to their feet. "Do you know what happened?"

"Bomb." He grunted.

"No shit." Fiona groaned. "Got anything else for us?"

"I think it came from the ground floor. I saw medics running downstairs."

Vincent walked over to the where the window had been a few moments before and looked down. Through the tons of pulverized concrete, churned to ash in an instant and floating through the air he could see a massive crater at street level. Fire rippled up from the crater and lapped up the side of the ruined building.

"We should go. This building is no longer safe." Zinvor urged. Vincent pulled himself away from the edge. Fiona led them out into the hallway where they were met with the terror filled eyes of hundreds of staff officers who lived on the same floor. They were attempting to file down the hallway towards the stairwell. A smoke alarm blared from somewhere on the floor and the air hung heavy with smoke. A glowing sign that hung from the ceiling directed the crowd in the right direction with a white arrow.

Zinvor pushed his way down the line.

"Make way for the Consul!" He commanded. He wasn't sure if it was his title or the fact a Mawr had screamed at them but it had the intended effect. The crowd jumped aside as if they were in a crosswalk and one of Fiona's trucks had been barreling towards them.

Once in the stairwell they quickly made their way down. They walked by the wounded from the blast. Those who happened to be too close to the windows when the bomb went off or people who had the bad luck to not be thrown clear of the shower of debris like Vincent and Fiona had. He saw people with faces disfigured by flying glass or skin blackened and peeling from burns. They had gotten as far as they could before collapsing, now they lay unmoving in the stairwell. As they went further down more of the wounded had gathered or dropped lifeless to the floor.

Vincent bent down next to one of them. He could see a khaki

uniform with the shoulder insignia of a Captain. He rolled them over to reveal a face that had been so badly burned he could hardly recognize it as human. Fiona put a hand on his shoulder and pulled him back to his feet.

"I don't think you can help these people." She said softly.

The ground floor of the building was in disarray. The blast had ripped away all of the glass and frames that made up the entry way of the building, throwing the deadly shrapnel inwards. A surging wall of flames had reduced the once flat grey surfaces to a charred black. Corpses of torn and broken soldiers lay all over. Medics milled about checking for any survivors, most were left where they were found. A few others were taken by stretcher to a waiting ambulance outside.

In the midst of the chaos was Aron, standing alongside a few officers that Vincent didn't recognize. His uniform was singed and his face smeared with dust. Aron noticed Vincent and ran over to him.

"Are you hurt?" He asked.

"No, I'm fine. What the hell happened?"

"It seems like the Grand Marshal made her move." He frowned. "A transport truck in EDF livery was parked outside. We had taken so many of them we didn't notice that it wasn't one of ours. I assume they knew that. It waited for a reaper to land outside before it detonated. They must have been watching it."

"A reaper?" Vincent asked. Aron bit his lip and motioned for him to follow, so he did. The glass crunched under their boots as they made their way outside. The flames from the crater still burned with enough heat to force them to give it a wide berth. A few soldiers were attempting to put it out using buckets of water but they were fighting a losing battle.

The twisted remains of a Reaper had been thrown across the street, impacting the opposite building hard enough to send spider cracks up its exterior. The windows of all of the surrounding buildings had been blown out, littering the area with glass. A few bodies lay in the street next to the reaper, cloaked with tin foil like emergency blankets. Several of Erin's Commandos stood around them, rifles in hand, on guard. Their faces were not ones of confusion, like Vincent's probably was. They were locked in a blind rage.

The Commandos saluted the approaching Marshals and their gesture was returned.

"Let the Consul see." Aron said to them and they nodded. One of the Commandos knelt down besides one of the bodies and pulled back the blanket. Vincent saw Erin's lifeless face staring back at him. Her eyes were still open, locked onto the last flash of light she would ever see. He felt his fists ball up and his fingernails dig into the palms of his hands. His throat went thick and his eye that was still able to form tears opened up the waterworks.

"We think they used their radar to track this Reaper from the *Olympus* to here and assumed it was you. Anyone else they caught in the blast must have just been a bonus." Aron said.

"I want them dead." Vincent seethed.

"Consul, we have to think about our response." Aron cut in, but Vincent could tell he wasn't convinced of his own words.

"This attack was like the one that took my eye." He spat. "The ones they used the target the Victorian civilians. Sure, they wanted to kill me, but if that is all they wanted to do it would be easy enough to shoot me on the street. They wanted to do more. They wanted to terrorize us. Make us feel like we aren't safe. Try to scare us. They're backed into a corner and this is all they have left. Lashing out like wild animals." He pointed at the Commandos.

"Get your men together. I want every person that can handle a weapon ready to move in a few minutes." The Commandos nodded and broke into a run back towards their barracks.

"*Sir.*" Aron said more forcefully. "I mourn for Erin as much as you, but we should think about this. This is the kind of response they want."

"I tried to do things Arai's way. We tried to co-exist with them. This is what it got us, Aron." He pointed back to the burning crater in the middle of the road. A few hundred stories above them one of the buildings floors gave way, collapsing onto the one below it. A plume of smoke rushed out from between them.

"Fine." Aron frowned. "But you appointed me Marshal to be your advisor, so let me advise."

"Go ahead."

"We send the Volunteers to search the EDF barracks. From there maybe we can find out who did this."

"You're kidding right? The fuck'n Grand Marshal did this. Send in my boys and we will make her pay." Fiona countered.

"We don't know that. Not yet anyway." Aron said. "We should do this the right way, maybe show them that we aren't the same as the Central Committee." He glared at Vincent.

"Fine." He said. "How fast can you make this happen?"

"We can be ready to roll in five minutes." Fiona said.

"Good, let's go."

The transport trucks turned off the central square of the committee dome and into a warren of narrow streets that made up the domicile units. Individual family homes, each identical with neatly manicured lawns measuring a few feet apiece. Every married couple would have been issued one once their registration paperwork was filed with the Marital Union Ministry. A larger house would be issued for every child the couple produced, with a max of three. Nobody ever said what happened if you had a forth.

Vincent grew up in a house much like most of the ones they drove by. Though in District Six they were markedly shabbier and more run down. To qualify for a house in the committee dome they had to be some of the most powerful or favored people at the highest echelons of Earthian political life. Not the people who made the government tick on a day to day basis, though those people may one day dream to reach these heights. At least, they used to. The Committee did not just hand out residency permits for Lunar City to anyone. It was something to be bought with years of loyalty, something people strived for their entire life, fighting their way up the rungs of power.

The curtains of the homes rustled as they drove by. The scared faces of civilians sneaking glimpses of the passing convoy, bristling with soldiers and weaponry. Behind them a Squadron of Volunteers marched. They purposefully sang as loud as they could and brought their heels down in unison against the concrete to make a sharp snapping noise with each step. Above them two Reapers flew low overhead, carrying squads of Commandos.

Beyond the domicile units was the military district. Identical grey building blocks, each a barracks for a different EDF unit. They were supposed to have been disarmed and confined to their district until the end of the occupation. The several ton bomb that had all but leveled the occupation office and killed Erin proved both of those things to be dubious at best.

Vincent rode in the back of a transport truck along with Fiona and her soldiers. Aron was with them, the scowl had not left his face since they had set out.

"Remember." Aron said. "let our regular troops secure the barracks before you send in your lot."

"What?" Fiona asked. "Worried we can't handle ourselves?"

"That isn't what I'm worried about." Vincent was worried about the same thing as Aron was. Fiona's soldiers were experts at rooting out hiding spot and war loot that could be pressed into service, that much couldn't be debated. But many of them were only a few months removed from being cutthroat street thugs. Most of them wanted to get their hands on the nearest EDF soldier and deliver a lifetime of payback many of them dreamed about since they were kids, Fiona among them. He wasn't against letting them have their vengeance, not anymore. First, he wanted to find the person responsible for the bombing first.

The Reapers swooped down even lower, their crew doors slid open and the Commandos swung out their mounted chain guns. Some EDF soldiers who were milling about outside, smoking and chatting in small groups, froze where they were standing, others took off running towards the barracks.

"By order of the occupation authority all EDF personnel are to exit the barracks immediately." Boomed a voice from a loudspeaker mounted from the nose of one of the Reapers. EDF soldiers appeared in the doorway, confused and only partially dressed. Just in time for them to see the convoy of trucks pulling onto the drill pad.

Fiona's soldiers jumped from the back of the trucks, their rifles held at waist level and screaming at the EDF to come out with their hands up. The reapers landed on the roofs of the barracks and dozens of Agents jumped out. Behind the convoy came hundreds of Volunteers, brandishing their rifles and yelling along with Fiona's soldiers.

One EDF trooper shoved by a soldier and took off running back towards the domicile district. A group of Volunteers tackled him, beating them with their fists and rifle butts before carrying them back towards the barracks. Another EDF trooper took a swing Volunteer, connecting with a sickening crack on the young lady's jaw, dropping her on her back.

The Trooper advanced on the downed Volunteer but was knocked unconscious by a rifle butt to the back of the head. The situation was quickly getting out of control when Fiona jumped up to the mounted machine gun that was mounted above the cab of her truck. She pointed it down at the ground and fired off a long burst, stitching it across the concrete drill pad. Hundreds of screaming voices all at each other's throats fell silent as they turned to look at who just nearly killed them.

"Anyone else takes a swing at a soldier of the Volunteer Army I swear on your Chairman I'll cut you in half with this gun!" She screamed. That seemed to have done it, the fight quickly left the EDF troopers, though they continued to hurl insults at the Volunteers. One group of Volunteers stood watch as another got closer to the EDF troopers to search them. The search produced nothing but a few knives and cigarette packs. Vincent saw more than one of these were also taken from the troopers, he didn't bother to order the Volunteers not to steal from them. He didn't care anymore.

Fiona looked on as her soldiers went to work, pouring into the barracks blocks to work them over with a fine tooth comb. This left Vincent and the rest of the Volunteers sitting outside, squaring off with the troopers across the drill pad.

"Why do they not fight us?" Zinvor asked.

"Because they don't have any weapons." Felicity said.

"They have their hands, their feet, their teeth. Do humans need a weapon to fight their enemies?"

"You don't fight people you surrender to." Felicity's tone of voice made it seem like she was quickly growing frustrated with Zinvor. He frowned.

"The bomb says otherwise." Vincent was pulled away from the conversation by shouting coming from the entrance of the military district. Aron was already quickly walking that way to see what the commotion was and Vincent jogged to catch up to him.

"I demand you step aside immediately!" Came an annoyed voice that Vincent recognized immediately.

"Shit." He sighed.

"We should have assumed the Grand Marshal would hear about this." Said Aron.

"I know. I just don't feel like dealing with her."

"I'm sure Fiona would love to deal with her if you don't." Felicity countered.

"Fair enough."

It would have been easy for the Grand Marshal to simply fly over the Volunteers guarding the district entrance had Aron not ordered to confiscation of every aero car in the city upon their arrival. Since then, the thousands of luxury model cars had been stripped down and parted out for the fleet. Because of that the

Grand Marshal had been reduced to riding shotgun in one of the few old model trucks that been left as a courtesy to the old government. A fact she did not look very pleased about.

She was surrounded by about a dozen armed Ethics Police Officers, standing at the district entrance demanding answers as to what was happening. Instead of being given the treatment she was used to and as afforded by her lofty rank, she was instead greeted by the sneers and jeers of around a platoon of Volunteers.

"Get fucked lady." Spat a Martian woman with the rank of a First Sergeant. "Nobody comes in without the permission of the Consul or the Marshal."

"I am acting under orders from the Chairman!" The Grand Marshal screamed.

"I'll tell you what." The First Sergeant laughed. "You go get the Chairman, bring him down here, and I'll tell him to get fucked too."

"First Sergeant." Aron called out to her. "What is going on here?" The First Sergeant turned on her heels and saluted.

"Sir, the Grand Marshal of the EDF is demanding to come into the district."

"You!" The Grand Marshal screamed, jabbing the air with a pointing finger in Vincent's direction. "this is in violation of our terms!"

"Yeah?" Vincent said, advancing towards the group. "So is setting off a goddamned bomb at my headquarters. Excuse me if I don't really give a shit about our terms at the moment."

"I had nothing to do with that." She folded her arms.

"I'm sure you didn't." Aron said, sarcastically. "But I bet someone in here will probably say otherwise."

"You have no proof." She scowled.

"Not yet." Vincent said. "But when I do, me and you are going to have a nice long talk. Now, listen to the First Sergeant and kindly get fucked."

"Listen to me, boy." The Grand Marshal seethed through clenched teeth. "This isn't the end of this."

She and her parade of Ethics Police climbed back into the truck and departed, leaving a black smoke trail in their wake.

"That could have gone better." Felicity said.

"It could have gone worse." Vincent shrugged.

"We really have set a low bar for ourselves, haven't we?" She laughed.

"Where the hell did she even come from? We took over their offices."

"You really don't read the intelligence documents that are delivered to you every day, do you?"

"You know as well as I do that I don't."

"You're lucky that I go through all of your shit then." She sighed. "The committee government moved into one of the other inner domes, probably surrounded by their favorite loyalists. I assume these people only stayed in our dome because they had no other choice. Before they killed her, Erin pinpointed the Chairman's location to the university. We can probably assume Grand Marshal Lagos is nearby."

"We are going to need someone to spearhead figuring out as much as we can about them now that Erin is dead." He rubbed his beard. "The job is yours if you want it, Felicity."

"You want to make me a Marshal?" She stammered. "I couldn't replace Erin."

"Erin was one of the most ruthless, intelligent, and cunning women I have ever met. If you can't do it, I don't know anyone else who could possibly fill her shoes."

"But what about my current role? Who will fill it?"

"I knew you were going to say that. I will accept anyone you nominate to be my aid, Felicity." He smiled. "Only the Union can vote on you becoming a Marshal, but I wouldn't worry about that. Until then, consider the job yours. Consider your last duty as my aid sending them the request." Felicity's almond eyes began to shimmer with tears and she grinned from ear to ear.

"I won't let you down, Consul."

"I know."

"Consul!" called the voice of the Martian First Sergeant. Vincent turned back towards her. "Sounds like they found something in the barracks." Vincent turned to Felicity.

"Sounds like you're already going to be busy."

19

The EDF soldiers were now sitting in the dirt, displaying a mixture of boredom and hatred. Their guards showed the same expression as they stood watch over them. The insults and jeering the two sides had been throwing back and forth had died down. Now, the commotion was coming from a collection of commissary soldiers.

They had emerged from a barracks building that was labeled with the building number *10005* in block lettering. The soldiers had several crates stacked up in front of them. They were nondescript black boxes that looked like they could be any low ranking officer's foot locker. Seated on the ground next to them was another dozen EDF soldiers, their hands bound behind their backs and more than a few bloody lips and noses among them. Fiona was crouching down in front of them, screaming at them and waving her Riten in their face.

"Am I interrupting something?" Vincent asked. Fiona glanced at him, turned back to one of the bound soldiers and slapped him across the face. Blood oozed out from his already damaged mouth and he yelped in pain.

"Check in the lockers." She said, standing up. One of the

commissary soldiers walked over and opened the locker. Vincent looked inside and was puzzled. He expected to see blocks of explosives, military grade stuff that they had managed to hide from the prying eyes of Fiona's soldiers. Instead, he saw large sacks of white powder.

"And what exactly am I looking at?" He asked.

"Homemade explosives. Mostly made from a kind of fertilizer." She sneered. "When we went through their barracks we only took the supplies that were on their inventory lists. They must have taken the components from the farmers so it wouldn't appear on any inventory that we could track. The farmers wouldn't have said anything because a bunch of these dick heads coming by and robbing them was just par for the course."

"They used fertilizer to nearly level an entire building?" Vincent asked, incredulously.

"Pack enough of this shit into the back of a utility vehicle you can blow just about anything up. And I imagine-"She said leaning down to look at one of the bound soldier's uniforms and pointed out a small badge they wore on their chest. "That a highly trained Pathfinder would know just how to do that."

"And." Felicity cut in. "You're not going to store several lockers full of explosives in your barracks without everyone else who lives with you knowing."

"Hence why we got all these pricks lined up out here." Fiona confirmed. "Should we just take them out back and shoot them?"

"No." Vincent snapped. "Do you really think a bunch of these guys, Pathfinders or not, randomly got the idea to blow up our headquarters on their own? We shoot them, we never figure out who was giving them orders."

"I think we fucking know who was giving them orders." Fiona frowned.

"I want to hear them say it." Fiona smiled and bent back down in front of one of the soldiers, grabbing their face in her hand.

"Oh. I can make them say whatever you want." A smiled crept across her face.

"Fuck you!" the soldier moaned through his bleeding lips. Fiona slapped him again.

"Not like that." Vincent sighed. "Felicity, take these fine officers into your custody and make sure nothing happens to them."

"Yes, Sir." She responded. She waved over several Commandos and without another word they hauled the bound soldiers away. Fiona slowly put what she was watching together and let out a chuckle.

"Her? You picked her to replace Erin?"

"Your personal aversion to her shined boots aside, can you think of anyone better?" He asked.

"No." She begrudgingly admitted. "You're right. I'm still going to hate her boots though."

"I know."

20

The sun rose above them, making odd shadows dance across the spaceport as its rays shined through the dome. The spaceport was crammed with as many soldiers that could fit. Vincent assumed it was thousands, he wasn't sure. They stood in their best looking uniforms in rigid formation, many were barely holding back tears.

"Volunteers!" Boomed the voice of Aron. Directly down the middle of the spaceport a path opened through the throngs of humanity. There he stood, staring back towards the dome exit. "Present, arms!" He commanded. At his order every person in the spaceport brought their hand up to their eye in salute. The exit opened and slowly Commandos appeared, bearing the body of Erin. Behind them came the bearers of the others killed in the bomb attack. There were no coffins, those would take up too much space. Each of the fallen was sealed into a plain black body bag. Erin's was obscured by an Elysian flag.

As he watched the dead parade by him Vincent felt his eyes begin to burn. At that moment he wanted to turn Fiona loose on the EDF officers in their custody. He wanted to join in on what happened next himself. A tear streamed down from his real eye. He pushed the ideas of revenge from his head. He tried to think of what Erik would do. He wouldn't shoot them on the spot, his *no white gloves in a revolution* rule aside.

He remembered back to when he helped Erik round up the Olympus gangers who had turned against him. He didn't shoot them, even though everyone probably told him to. He made them stand trial for their crimes for everyone to see. Vincent knew the substance of the trial wasn't the fairness of the event. Erik knew every single person who stood before his court was going to hang before the trials even started. It was to show everyone else that he was not to be fucked with. The old order was dead and there it was, swinging in front of you.

The funeral procession made it to the end of the path where three Reapers were waiting. One by one their bodies were loaded into the cargo holds. Once they were done their pallbearers stood shoulder to shoulder and saluted as the cargo doors were closed. Slowly the Reapers lifted into the air and entered the dome's airlock system. Small groups of soldiers continued to watch while others began to make their way towards the exit.

"Consul." Said Felicity. Her eyes were bloodshot. She had cried in loud sobbing heaves during the procession and her attempts to smother them with her sleeves had failed. "The interrogations are going well." She sniffed. "I should have answers for you by the end of the day."

"Good." He nodded. Felicity began to walk away and he stopped her. "Oh, before I forget. The Union approved of your promotion."

"Congratulations, Marshal Haagen." Fiona said, her voice only slightly mocking.

"I wish I felt good about it." She said, her eyes beginning to well back up with tears again. Fiona recoiled at the open show of emotion.

"Jeeze. I'm sorry."

"You're at a funeral. Can you at least act sad?" Vincent scolded.

"Why?" She frowned. "Erin can't see us crying. She's dead. You knew her, she was tougher than rationed meat. You think she would want us all standing around hugging and crying over her?"

"No." Felicity sobbed.

"You're fucking right she wouldn't. She would want us to get mad. She would want us to root out the little shits who did this. You probably don't think you're worthy to take her spot, do you?"

"Fiona, take it easy." Vincent said protectively.

"No. It's okay, she's right." Felicity wiped her nose with her sleeve.

"Then fucking work until you do." Vincent couldn't believe it, but Fiona's mean motivational speech seemed to be working.

"You're right, I will." She stormed off in the direction of the exit.

"Did that just work?" Vincent asked, confused.

"Of course it did. She was a rich kid who went to the military academy and nobody has ever talked to her like she was a piece of shit before. She just needed some tough love. I do that to you all the time and look how far you've come."

"That doesn't sound as good as you think it does." He thought for a moment. "We should go check on her. I'm worried your little pep talk is going to drive her to act like well, you."

"You say that like it is a bad thing."

"It is."

The Public Order Cohort, now under the command of Felicity, had set up a small jail in the basement in the former Ministry of Communications building. They hadn't intended for it to look or feel like the dark, miserable, hole. The room just ended up being the only place in the entire building that didn't have any windows. The rest of the building had been turned into their headquarters and billet area.

The basement was never meant to store human beings and as such the Officers standing guard over the newly arrested EDF soldiers had to make do. Several of them sat on the floor with ropes tied around their arms and legs, joined together with a knot, and then secured around a pole in the middle of the room. A few discarded ration packs sat on the floor next to the prisoners, uneaten.

The two Officers on guard saluted Fiona and Vincent as they entered the basement.

"Where is Marshal Haagen?" Vincent asked.

"In the next room, Sir." One of the Officers said. "Follow me." The young woman in a far too large peaked cap led them down a badly lit hallway and to a small door. She knocked on it and then entered. Inside Felicity sat in a chair across from a prisoner. He was bound with his hands behind his back and his face was crusted with dried blood.

"Are we interrupting?" Vincent asked.

"Hm?" Felicity looked up from a data display she was taking notes on. "Oh no, we were just finishing."

"I see you used some of my old tools, eh?" Fiona said gesturing at the man's damaged face.

"No, Marshal. You did that."

"Oh, right." Fiona laughed.

"So, what do we have?" Vincent asked.

"The soldiers outside broke easy enough, fingered this one as the commander of the bombing." Felicity said. "All we had to do was promise them passage to Elysian."

"You're going to let these pieces of shit into our home?" Fiona screamed. "You can't let her do that!" She turned to Vincent.

"She is a Marshal." He shrugged. "I expect the Commandos will keep tabs on them for the foreseeable future."

"Of course." Felicity nodded.

"And are we supposed to believe this dick is the ringleader?" Fiona snarled.

"This is Lieutenant Colonel Arnsholt Aliyev." Felicity said without looking up from her display. "Commander of the Lunar Pathfinder Brigade. Born on Earth, posted to Lunar City three years ago. Veteran of more than one Martian Rebellion. Though the service records I was able to find from the EDF servers is missing some years here and there. Nothing I wouldn't expect from Pathfinder, though."

"And?" Vincent raised an eyebrow.

"He married a local two years ago and is a father of one."

"We don't care about his goddamn family life, Felicity." Fiona spat.

"You should, Marshal." Felicity glared at her. "It is called leverage. I threatened to dispatch a team to detain his family unless he told us who gave him his orders." She turned back towards the man who by now looked like he would do anything to escape his bonds and murder Felicity with his bare hands. "And?" She asked.

"Chairman Han." The man said through broken and bloody lips.

"The Chairman?" Vincent asked. Through everything that had happened so far Chairman Han had seemed almost relieved to surrender Lunar City. After his sob story about his child and his speech about being tired of war, why would he order something he had to know would bring them more war? Even if his plan did end in Vincent's death as he planned, he had to know that wouldn't have chased off the Volunteers. If they had succeeded Arai would have ordered the entire city razed.

"Can I talk to you outside?" He asked. "I don't think he is going anywhere." Felicity nodded and followed him out of the basement.

"I assume you think it was the Grand Marshal too." Felicity said.

"Well, yeah. You were in that meeting with them. She wants us all dead."

"True, but she is still a career military officer. She didn't make it this far by going rogue and disregarding orders. Especially orders from the Chairman himself." Felicity said. She was right. Disobeying the Chairman and launching what amounted to a coup would be unthinkable for any Earthian officer.

"So, you think Han's entire speech in there was an act?" He asked. "It seemed so real."

"You should know as well as anyone how well politicians lie." Fiona scoffed. "You think he got to where he is now by being a paragon of moral character?"

"Fair."

"I think you sat down with the Chairman and got played." Felicity added.

"But to what end? He still surrendered."

"Maybe he saw what happened to his armies on Mars and his fleet when they tried to stop us and realized standing up to us in the field was a bad idea." Felicity pinched her chin. "Drag us into the city and fight a guerrilla war?"

"Worked for Mars." Fiona added. "Levels the playing field a bit. And as long as our soldiers are in these streets they know they don't catch the Victoria treatment."

"Okay, fine." Vincent sighed, rubbing the bridge of his nose. "I got played and then the asshole killed Erin."

"He was trying to kill you." Felicity said.

"I know. I know." He waved her off. "What is our next move?"

"You're kidding me, right?" Fiona laughed. "We fucking kill him." He turned to Felicity.

"Ideas?"

"We could do what Fiona said or we could let the Lunas do it." She shrugged. "He may have killed a few of us, but there is no telling the misery and death his policies have brought them. The end result is the same, but now the Lunas will be on our side should we need them."

"You got good at this job in a terrifyingly fast amount of time." Vincent laughed. "But we need to actually detain him first." Fiona slapped Vincent on the shoulder.

"You better call Aron before I do this shit on my own."

The Volunteers entered Inner Dome thirteen in force. A dozen trucks packed tight with soldiers flanked by armored personnel carriers bristling with machine guns poured in from the tunnel. Vincent wasn't sure if it was the shock or the overwhelming amount of firepower on display but the Ethics Police on guard did nothing to stop them as they drove by.

The Dome had originally been laid out to be something of a university district. The University of Lunar City was one of the most prestigious in all of Committee controlled space, back when that was a thing. Only the best and most privileged students of the human race could ever hope to enter its halls, at least that is how it was described to Vincent as it was explained to him by several of his teachers as to why he would never be able to get in. Instead, what it had become was a place for the Committee's upper crust to dump their kids in order to incubate the next generation of the ruling elite.

Now, as he stared over the cab of the truck, the university had been abandoned. There was no obvious student life to see. The lush green parks that had drained away so much of the city's water supply were empty. He was curious if the students had been evacuated back to their homes as the Central Committee took over their school as a new seat of government or if they had become pilots or Officers and been killed in battle.

Vincent had never been to any university before, they had all rejected him once he graduated with the lowest possible grade, but he assumed they were normally more lively. The brochures he saw always showed throngs of happy students doing happy student things. Now all he saw were some angry looking cops and soldiers standing watch over the double staircase that led up to the university's front doors. Cops and soldiers who were raising their weapons on the convoy.

A slug sparked off of the cab of the truck Vincent was riding in and he ducked back into the bed for cover. He unholstered his Riten and rose back to the firing platform and all around him soldiers were doing the same. The bass of a heavy machine gun began banging away from one of the APCs as a chorus of rifles joined in. By the time he raised his Riten to fire the entire front of the University was exploding with splinters of concrete and he had lost sight of his targets.

The soldiers standing guard over the university had been left out in the open and stood no chance. Several of them had tried to run when they came to the same realization but it did no good. When the Volunteers finally stopped shooting and the smoke cleared the defenders had been reduced to little more than blood spatters on the surrounding decorative pillars.

"Well, this could have gotten off to a better start." Fiona commented.

"Why the fuck would they shoot at us!" Vincent shouted. "Look how outnumbered they are!"

"Did you think they would respond to us barging in through the gate like this by lying down their weapons? Come on now." Fiona turned back towards the soldiers on the truck. "What the fuck are you waiting for, eh? An invitation? Get in there and arrest that old bastard!"

All around him the soldiers jumped off of whatever vehicle they had rode in on. Sergeants and Officers yelled out commands and slowing they advanced up towards the doors of the university. At their flanks the APCs trundled slowly. Vincent made to climb off of the truck to join them when he felt a pull at the tail of his jacket. He turned and saw Zinvor.

"This is not a battle for you."

"Since when do you think any battle isn't for me?"

"Since I was ordered to keep you from getting yourself killed."

"And who do you take orders from other than me?" Zinvor turned and nodded to Fiona who smirked.

"Love ya." She winked and jumped off of the truck to join the advance. Vincent thought about running after her. He knew he could outrun the Zinvor, or any Mawr for that matter, but he wasn't sure he had the strength to break from his vice like grip in order to do so.

"You take orders from Fiona now, huh?"

"Any wise Warrior would." Zinvor said and Vincent was forced to agree with him. The wrath of Fiona was enough to scare anyone, even someone who died for several minutes once already. "She is right though, your place is not on the frontlines. Not anymore."

"Would you say that to Arai?"

"You are not Arai. Without Arai, we Mawrs would go on doing what we have been doing for generations. Without you? I do not think Humans would be able to do the same thing."

"That is both the nicest and scariest thing you've ever said to me." Before Zinvor could respond the doors to the university swung open. The advancing soldiers dropped to the ground, preparing for a fight, their weapons coming up in front of them as they did. Soon, hundreds were laying in the prone or kneeling, weapons drawn. The APCs moved around to cover them, their machine guns swinging over to cover the doors.

"Please!" Called out of a voice. "Do not shoot!"

"I recognize that voice." Vincent said to nobody in particular.

"Nobody else must die here today!" The voice said. At that Vincent quickly leapt over the side of the truck, too fast for Zinvor to grab him. He hit the ground running, sprinting between soldiers.

"Hold your fire!" He yelled. "Lower your goddamn weapons!" Soldiers exchanged confused looks but dutifully obeyed his order. Felicity and Fiona jogged over to him.

"I swear nearly dying made that Mawr useless. I told him to not let you off of the truck." Fiona said. Felicity ignored her.

"What is going on?"

"I know that voice. It's Chairman Han. He is surrendering." Vincent panted, trying to catch his breath.

"Sounds like a trap to me." Fiona countered.

"If they were planning a trap they would have lined this entire rooftop with machine guns. Hit us when we came into the dome, wouldn't you?" Felicity asked. Vincent glanced nervously at the roof of the university, suddenly unsure if he was sitting in someone's sights as they spoke.

"Fair enough." Fiona turned back towards the still open doors. "Alright, come on out, but any more of what these idiots out here tried and we go into that school and reenact what we did to your people on Mars. Got it?"

"I'm coming out! I am unarmed!" Han yelled. Slowly from the darkness of the school appeared Chairman Han. He was still dressed in his grey tunic and pants, which were still so flawless they looked like he had just had them treated. His black shoes gleamed with an attendant's labor until he stepped out onto the stairs and his feet landed in the remains of two of his guards. His face recoiled in horror as the coppery smell of blood curled its way up his nostrils.

Vincent, flanked by Fiona and Felicity advanced on his.

"Marshal Haagen." Vincent said. "Place Chairman Han under arrest."

"Yes, Consul." Felicity answered. She motioned two of her agents to grab him. His hands were placed behind his back and plastic restraints were tightened around his wrists.

"Chairman Han, you are being placed under arrest for the bombing attack against our headquarters leading to the deaths of dozens of my soldiers as well as the targeted assassination of Marshal Erin Olympus. You are also being charged with various crimes against the Lunar people."

"Consul Solaris, in all due respect I have no idea what you're talking about and I do not recognize your authority to charge me with any crime." Han's words were defiant but Vincent knew fear in a man's eye when he saw it.

"I am not charging you with anything nor will I try you for any crimes. This is not my planet or my city and unlike the Central Committee taking over someone else's world and bending them to our laws is not something we do. You are being charged by a representative of the Lunar people and they will also conduct any trial and punishment they see fit."

"So, you're going to kill me." Han bit his lip.

"Have you thought, maybe, just for a second, that if you didn't treat the farmers in the outer domes so badly for all those years that perhaps you wouldn't already know how this ends?" Fiona raised an eyebrow.

"Let's get out of here before the soldiers waiting inside decide that they want our little fight here to continue." Felicity nodded and the Commandos led Han away back towards the trucks.

23

The entrance into the outer domes was much different than the last time Vincent had gone there. Every barricade and sign had been torn down. Previously the road had been totally empty, populated only by the occasional military checkpoint. Now farmers with carts and trucks crowded the streets. Still others had opened stands on the side of the road, bartering with others as they made their way towards the inner domes. They and the Volunteers exchanged waves as they passed by one another. He was shocked to see a diminutive soldier, clothed in grey, and carrying a rifle also exchange greetings.

"What the hell?" Fiona spat.

"That was a Luna, no doubt about it." Felicity asked.

"Why were they wearing an EDF uniform?" Vincent asked.

"We leave the goddamn place for a week and we have no idea what is going on." Fiona complained. "Isn't this your job?" She glanced at Felicity.

"You'll have to excuse me." Felicity said, her voice dripping with sarcasm. "In the seventy-two hours since I have taken command, during which time I have not slept mind you, I have not had a chance to check in with every spy that Erin had on her payroll which I assume is probably in the thousands by this point." Fiona rolled her eyes.

"Don't give me that attitude. I didn't have that problem."

"You didn't take over from anyone!" Felicity yelled, throwing her hands up. She groaned and sat down heavily on a crate of ammunition. "Why do I even bother with you?"

"I could ask you the same thing." Vincent laughed.

The unmistakable stench of the farms hit his nostrils as the trucks pulled alongside Shay's office. While their world had obviously changed, the farmers of the outer domes had continued on living as they had been. Groups of people were working the fields while others tended to the various animals. Though now they went about things differently. Their clothes were no longer home-spun rags, their moved with less pain and more energy, it seemed as if the entire dome and been reenergized. Vincent wasn't sure if it was from the relief of having the Chairman's boot off of their neck or being able to eat as much as they wanted for once in their lives. Either way, he liked it.

Shay waited outside of his office, flanked by Akabi. She was no longer wearing the khaki uniform of a Volunteer, but rather the grey of an EDF soldier.

"I've been waiting for you." Shay said, smiling. Vincent climbed down off the back of the truck and splashed down on the muddy road.

"That makes two of us. I didn't expect it to go as smoothly as it did." Vincent looked at Akabi. "Did I miss something?" Her face went red.

"We were going to talk to you about that." Shay cleared his throat. "I spoke to other representatives of the other outer domes after what happened before. I spoke to her as well and what those Ethics Officers said is very true. If we leave things the way they are now, when you leave, they will come back for us. Probably kills us all for working with you."

"We wouldn't let that happen." Vincent said, but honestly he wasn't sure if that was true. As independent as the Volunteers are, he had no doubt Arai didn't care about a civil war on a moon thousands of miles away from Elysian when she wanted to focus on the Anarchs. Shay held a hand up.

"You Marshal-" He motioned at Fiona. "Made a very good point. This city belongs to the people. To us. The representatives of the outer domes no longer recognize Chairman Han or his Central Committee as our governing authority. We instead voted on our own Committee and Chairman to take their place." Shay motioned towards the Eagle and Star pin that decorated the area over his heart. It was now adorned with a golden wreath.

"So, I supposed I should call you Chairman Shay now, eh?" Vincent smiled. Shay nodded.

"I am grateful for you letting my daughter into your ranks, but I formally request you transfer her to our new Lunar Defense Force. As well as any Luna soldiers within your ranks that wish to join us."

"Of course. I'll let Marshal Victoria know."

"So, where is Mr. Han?" Vincent noticed he had already dropped the formal Chairman title. Shay moved fast. He knew the man was a functionary of the Central Committee through and through. Even a district farm manager and a Luna would have taken part in cut throat politics to make it as far as he did. Erik kept telling him he couldn't do a revolution while wearing white gloves. He already had his hands stained with Victoria. There was something visceral about seeing the violence his orders caused. Smiling and handing power to someone like Shay hurt him in a much different way.

"Marshal Haagen's people have him detained at their head-quarters. We figured it would look better if you brought him back to the outer domes, rather than us."

"Of course. I'll get an escort together and send them right

over."

After a few minutes of shouting, the newly established Lunar Defense Force had loaded themselves into a truck and followed Vincent out of the dome. Before long they were at the Public Order headquarters.

Since capturing Han, the Commandos and Volunteers had spent their spare time reinforcing the area for any possible EDF counter attack. APCs were lined up outside, providing cover for the multiple platoons of soldiers that stood behind them. Various trucks and aero cars had been used to block off all coming approaches and a soldier had been asked to move a truck out of the way to allow Vincent and Shay's vehicles through. Reapers hummed along in the air and a slow speed, making a lazy orbit of the entire dome.

"Expecting company?" Shay asked.

"Something like that." Vincent responded. "Have you met the Grand Marshal?"

"Grand Marshal Lagos?" Shay frowned. "I haven't had the pleasure, we have all heard stories."

"Trust me, if you had, you would understand." He sighed. The truck came to a stop and his newly christened soldiers walked towards the headquarters' door. Two soldiers quickly opened the door from which another squad appeared. They were members of the *Quick Reaction Force* of the Public Order Cohort. Between them was the restrained form of Han, with a black bag over his head.

The Officers walked him over to the Lunar Defense Forces truck and handed him to the soldiers before quickly retreating back into the building. The soldiers roughly loaded Han into the back of the truck, jumped back into the cab, and sped off back towards the dome exit. The rest of the convoy hurried to catch up to them as the dome door slowly cranked open. As it did, they were greeted by a torrent of gunfire.

The Lunar Defense Force truck exploded in a brilliant fireball and burning human shapes cartwheeled into the sky. Vincent's driver shook violently as bullets slammed through the windshield and tore into her body. Shay tumbled out of the back of the truck, trailing blood. Bullets cut through the convoy of unarmored trucks as if they were cloth. Most soldiers were killed or wounded before they could jump out but the few who did landed in unorganized piles on the ground. Vincent was picked up from his seat and tossed to safety by Zinvor, who came crashing down on top of him soon after.

A rocket streaked into the dome, cutting through the air directly above his head, and impacted the truck behind them. It detonated, throwing pieces of metal in every directly, cutting through fleeing soldiers like a scythe. Slowly, the shock of the ambush wore off and the soldiers began listening to their commanders who began desperately screaming orders to form a firing line. The patrolling Reapers swooped down and unleashed their rockets and machine guns against the ambushing force. Confronted, their gunfire died away slowly.

Vincent picked himself off of the ground and quickly looked himself over. His uniform was wet with blood but none of it was his. He crawled over to Shay who was laying slumped against the back tire of the truck and rolled him onto his back. The old man groaned and pushed him away.

"I'm fine." He complained. "It's my arm." He held up his left arm where it had been mangled below the elbow. It hung at a sickening angle.

"That doesn't look fine." Vincent said. Soldiers were rushing by to press the attack when he saw a medic amongst them and waved him over. The medic took a look at Shay's arm and wrapped a black tourniquet around it, tightening it while ignoring Shay's whimpers of pain.

"Make sure you get him to a doctor in a couple hours, yeah?"

The Medic said before glancing at Vincent, recognizing him and quickly adding "Consul, Sir."

"Thanks." Vincent said and the medic ran off. Felicity appeared from behind the burning hulk of the third truck. Her face was blackened with smoke and she was reloading a carbine.

"You okay?" She asked as she fished around in a pocket for another magazine.

"Yeah." Vincent said looking down at all of the blood. "None of this is mine. You?"

"I'm always good, sweetheart." She smirked. "Is he going to be okay?" She motioned towards Shay.

"Yeah. I don't think the same could be said for Han though." The Chairman had been in the first truck when the attack had begun. The first truck now lay on its roof and burning, there was no way anyone would crawl away from that wreck alive.

"Oh." Fiona whistled. "He's fucked. So much for their rescue mission." Felicity appeared from the smoke. She normally flawless uniform had been ruffled by the fighting, even her boots were scuffed.

"That was no rescue mission." She scowled. "That was a hit." Vincent raised his eyebrow.

"Why the hell would they kill their own Chairman?"

"Follow me." She said and stormed off, back towards the Public Order headquarters.

"Shouldn't I meet up with the soldiers chasing down the people who just attacked us?"

"That is what you have commanders for, come on."

The Public Order headquarters had turned into a triage area for those wounded in the ambush. While the Lunar City Central Hospital had plenty of beds, they were generally unprepared for dozens of people to be shot or blown up at once. Medics sent off the most serious cases first and stayed in the front lobby, tending to the ones who could be treated without a doctor or making the lost causes more comfortable as they slipped away.

Since breaking during their interrogations, the Pathfinders had been moved to the Public Order building. They were no longer considered under arrest, but until transport could be arrived for them to move to their new lives on Elysian, they and their families had quartered there for their own safety. It wouldn't have taken long for people in their old neighborhoods or barracks to figure out they had talked. Not too long after that they would have found their corpses in the street.

Felicity led them up through an elevator and down a few different hallways until they came to a doorway. She knocked and after a few moments they entered. Sitting on a couch and nursing a cup of Kaff was the Pathfinder from earlier, Aliyev. His children were sitting on the floor around a table drawing or coloring as his wife cooked something in the small kitchenette. It dawned on Vincent that somehow this was the most normally functioning family unit he had seen since he left Earth.

"Consul." Aliyev said, rising to his feet. "Would you like a cup?" He motioned to the Kaff.

"No thanks. You'll have to forgive my manners, I was nearly just killed again. I assume by your people."

"They were no people of mine, Consul. We surrendered."

"Yeah well, so did the Chairman before he sent you to kill me." At this Aliyev sighed and sat down heavily. His face sank into his hands and this wife took that as a signal to grab the children and leave the room. Once they had closed themselves off in an adjoining bedroom Felicity pressed him.

"Tell him what you told me."

"The Chairman didn't order me to do anything. Our orders came straight from the Grand Marshal. All of them did. We were told if we were captured to blame the Chairman. She knew you would go for him, then she could make her move."

"Her move?" Vincent asked. What could she have to gain from killing Han?"

"Han was a puppet." Felicity said. "It was a theory I was working on but we didn't have proof. Once we had Han I assumed we could work with the Lunas in getting the information out of him."

"What information?"

"That he wasn't really in charge."

"You have got to be kidding me." Fiona sighed. "So, you're saying after the last Chairman killed himself, Lagos took over and then put that idiot Han in as a figurehead for some reason?"

"Historically, the Chairman isn't a military figure and Lagos knew that. She knew a civilian leader would need to take the seat and Han was popular with the Committee. The Committee was in no place to argue after the Chairman wasted the rest of the fleet on that botched attack on us. Lagos had the only muscle left in town directly under her command."

"And all of this rested on the Chairman just so happening to kill himself." Vincent said in disbelief.

"he didn't kill himself." Aliyev interjected. "After his plan to ambush your fleet failed, Lagos was furious. After a meeting with him she told us he killed himself, but I know what a murder looks like when I see one. At that point nobody was in the position to stop her. After you offered the olive branch that gave her the chance to find a way out of this mess. She'd deal with you hanging around for a bit, during which time she would solidify her power. Of course, she didn't expect you to empower and arm the Lunas. That certainly chucked a wrench into her plans. Once that happened, she knew whatever she needed to do to hold onto power would be opposed by Han. So, she turned you against him."

"With your bomb."

"Yes. She assumed you would have killed him immediately

rather than capture him. Since he lived the possibility of him telling you everything I'm telling you now was a risk she couldn't take. So, she sent her forces to kill him."

"So why are you telling us this?" He sipped from his cup.

"I assumed after I told you it was the Chairman, regardless of whatever Marshal Haagen told me, my soldiers and I would be taken outside and shot. It is what we would have done, after all."

"We aren't the Central Committee."

"Obviously." Aliyev nodded. "That became apparent when Marshal Haagen quickly got our papers in order, sent for my family, and put us all up here until we can be moved. You did good by me, I figured I owed you the truth. On my honor as an Officer. I understand if you want to take back our deal, but please allow my family to move to Elysian after you're done with me."

"I said we aren't the Central Committee." Vincent repeated. "Thank you for your candor, Lieutenant Colonel. Hopefully going forward as a citizen of Elysian we can all be a little bit more honest."

"Of course, Consul." He nodded at Aliyev and turned towards Felicity.

"Until then, what do we do with this information?"

"I think it's obvious at this point, Consul. Any idea of working with the old Committee should be discarded. We should recognize Shay's Committee as the government and allow them to do what they need to do in order to secure power. It would be aligned with the Warlord's wishes to transfer power and avoid any further conflict."

"By avoid further conflict you mean avoid further conflict *for us*." Fiona said.

"Yes."

"What about the Lunas? Just leave them to rot?"

"Shay said they formed a new government. Let them govern."

24

Occupation General Order Sixteen:

By order of the Office of the Occupation the recognized representational government of Lunar City is the Lunar Central Committee chaired by Chairman Shay Daniels in accordance with local agreements and elections. All governing authority previously held by the Occupation Office per the Instrument of Surrender signed by Former Chairman Gideon Han is hereby transferred to the Office of the Chairman.

Signed,
Consul of the Human Office, Vincent Solaris

"Are you sure about this?" Aron asked. He was looking over the order that had been published across the Lunar intranet.

"Arai didn't want us to get bogged down in Lunar affairs. Now we aren't. This whole mess is Shay's problem now."

Vincent leaned heavily against his desk, reaching for a flask of an unknown substance that Fiona had left there. He sipped it and was relieved to find the liquor was not of Martian origin. He offered the flask to Aron who refused.

"I don't think we should be celebrating."

"I'm not. I'm coping." At that Aron reached over and grabbed the flask, taking a shot.

"The problem with big ideas is that people tend to ruin them eventually."

"I'm learning that." As if to underline Aron's words the ground shook violently. He didn't flinch. Aron walked over to the window and glanced out.

"It looks like Shay is getting rid of some of those people." Vincent pulled himself to his feet and looked out. From far away at night it was hard to tell where one dome ended and another began. Without the sunlight shining through them it was hard to tell them apart. From where he was standing, for as far as he could see, there was fires raging in some domes, tracers arced into the air in others. From somewhere out near the military district a bright flash lit up the and night rattled the walls.

Over the next several days Shay's newly established Lunar Defense Forces went on a tear across Lunar City. The new Committee government put out a blanket amnesty for all serving members of the Earth Defense Forces, assuming they showed up at a warehouse to turn in all of their gear to be used for the new army. As soon as they showed up, they were arrested and marched away.

All members of the old committee government had arrest warrants issued for various crimes against the people. Most people assumed something like that would happen to anyone even remotely connected to Han or Lagos, but Shay did not limit himself. Entire payrolls from every major and minor Ministry were turned into warrant lists. Soon, the same faceless worker bees that made every layer of government possible in the city were walked out of their houses in handcuffs.

Then came the Committee Orders.

Committee Order #1 ordered that all residency permits for Earthians within the City revoked.

Committee Order #2 ordered that all people without a residency permit must leave the City within a week or face arrest.

Committee Order #3 made membership or former membership in the Earth Defense Forces illegal.

Committee Order # 4 reinstituted the old Committee Guilt by Blood law meaning if someone had violated a law, so had two generations of their family.

Within four orders Shay had made being Earthian in any way illegal, the Volunteer Army having a waiver for the time being. This caused a rush of people to the Spaceport. Willing to trade or sell anything in order to get on one of the Volunteer flights back towards Elysian or Mars. There was no real law about moving to Elysian, so the Volunteer fleet opened their doors to anyone willing to leave. Not everyone would be so lucky though.

For the people who couldn't make it to the spaceport, the Lunas were waiting for them. Sometimes it was just groups of vengeful civilians, wielding whatever weapons they had. Other times it was the Police or Soldiers. Either way their dead bodies would be vented out of the domes via trash chutes. Within weeks so many bodies had been thrown out of the domes the lunar surface looked like a badly concealed mass grave.

Fiona tapped took a deep drag from her cigarette and exhaled a cloud of smoke. It swirled around in the space above her head and the ceiling.

"I have to give them credit." She said, looking out the window. "They went a lot harder than I thought they would. I thought Shay would just turn the tables on them but, damn."

"I'd rather you didn't give them credit." Vincent sighed. A knock on his door distracted him momentarily from the horror show going on outside of his window. Zinvor entered, holding an envelope.

"From the Chairman." He said, handing it to him. Vincent tore the envelope open and unfolded the letter within.

To the Office of the Human Consul,

The fugitive former known as Grand Marshal, Anit Lagos, has been captured due to the heroic efforts of the Central Committee's Security Forces. She is currently detained in an undisclosed location awaiting charging and sentencing regarding the enclosed arrest warrants.

Due to our government's close relationship and the crimes committed by Inmate Lagos the Office of the Exalted Chairman has gratefully invited Consul Vincent Solaris to attend the proceedings.

-Office of the Central Committee

"Exalted Chairman?" Fiona laughed.

"He got comfortable real fast didn't he?"

"I will send for your new aid to get your dress uniform together." Zinvor said. Vincent held up a hand.

"Don't bother, I'm not going."

"What?" Fiona gasped. "You don't want to watch that bitch hang?"

"I do. But not with the 'Exalted Chairman'" He shuddered. "I can't get out of this damn city fast enough."

"What was it that Commander Erik said? it would have been diplomatically unwise to ignore an invitation to your wedding?" Zinvor asked. "I think this might be one of those situations." Vincent frowned.

"Are you comparing my wedding to a mass execution?"

"Man, that would have been awesome." Fiona thought aloud.

"If you were the Martian Commander would they really be

any different?" Zinvor mused. Vincent tapped out his cigarette on an ashtray and leaned his head back. Zinvor was right, it didn't matter how he felt about it personally. They needed Lunar City, it was hardly the time to snub them.

"Goddamnit, Zinvor." He sighed. "Why do you have to be right." He got to his feet and went to the closet where he stored his rumpled dress uniform.

"Shouldn't you get that ironed first?" Fiona asked.

"Just because I'm going doesn't mean I'm going to make an effort to look presentable."

25

As the occupation forces had been slowly withdrawn, several buildings that had been used to billet soldiers were ceded back to the Lunar government. Shay's functionaries quickly moved back into them. Their uniforms and symbols were even the same. If it wasn't for the fact that most of the new Lunar representatives were still recovering from years of being starved, the transition between the old central committee and the new one would have been seamless.

They Ministry of Justice had seen better days. Over the course of the previous weeks violence sporadic bursts of gunfire and the occasion explosion had worn away its stately veneer. While Shay wanted it to look like his government had everything under control, it was clear old regime holdouts still survived somewhere in the city waiting for their turn to strike back. Grey uniformed soldiers in full combat gear waited by the doors of the Ministry.

The soldiers nodded to acknowledge Vincent and opened the doors for them. In the doors where glass would have once been was instead replaced with particle board. Another soldier led them within the building where there were armed guards in front of every door and staircase. Government workers hurried back and forth. Every part of him wanted to leave the building immediately, all of the grey uniforms and eagle and star badges on everyone's chest reminded him too much of Earth.

As they moved further and further into the building security only increased. Every few feet they had to be buzzed through another locked door, before each one they were eyed suspiciously by armed soldiers or Police. Shay had at least done away with the title of 'Ethics Police'. Now their identical uniform patches read 'Ministry of State Security' above the sprawling form of an eagle.

After making their way through countless security checks they were brought to an empty chamber. It had high vaulted ceilings and its bare walls were covered in Committee flags. Vincent squirmed uncomfortably before producing a cigarette and lighting it.

"I doubt they want you smoking in here." Felicity dead-panned. Vincent glared at her and exhaled smoke. "Everything okay?"

"No." He said more harshly than intended. "Sorry. This fucking place just reminds me of when I was sentenced."

"Oh." Felicity said. "Right. I'm sorry."

"Hey at least you got your day in court." Fiona said.

"My day in court was about as fair as you being sentenced by being born." Felicity grimaced.

"I have a feeling we are about to see the same thing here."

"What would you do if you were them, uh?" Fiona shot back. "Join hands and be friends. Maybe do like the Mawr and start a damn book club?" She sarcastically flourished her hands by the side of her face.

"No." Felicity scowled. "But I imagine it wouldn't involve throwing so many people out of airlocks."

"Remind me never to let you end up in charge." Before their argument could continue further off the rails the door to the chamber opened. Akabi stood in the doorway, her brows furrowed.

"Smoking isn't allowed in Ministry buildings, Consul." Vincent sighed and stubbed out the cigarette under his boot. The person who greeted them in the chamber was not the same meek young girl that had left the Volunteers to join the new Lunar Defense Force a short time before. She stood ramrod straight and her cold eyes reminded Vincent of any cop he ever had a run in with back home. She had moved into her role in the old power structures as quickly and seamlessly as her own father.

"I'll send someone to clean that up." She said, looking down at the crinkled cigarette butt that had smeared black ash across the polished floor. "Follow me." She exited and led them into a courtroom that looked copied from the one Vincent had once stood in back in District Six. A high, elongated judge's bench lined the back wall of the great hall. It was tall enough that regardless of the size the defendant that was forced to stand before them the panel of judges would always tower over them. Above the bench on the wall an inscription read *Equal Justice Under Law* and flanked by eagle and star flags on either side.

The courtroom back in the district was a small room with only a few seats outside of the bench for those who presided over it. This courtroom had auditorium seating, enough for around one hundred people. Clerks in grey uniforms busied themselves, placing data displays on the judge's bench while others swung down cameras and microphones that were mounted to the ceiling. Akabi led them down two sets of stairs to bring them to their seats in the auditorium when they saw a familiar face.

Erik sat alongside his normal staff of solemn faced attendants.

"I assumed you would be more comfortable in the foreign dignitary section." Akabi said. Vincent nodded, she left them and they took their seats next to the Martian delegation.

"Consul Solaris." Erik smiled. "It is good to see you again." He reached out his hand, Vincent grabbed it.

"I have to say I never thought I'd see you in the city."

"Yes, well. Times are changing I suppose."

"Are they?" Fiona asked.

"Yes, but not in the way we would have hoped." Erik laughed. "I have little doubt Shay hates me and my people as much as his predecessor. That kind of thinking doesn't go away overnight."

"What has changed is now Mars can crush him at will." Vincent interjected.

"Correct." Erik nodded. "Sure, we will fight as comrades until the Anarchs are defeated, but after that? If I was him, I'd be worried about that too. Hence the diplomatic niceties."

"And?" Vincent slid his face a bit closer to Erik's. "should we have something to worry about after that?"

"Of course not. But if that fear is what makes this new Central Committee leave Mars alone, then so be it." The door to the left of the bench swung open and a man in a state security uniform stepped out. "Oh boy." Erik sighed. "here we go.

"All stand for the playing of the Anthem of the Bringers of Justice!" The man announced. Everyone in the auditorium rose, placing their hands over their hearts. The Martian and Elysian delegations did not follow suit. A rousing bit of orchestra music began to play from a set of speakers.

"I don't remember any anthems when I was in court." Vincent said quietly.

"Your day in court wasn't being watched by every person in Lunar City" He motioned to the people working the cameras. The swing arms panned over the audience in the auditorium as they stood for the anthem. Vincent made sure to scowl at the lens as it reached the foreign dignitary section.

"Did the Committee always do that?" Felicity asked.

"No. Well, they probably would have if they would have

survived long enough to capture Vincent. Have you marched out in front of a billion eyes of eyes in chains? They would have loved that."

"Guess you have to show the people how strong you are and what happens to your enemies and all that." Vincent said.

"We both know a little something about that, hm?" The anthem finally came to a close and the camera quickly spun back to the door of the great hall.

"Remain standing." The man called out once again. "For the Central Committee of Lunar City." Slowly nine grey uniformed men and women filed into the hall, taking their seats behind the bench, leaving one seat at the center vacant. Trailing behind the Committee itself was Chairman Shay who took his seat in the middle. Shay still moved slowly, but he no longer used a cane. He wasn't hunched over like he was before either. Instead, he walked upright, his chest puffed out in front of him.

"The *Exalted Chairman* should looks better than he did last time we saw him." Felicity observed.

"Food will do that to a man." Vincent said, half joking. Erik placed a hand on Vincent's shoulder.

"Or he played a weak old man so you would think him trustworthy and hand him power." He said.

"No fucking way." Vincent jerked away.

"He is a Luna but rising to be head of Outer Domes means he had to be trust worthy enough to the old Committee. You know, there were Martian functionaries to the Committee. Savage little fuckers too, would dime out their own kids if it meant getting into the good graces of the Committee. Once he saw you, not knowing a single thing about city politics, stride in with in army at your back he probably saw an easy mark. No offense."

"I fucking hate this city." Vincent said, folding his arms across his chest.

"ladies and gentlemen. Lunas and dignitaries." Shay began.

Thank you for being here. As all of you know our city has been going through the trials and tribulations of revolutionary change and progress. The people of Lunar City have thrown off the yolk of their history and stepped boldly forward onto their own. We have grasped our own destiny in our hands and are now on an unceasing march forward towards our future!"

The auditorium lit up with applause. Not the sternly regimented three caps and stop type of applause he had seen in some military ceremonies on Elysian or even back in Ethics School. The gathered crowd of the hall went wild. What sounded like empty platitudes any politician would say to him played the crowd like a fiddle and they cheered like they were at a concert.

"I definitely don't remember any cheering in court." Vincent said, more loudly this time around so Erik could hear him over the rapturous applause.

"No court chaired by the Head of State is actually a court. Shay is a politician, not a lawyer." Erik shrugged. "This is a political rally with an execution after party."

"In order to turn the page completely on our past, we must confront it directly. Which is why we are here today. While the traitorous Gideon Han is beyond this court's reach, the person that made his accension to the Chair possible is yet to be sentenced." The crowd booed at the mention of Han's name. "Please, present the defendant to the court." The man once again returned to the door and opened it. Several state security agents entered, marching in lock step with one another. Between them, hooked by her arms and secured at the wrists and ankles was Grand Marshal Anit Lagos.

Her gait was reduced to a pitiful shuffling by the ankle chains but she remained defiant. Lagos still wore her uniform and cap, her greying hair pulled back into a tight bun. She regarded the gathered crowd with utter contempt and fired a venomous glance directly at Vincent. Her guards guided her to a small carpeted red circle, directly in the center of the bench.

"Defendant Anit Lagos, you stand accused of crimes against the state, treason, murder, deprivation, and sedition. How do you plead?" Shay read from a list.

"Grand Marshal." She said without elaborating.

"I'm sorry?"

"My title is Grand Marshal, not *defendant*."

"Your military rank was stripped from you by order of the Committee. You are a civilian." This, somehow, seemed to infuriate Lagos more than anything else.

"I don't recognize your fucking Committee, you shit fingered dirt farmer." She spat. Shay balled his fists, not wanting to engage in a screaming match with someone brought before him in chains. He probably wanted to keep the thin veneer of professionalism over the court he had managed to put together. Lagos gathered herself, straightening back up and clearing her throat. Shay had made her losing her bearing, something she obviously regretted.

"I take this to mean you plead not guilty." He said flatly.

"I'm not playing this game with you. We both already know how this ends, just get on with it. Find me guilty and vent me out of an airlock like you did with all the others. I'm tired of this charade." She cocked her head to the side. Vincent hated Lagos and knew she was certainly worthy of the sentence that was about to be passed onto her, but he had never seen anyone face their impeding death with so much indifferent defiance. He watched the Gangers of Mars get strung up one at a time and each of them screamed and cried for their life until it was finally snatched from them. Not her, though. She was facing it head on. He wasn't sure if he could ever do the same thing.

"Defendant Lagos, the Central Committee of Lunar City finds you guilty on all charges. The mandatory sentence of aforementioned crimes is death to be carried out after the adjournment of this court. Would you like to take this opportunity to address your peers in the audience before this sentence is carried out?"

"These people aren't my peers. My peers are all dead. I'll see them on the other side of the airlock." Shay looked disappointed that he wasn't going to get the dramatic exchange that the cameras and his audience demanded. Lagos knew what was happening and it was clear she didn't want to take part. She accepted her death like it was just another part of her job.

"Take her away." Shay ordered. The state security agents hooked Lagos under her arms once again and led her away back through the door. As she shuffled back she held her head up high as the audience rained boos down onto her.

"I thought I would like this." Fiona said. "But it feels kind of unfair."

"How do you mean?" Vincent asked.

"I hate that cold bitch, but just kicking her out of an airlock doesn't seem right." She pinched her chin. "It's all too clean."

"You mean you respect her and want her to die a soldier's death?" Erik mused. Fiona screwed up her face, Vincent wasn't sure if she had ever openly admitted to respecting another person before and she was clearly having a hard time coming to terms with it.

"I just hope if I ever have to face down a death sentence." She changed the subject. "I go down like she did. Look at Shay, he is pissed" She gave a little laugh. "He was hoping for some grand spectacle for the hooting masses watching at home and she denied it. Somehow, she got walked in here shackled up like a common criminal, facing all of those charges, and made Shay look like the bad guy. Just incredible."

"You sound like you admire her or something." Felicity frowned. "Am I the only one who remembers that she killed Erin?"

"I just wish I had the chance to kill her on the battlefield is all." Fiona shrugged. Vincent put his arm around her shoulder.

"I'm starting to think you have been hanging out with the Mawr a bit too much.

The occupation of Lunar City ended almost as swiftly as it began. Originally Arai and Pharos wanted to occupy the city until the end of the war against the Anarchs, but their opinions rapidly changed once Shay took over. Vincent was starting to believe what Erik said was true, and he was really a conniving political mastermind rather than just a liberated farm manager.

In the one meeting Shay had, with Vincent attending in role as Consul, he had watched the 'Exalted Chairman' who had just presided over a kangaroo court and ordered who knows how many others to be sentenced to the airlock, turn right back into the man Vincent first met. Knowing that he was going to be on a video conference he chose not to wear his best uniform and he made sure to leave his eagle and star badge at home. Shay was smart enough to know what that badge symbolized to the Warlord.

When the meeting began, he was deferential to Arai to the point of it being overkill. Vincent wasn't sure if he had even seen Cohort Leaders grovel in such a way before her. It was clear what his goal was, show the Clan that the city was in no way a threat to them. While at the same time promising to bring the full weight of their military against the Anarchs when the Warlord called for them. With one small request: The Volunteers had to be withdrawn.

The reasoning was simple enough, the influx of tens of thousands of new residents in the city was straining its resources and taking up governmental buildings that Shay would need. Vincent didn't bother to raise an objection. He was sick of the city and was ready to return to Elysian. He knew there was more than enough room in the city, as Shay had expelled hundreds of thousands of Earthians, but he didn't care enough to point that out. The Earthians were Elysian's problem now.

Whether they were convinced or not by Shay's display, Arai agreed. Her choice was as practical as Vincent's want to leave the city as soon as possible was impractical. The Volunteer's problems in training and logistics were not a secret. The sooner she could get her wayward Human Army back to Elysian to prepare for the fight against the Anarchs the better.

Vincent and his staff stood in the spaceport, watching the last few units of Volunteers load themselves onto the shuttles that would take them back up to orbit.

"Why does it feel like we didn't do anything here?" Vincent asked nobody in particular.

"You wanted a liberation. You got one." Felicity said flatly. "Unfortunately, history shows us that sometimes the liberators are assholes too."

"Assholes or no, we accomplished our mission." Aron pointed out. "We should make sure our soldiers are awarded thusly." Vincent sighed.

"What mission did we accomplish exactly?"

"We replaced an enemy government with one that suits our needs. At least for now." Aron said. "What Shay does with the power we gave him is on him. You didn't tell him to go on a tear through the city, he did that on his own. That blood is on his hands."

"Is that what you tell yourself, Aron?"

"It is if I want to sleep at night." He smiled somberly. "How do you manage?"

"I don't."

One of the shuttles slowly took off through the series of airlocks that would eventually take them back towards the fleet. A Lunar delegation entered the spaceport, stepping over the lazing Volunteers who were lounging around or playing cards waiting for their turn to enter a shuttle. Among them wasn't any member of the Committee, not even Shay. Instead, Akabi led a group of older Lunas, each of them dressed in the uniforms of staff officers.

"Consul." Akabi said in greeting. It wasn't a warm welcome, she looked like she had never even met him before. If it hadn't led to so many people dying Vincent would have been impressed at her rapid transition from scared, raw soldier to cold, unfeeling government representative.

"Akabi." He nodded. She glanced down at the stars that lined her collar.

"That is General Daniels now, actually."

"They made you a General?" Fiona laughed. "You were a private like two weeks ago. Shay's really dialed that nepotism up to eleven, huh?"

"And you were made a Marshal." Akabi deadpanned.

"She got you there." Aron admitted.

"The *Chairman*" Akabi continued. "Sends his best wishes but as you can imagine he is very busy and cannot come himself. He thanks the Elysians for the sacrifices they have made in their valiant efforts to topple the Central Committee of Earth."

"Yeah, sure. Great." Vincent said. "I don't care how thankful he is. I care that your new Lunar Defense Force is ready to hold up its side of our deal." Felicity nudged him with an elbow.

"Consul!" She scolded. He shot her a glance and she backed off.

"We've been lied to enough in this city. You're not my ally, you're not my comrade, you're not in my Clan. You're paying us a debt that you owe. Tell your Chairman if he fucks us on this, we will be back and there won't be able liberating going on."

"Is that a threat, Consul?" Akabi frowned. The rest of the staff officers around her expression's all looked like they had suddenly smelled something foul.

"Yes." He said, making eye contact. "I thought I made that very clear." He turned and began to walk towards the *Shanna II*. Tyr was pacing around the ship, making last second checks.

"That is one hell of a goodbye." Felicity said, walking quickly to catch up.

"They might have tricked Arai into thinking they were groveling subjects, but not me." He said. "Probably thinks he outsmarted aliens that are below him. I had to remind him we are watching him."

"Are we?" Fiona asked. "Do we have spies in the city?"

"No comment." Answered Felicity.

Tyr jumped into the cockpit and fired up the ship's engines. They sat down and closed the crew compartment and as the ship slowly rose into the air Vincent sighed with relief. He had never been happier to leave anywhere than he was at that moment leaving the orbit of the Moon. He wasn't sure if he wanted to curse Arai for sending him there or the Central Committee for making the city its second home.

Space above the Moon was crowded with ships. With the old Committee deposed and replaced, technically the war against the Clan, Mars, and Titan was over. Before the ink even dried on the pages of the treaty Titan and Mars had flooded the area with trade ships. Now the thousands of traders competed for room with the Volunteer and Martian Fleets. Several of the trade ships docked with the fleet, exchanging both illicit and legal goods. Only Fiona could be sure of how much of which were flooding the *Olympus*.

The *Shanna II* pulled into its assigned berthing, leaving Lunar City behind them.

In the weeks since they had been gone an unceasing stream of Mawr and Rhai Cohorts had made their way back to the planet and the surrounding moons. Arai had put out a general muster order in preparation for the coming campaign against the Anarchs, swelling the population of the Elysian system.

After that, came the waves of Human refugees from Lunar City. Many were Earthians, fleeing their probable executions at the hands of Shay's new government, while still others were Luna looking for a fresh start somewhere far away from the fields of the outer domes. The Unions had assigned them all workplaces and duties that corresponded with their previous work experience and a home. By the last count they numbered more than two-hundred thousand.

When the *Shanna II* touched down at the spaceport it felt like every person who had crowded onto the planet had come to greet them. It was the largest reception any of them had ever seen. Various Elysian, Union, and Clan flags fluttered in the wind. Families gathered to welcome their loved homes, kids held up signs with their parent's names scrawled across them, and even individual workplaces came to see their coworkers return. The only thing keeping the Spaceport from being over-whelmed entirely was a few Public Safety Officers who managed to cordon off a space just large enough for a shuttle to land.

Tyr flipped a switch and the compartment door slid open. The deafening cheers of the gathered masses mixed with the rising music of the Volunteer band. Vincent recognized the tune they were playing called *Pour the Wine*. It had begun life as an old EDF drinking song and had been adopted as something as an unofficial anthem for the Volunteers. It followed a common trend of most of their ceremonial music being originally born in a bar somewhere.

Waiting for them on the tarmac was Arai and Pharos, flanked by various Clan officials whose names Vincent couldn't remem-ber. Arai was wearing her ceremonial armor for the occasion, ribbons fluttering from her chest and pauldrons. Vincent had a feeling they were going to be walking into some kind of parade or another so he and Fiona made sure to dress in their battle armor for the occasion.

"Welcome home, Liberators of Lunar City." Arai croaked. Her voice was always a pitch above a grumble, but now it just sounded exhausted. Her eyes were sunken into their sockets and it looked like she hadn't slept as long as they had been gone. Not a great sign in regards to the planning of the Anarch campaign. She bowed, and held out her hands, showing two grey ribbons. Vincent and Fiona took them, affixing them to their armor next to their others.

"Liberators is a bit of a strong word, but thank you." Vincent said.

"We are glad you are back." Pharos said. "We have much to discuss and plan."

"Of course we do." He groaned. "Can't a returning liberator get a weekend off?"

"What is this week *end?*" Arai asked, glancing at Pharos. Pharos shrugged. Vincent turned to the Marshals behind him.

"Make sure all of the returning soldiers get awards and time off. I'll see everyone when the Rhai invent a day off for the first time." The Marshals saluted as more shuttles began to land behind them. The crowd went wild at the scene and Vincent was led away to a special shuttle. He assumed they were going back to the Government Quarter, but they kept flying. He had never visited the Rhai Quarter, which laid beyond. There wasn't any rule against Humans from going there, it was just that there was nothing to do there. As a specie they didn't really have any recreational activities that Vincent had ever witnessed and as such, their Quarter was nothing but various workspaces that he wanted nothing to do with.

"Where are we going?" Vincent asked.

"My Cohort office." Pharos answered. The Special Activities Cohort was as secret as anything within the Clan got. Even though he had been Consul for years, he had never been invited to visit their office. Occasionally he wasn't even allowed to sit through their briefings to the rest of the government. Their work was for the eyes of the Warlord only, and very few other select individuals. It turned out, Vincent was now a select individual.

"Oh is this about-"He began, but Pharos spun around in their seat, cutting him off.

"Don't finish that sentence." Vincent bit his lip. "The subject of which you speak is considered the highest of security to the Clan. Those who are not cleared and happen upon such information will have to be liquidated in insure the spread of said information to other uncleared individuals does not continue unabated and if you don't mind I would rather not shoot my pilot." The pilot glanced back, a look of concern on their face.

"Sorry." Vincent said. "I promise I won't make Pharos shoot you." He smiled nervously to the pilot.

"Do not make promises you can't keep." Pharos scowled. The shuttle swooped down through the spaghetti strand madness of elevated walkways. Thousands of the tunnels snaked from every floor of every building to the one next to it, hundreds of stories above the ground, the sight of which was blotted out by the metallic forest of Rhai skyscrapers that jutted into the air. Few other shuttles clogged the airspace. In the Rhai Quarter they were restricted to only those who needed to use them and every one would have to take off from the same spaceport. Each flight time was strictly regimented and rationed in the name of efficiency. They didn't complain, most Rhai were at work so much that they would never have a reason to leave the Quarter anyway.

The shuttled dipped down low, the pilot expertly guiding it through the walkways and back towards the surface. The light faded as they dove lower and lower until soon the entire cabin was pitch black other than the glow from the pilot's instrument panel. He wasn't sure if the Cohort building was somewhere down here because of the darkness or if that was just an added benefit. After a few moments of not being able to see an inch in front of his face a blinding light filled the shuttle.

A flawless white tunnel had opened in front of them. It was narrow, only large enough for the shuttle. No physical security greeted them but he had no doubt that the approaching shuttle was being watched by around a thousand cameras. Knowing Pharos, there was no less than eight different ways they could be blown out of the air should they be deemed an unwelcome presence in their underground headquarters.

"You're the first Human to ever visit this place." Pharos said. They must have seen Vincent's slightly disappointed facial expression because they followed it with "Do not be insulted, the only non-Rhai to ever come here before you was the Warlord."

"And I've only been here once or twice." Arai said. "I do not feel the need to hover over the various parts of our government."

"You're in the Human Quarter all the time." Vincent countered.

"In our defense." Pharos added. "the Rhai have never started a rebellion against the Clan." Vincent had to give it to them, in the Human race's short amount of time as members of the Clan they had started entirely too many problems.

"Fair enough." He said. "But we are happy to have you in our Quarter."

"I only go because I believe it to be necessary." Arai frowned.

"Great." He sighed.

The shuttle left the tunnel and was deposited into what looked like a hanger bay. Dozens of other identical shuttles were parked immaculately, wing to wing. If any Human pilot other than Ezra tried to do the same thing, they would have caused a dozen ship pile up within seconds. They glided along and parked next to another unmarked shuttle and landed a second later. As they exited the shuttle Vincent noticed the pilot was staying in their seat. And then that every other ship in the hanger still had a pilot sitting in the cockpit. It turned out Pharos wasn't kidding about the pilot not having clearance.

Pharos led them out of the hanger bay and down another featureless white hallway. In any Human or Mawr office dozens of people would be walking around going about their jobs. The offices felt alive, because they were. Whether he liked it or not they spent more time working than they did doing anything else. The Rhai office felt like a morgue, even down to its sterility and temperature. He could see his breath cloud up in front of him as they went.

He saw the first sign of life other than them standing in front of Pharos' office. Two black clad Agents stood on either side of the door, their faces obscured by the Rhai targeting helmet and paired with a plasma weapon they wore over their left arms like a sleeve. Neither Agent made any acknowledgment of their approach and the door slid open silently as Pharos walked through it.

As they walked into the office displays automatically triggered and lit up across the walls. Within seconds dozens of different screens lined the room and hundreds of lines of data scrolled by so quickly that even if Vincent could read the Rhai language there would be no way he would have been able to keep up with it. Pharos rounded their desk and had a seat, as they did so more displays flickered on in front of them.

"I assume all of this has something to do with why you both look so tired." Vincent said nodded at the collection of scrolling text. "I can't even read it and I'm ready to fall asleep."

"Your assumptions are correct." Pharos said. They swiped their hands in the air, moving around the displays. They shuffled through dozens before finally grabbing one, enlarging it, and turning it to face Vincent and Arai. He assumed Pharos either didn't hear or care when he said he couldn't read is language. "During your operations in Lunar City my staff and I have been pouring over the data we secured from our recaptured home world. It was much harder than I originally believed it would be. It seems as if the Anarchs knew how compromising this information was and made efforts to destroy it. Thankfully, underground resistance to the Anarch occupation made efforts to preserve it over the years."

"But they never tried to get it off of the planet?" Vincent asked. "Maybe to bring it to the Clan?"

"Coming out of hiding meant certain death for them." Arai said. "There is a reason why the Clan stayed hidden until we believed we may actually be able to win and even that was a longshot. I doubt they ever had such a chance. Their resistance was simply survival."

"We should all be grateful they were even able to do that."

Pharos hissed. "The information we were able to gather shows that the Anarchs are an engineering marvel. The old Rhai Ministry of Technology struggled and worked for decades in order to perfect their prototypes before coming up with what we now know to be Type As, or the line Anarch soldiers we have all fought. Other such designs didn't work so well and were discarded after failing field testing." Pharos pulled up a screen that showed an old schematic, a several stories tall, six-legged tank, each leg housing a weapons pod. A shiver ran down Vincent's spine, imagining the horrors it would be able to inflict on the battlefield.

"Instead." Pharos continued. "The decision was made to streamline production to just the Type As. In the event of war Rhai support like fleet and air support would be used, leaving the ground fighting to the war machines." Vincent pinched his chin, squinting at a different design that scrolled by, a sleek black ship the size of a destroyer.

"But we both saw they learned how to fly." He said. "How did that happen? Are they learning and adapting?"

"It does not seem that way." Pharos said, relieved. "of all of the problems my ancestors built into the Anarch design true artificial intelligence isn't one of them. Instead, it seems like they underestimated their creations ability to do their own job." They pulled up another screen. "I told you before that eventually, after years of peace, the government eventually assigned more and more duties to the Anarch weapon system. Of course this ended with their own production and maintenance. In order to do this they built what we are now calling the Hive Mind. An Anarch computer that could their production facilities. When they did this, they gave the Hive Mind access to their own servers which almost certainly contained the unused schematics for old programs. It didn't take very long for the Hive Mind to start building those as well. Soon, their ground based war machines were churning out fleets and logistical abilities totally independent from their own masters."

"The Rhai got outsmarted." Vincent commented. "I didn't think that was possible. What happened when the Rhai found out the Anarchs were beyond their control?"

"Of course, there was a dead switch built into the original models. However, since the Hive Mind took over it had streamlined models in order to speed up production. To do that they cut off pieces that were not directly related to combat function."

"You mean." Vincent shook his head. "their own production system eventually cut out the dead switch the Rhai put there to protect themselves."

"Yes." Pharos nodded. "By the time they flipped the switch only a fraction of models were impacted. The ones that weren't quickly reacted to the Rhai as if they were an invading force. Any that didn't flee or hide were killed outright. The conquest of the home world only took a few days."

"But you reconquered the home worlds, shouldn't that have been the Anarch home world too?"

"If only it had been that easy." Pharos said, spinning another display to face him. "After eliminating the Rhai threat they left a garrison to occupy the planet but at the same time picked up and moved their production facilities to a different planet, where the Hive Mind is now believed to be located." He switched displays again, this one now showing a small planet surrounded by several moons.

"One of the reasons why the Rhai leaned on the Anarchs so heavily for defense is our world is naturally indefensible" Pharos showed a map of their home world, sitting alone in orbit. "It has no moons nor any kind of belt to keep an enemy fleet away. So, they moved here, a rock we are calling Baki Prime, a planet the Rhai previously deemed uninhabitable due to soil composition. As the Anarchs do not have to eat or grow crops, that is not a problem for them. It also has an asteroid belt and several moons to ward off invasions and make them a nightmare for the enemy that might be planning them."

"So, that is why you're building a weapon to vaporize that piece of shit to dust, right?"

"We wish it was that easy." Arai grimaced.

"Unfortunately, my ancestors made sure it wouldn't be." Pharos said. "Our home world was under threat from the Mawr, which was the primary driver of the creation of the Anarchs but not their only function. A few hundred years before their creation, data shows an asteroid impact badly damaged the planet, nearly wiping us out."

"You're telling me they also built the Anarchs to protect them from another asteroid? What does that have to do with us?" Pharos turned another display that showed a computer graphic of the Rhai home world. The graphic began to move, showing an asteroid moving in, within a few seconds, hundreds of thousands of small dots leapt from the planet into the path of the asteroid, knocking it off course.

"Those dots." They said tapping the display. "Are Anarchs." They turned the graphic off. "If we complete our dark energy projector and fire it, we have reason to believe that they will react the same way, absorbing the blow, rendering it useless. At this point the Anarchs will see our continued existence as a threat and burn Elysian to the ground much like they did to Earth."

"Right now." Arai said. "Our current theory is that we will need to distract as many Anarchs as we can all at once if there is any hope of the energy projector working."

"Which is where you come in." Pharos pointed at Vincent. "Not just you, but everyone else not needed to fire the projector."

"How do you expect us to distract the Anarchs?" He laughed. It was mostly a nervous laugh, though it also helped him not think about how scared he was at the idea of fighting them again.

"Our scouts have been gathering as much information as they can about Baki and its moons. We have found one that will be suitable for all of our races, though Humans will have to wear a filtering apparatus to protect their respiratory system."

"Protect it from what?" He asked, panic in his voice.

"There is not a word for the particles in the air in your language that I am aware of. Though the Doctors we have consulted have assured us it would turn your lungs to something akin to a jelly. Which I believe is bad." Vincent bit his lip.

"Yes, that would be very bad." Arai continued.

"Baki Two is the bigger of the two moons." She gestured at the map of what looked like a rugged hellscape. Jagged mountains and valleys as far as he could see. "In this particular valley." She zoomed in. "Is protected on all sides and has only one way in or out. If we inserted a force here, they could hypothetically hold off a superior enemy for hours."

"Wait." Vincent held up his hands. "You're talking about us invading the Anarch home cluster?" Before Arai could answer it dawned on him. "Hold on, *we are the distraction.*"

"Yes." Arai nodded. "In order for this to work we will have to deploy all forces available to us from the Clan all the way down to Lunar City. We dig in at the end of this valley and force the Anarchs to commit all of their forces in order to defeat us. When they are fully involved, Pharos will fire the projector."

"Against how many?" He asked. "And for how long?" He noticed is voice was rising in pitch as he spoke, that tended to happen when he was scared.

"We don't know." Pharos said, unhelpfully. "We can assume the Hive Mind will direct all available military resources into driving you from their moon. You will be fighting the entire Anarch Military they will not hold a single thing in reserve in this fight. That is by design."

. . .

"By design?" He asked. "You didn't even plan on giving us a chance?"

"Consul, you misunderstand." Pharos moved a few more displays around, eventually showing him a scene in the same valley with dozens of layers of defenses all the way back to the dead end. "The purpose of this is as a distraction, so we have to make it convincing. We must trick the Anarchs into thinking that this is a foothold we will eventually use to invade their home world. They will have no choice but to treat your deployment as a treat to their existence and react accordingly. If they do not commit fully, the projector may not work."

"We are working to make sure our forces can survive long enough on the ground to make this possible."

"I noticed the end goal wasn't survival." Vincent said but nobody pretended they heard him.

"As we have poured everything we could into the projector, we seconded the process of weapons manufacturing to Mars." Arai continued. "This was their mission to distract them from our work on the projector. Against the wishes of Pharos here."

"Of course, my plan was to outfit every soldier taking the field with cutting edge plasma weapons." Pharos pointed out. "But it ran into problems."

"We lack the resources to build millions of plasma weapons." Arai said, somewhat annoyed. "And Mars even more so, who still cannot manufacture them at all. Instead, we will distribute the plasma weapons we do have to the units we believe can cause the most damage with them and everyone else will be armed with the new Martian rifle."

"What was wrong with the weapons we have?" Vincent asked. "Or were you only trying to distract Erik?"

"As someone who fought the Anarchs you know how much it takes to kill one." Arai said. She was right. Firing a weapon at a human, Rhai, or even a Mawr meant you had a good chance of dropping them with a single round, assuming the person firing had decent enough aim. The Anarch were armored head to toe and absorbed punishment that required hundreds of rounds and explosives to even give someone a small hope of taking one out. If they were about to dig in against the full weight of the Anarchs it would be hopeless if they couldn't actually kill one.

"Erik came up with this." The door to the office opened and a Rhai technician entered. In their thin arms they were carrying a rife that was nearly four feet in length and looked like it was welded together from spare parts. The technician handed it to Mawr who hefted it up in her hands. The rifle had no magazine, instead a sliding bolt covered the top of it. Arai gripped the bolt handle and pulled it back. It clicked loudly and she produced a bullet from within. The bullet she held up in her hand was the same length as Vincent's forearm. Its end twisted around and came to a point.

"Do not let looks fool you." She smiled. "We tested his creation against captured samples of Anarch skin and it worked flawlessly."

"Arai, it's a bolt action rifle." Vincent rubbed his temples.

"An automatic gun doesn't matter if it won't kill an Anarch." She grunted. "This, this will kill an Anarch."

"So, you want my soldiers to face down the entire Anarch military armed with bolt action rifles Erik and his people banged out in their backyard within the last few weeks?" He groaned. "Can you give me something to be optimistic about? Like how about how great that projector of yours works?"

"In the lab it has worked flawlessly." Pharos beamed.

"In the lab." Vincent repeated.

"Yes."

"So you haven't really tested it?" Pharos pursed their beak like lips.

"We cannot conduct a live test of the projector. If we fire it off the Anarchs will certainly catch on to our capabilities and set Elysian on fire."

"You're asking all of us to throw our lots in with a weapon we won't know works until you pull the trigger and find out yourself?"

"No." Pharos shook their head. "Don't be ridiculous, outside of this room nobody taking part in the battle will know about the weapon at all. They will assume they really are taking part in taking a foothold for a future invasion of Baki."

"That is worse, Pharos. You do understand how that is worse, right?"

"Consul, I understand I am asking a lot of you and your people." Arai cut in. "But rest assured we will all be there together. All the races of the Clan on our allies will be shoulder to shoulder facing down this threat. Some subterfuge that even I am uncomfortable with is being used, I know, but to us it won't matter down on Baki Two. We will dig in and hold until Pharos and his Cohort carry out their duties. It is that simple."

"And if they don't? What if the projector fails?"

"Then we have nothing to worry about as we will have been killed on Baki Two and we'll have no idea." Arai laughed and slapped him on the shoulder.

2 8

It had been two days since Arai and Pharos dropped their plans onto his shoulders. As they made him promise, Vincent had not told another soul about the projector. Not even Fiona. Though she was smart enough to know something was going on, she knew not to pry too hard. Though Arai's words rang true: in the grand scheme of things, Pharos' secret weapon didn't matter much. He would still order his Volunteers into battle and they would still fight. In the blood, guts, and misery of war as a ground soldier whatever was happening beyond what he could see at the end of his rifle felt very unimportant.

Aron had promised the Volunteers time off when they had gotten home. Aron did that because Vincent had told him to, which of course meant only hours later after his meeting with Arai and Pharos, he had to tell him to put them all back to work. If the entire army and fleet was going to be deployed to war for the first time there was a lot to be done.

Vincent couldn't tell anyone about the projector, but he could tell them other things. He warned the Unions that a full mobilization could be coming as soon as two weeks from then and to prepare accordingly. That led to a never-ending chain of complaints and requests from every Union Representative that he knew and some that he didn't. There still wasn't enough uniforms, enough food, the water filtration systems needed work, and various other requests that all blurred together after a while.

Things moved so quickly, it seemed as if he hardly saw anyone but his new aid. A young Sergeant named Ibram, who functioned mostly to deliver one request after another to remind him of an appointment that he had scheduled and then forgotten about. He worked late and Fiona seemingly never stopped working. She returned back to their apartment at odd hours of the day and night to shower and occasionally crash headfirst into the bed to steal a few minutes of sleep at a time.

One night the door opened and she walked in, trailing her uniform top and only wearing a tank top. She stubbed out her cigarette in an empty beer bottle that sat on the counter and plopped down into bed next to him.

"I can't believe I let you promote me to this goddamn rank." She sighed. Vincent propped himself on is elbow, leaning over and kissing her. Despite her exhaustion she still smiled and kissed him back.

"Sorry." He faked an apology. "I just wanted to share the misery as much as possible." He snuggled up close to her, unsure of the last time they were able to share a bed.

"Sorry, I probably smell like a warehouse." She wrapped him up in her arms. "You wouldn't believe how many crates of those damn rifles the Martians are sending us. It is taking up so many of my damn ships I can't even use any to haul booze."

"You do know that using your ships for smuggling is still illegal right?" He said, not really caring.

"Yeah, well who is going to catch me?" She laughed. "Me?"

"I don't know." He smiled. "I might have to turn you in." She rolled over on top of him, pinning his arms to the bed. She smirked the way she always did.

"I'll just have to keep you quiet."

Both of them slept in way too late and woke up in a hurry. Fiona got dressed, grabbing her clothes from the day before. She gave them a quick sniff, shrugged, and then slipped them on anyway. Vincent did the same thing and they managed to sneak a quick kiss before both of them went back to work.

Rather than return to his office, Vincent got on the tram and went to the Volunteer Headquarters. Aron had situated the headquarters near the spaceport for ease of access and travel. He had crammed the entire working staff structure into a converted warehouse that had once been a food storage facility. Nobody could tell them what kind of food the Clan had stored there, but it smelled like a mixture of old fish and rotting vegetables.

Aron, as usual was unhappy to see him. Not because they had any personal animosity, but because as Consul he immediately became the sponge for any abuse the Marshal wanted to fire in the direction of the Warlord.

"I can't believe they let the Martians build these things." He cursed at the crates of rifles sitting around in piles. "Did they raid a museum for these?"

"Arai seems confident that they will work." Vincent said. "I don't have any reason to doubt her."

"You don't?" He laughed. "Have you ever taken even a glance at the old EDF infantry training manual?" Aron didn't wait for an answer, because he already knew it. "Take away our volume of firepower and all of that old shit is out the window. We have to retrain everyone a week out from a possible invasion. So, excuse me if I do have a reason to doubt her."

"You're retraining everyone?"

"Yeah." He got to his feet and led Vincent through the building and the streams of officers and aids that milled back and forth. They exited the building to the rear, showing a decent size drilling pad. Not that such space had been given to the Volunteers.

It was simply an unused part of the spaceport and after Aron had moved in Clan authorities figured it was easy to give it to them then kick them off.

On the drilling pad lines of Volunteers stood, their Martian built rifles held up at the shoulder. A Sergeant was yelling commands.

"Load!" They called out. The soldiers all dropped to a knee and began fishing their free hand into a satchel they wore over one shoulder, produced a single bullet, and inserted it into the rifle. They slammed the bolt forward in unison.

"Aim!" They brought the rifle up to their shoulder, staring down the length of the barrel, nearly double the length of the weapon they had all trained on previously. He noticed that several of the rifles swayed unsteadily as they did so, unable to control the added weight of the thing.

"Fire!" A deafening thunder clap cut through the air as a dozen of the guns fired in unison. Though one soldier flung themselves back, blood streaming from their face which had become blackened and burned. In their hands was the twisted remains of their rifle, exploding at the bolt and sending a geyser of burning powder and shrapnel directly into their face. The soldiers stopped what they were doing and turned to render aid for their fallen comrade.

"Does that happen a lot?" Vincent grimaced.

"More often than you would think." Aron folded his arms. "Got at least a dozen in the hospital after drilling with these pieces of shit for the last day and a half." The Marshal rubbed his eyes and took a deep breath. "No matter how much I bitch about these we are going to use them, huh?"

"You got it."

"Well, I'll tell the boys to look on the bright side. If they maim themselves with their malfunctioning weapons they won't have to take part in the invasion."

"Can't be any worse than riding in the freeze back and forth from Lunar City. By this point the Volunteers are tougher than anything we can throw at them." Vincent smiled, putting a hand on Aron shoulder. He wasn't sure if he was growing up, or Aron was just in a worse mood than he had ever seen him in. It was a strange time to find him of all people reassuring the stoic former Sergeant Major.

"You're right." Aron nodded. "I only complain to you because all the other Marshals are busy and I'm sure as hell not cluing any of the troopers in on the fact that I'm stressed. You're my blow off valve."

"You know, some people get hobbies. Or a girlfriend or something. You should try that instead of yelling at me all the time."

"I'll get right on that." Aron laughed. "Right after we get back and I drop my retirement packet on your desk."

"Finally had enough of being a soldier?"

"More than enough, I hear they are letting retirees settle on some of Elysian's outer worlds. I could do that. I suspect you're planning on doing the same in regards to being Consul." As Aron spoke the wounded soldier had been walked over to a medical station and the rest of them took back up their rifles, practicing their firing drills again.

"The thought has crossed my mind." Vincent admitted. "Fiona isn't much for a normal life, but I could see myself with a little place out there with you. We could get Ezra to retire and keep the whole band together." He laughed.

"I think we both know Vorbeck is going to die of old age behind the controls of a ship. Or from a heart attack, which ever happens first. Do you even think Arai would let you resign?"

Vincent did know, because they had already talked about it. During one of their many meetings he had informed Arai that he intended on resigning as Consul once the war was over. To his surprise, she accepted that without question. Not under any personal or moral grounds, but with the understanding that human life is comparatively shorter than the Rhai or Mawr and she assumed he didn't want to spend the rest of his locked into various meeting rooms. He didn't want to tell her he was actually still young, and just didn't want to do the job anymore. She said she would promise to accept the vote of the Unions to appoint the next Consul and he believed her.

"Wow." Aron said. "I didn't think she would take that."

"The Mawr believe in living a full life of self expression and discovery. Normally for them that means finding a battlefield to die in, but every once and awhile it isn't. I think that is how she sees it for me."

"And what about Pharos?"

"We had to tell him what the world 'resign' meant." Vincent said and both of them laughed. After a few moments an odd silence fell over them. Aron cleared his throat.

"I'm ready to get this over with." His voice was uncharacteristically unsteady.

"Me too, Aron." He nodded. "For better or worse, this is the last time."

Further across the spaceport was the utter chaos of Ezra's Volunteer Fleet. His flagship, the *ESS Olympus* had mercifully been towed back to Mars for further retrofitting and repair after their run in with the last remnants of the EDF. That left Marshal of the Fleet Ezra Vorbeck trying in vain to instruct his force of still largely green pilots.

The interceptor pilots that had managed to survive the battle outside of Lunar City had become the grizzled veterans of the fleet. Even they only had a few hundred training and flight hours under their belt. That fact alone made Vincent wonder just how the hell they had managed to escape from that battle alive and not be reduced to dead space debris.

In the several weeks since they had left, Titan and Mars sent more and more pilots back to Elysian, freshly graduated from their abridged training. Equipped with just enough knowledge to severely injure or kill themselves upon takeoff and landing, it was now up to Ezra to organize them all once again. More importantly he had to turn them into a force that could square off with the Anarch Fleet. Vincent had no idea how Ezra was going to turn a fleet of barely trained liabilities into something that could hold off literal war machines, and by the looks of it, either did he.

Ezra was sitting in his office that overlooked the entire spaceport. It was a small room at the top of a tall tower, surrounded by windows on all sides. All around him he watched displays that spat a constant stream of data at him as his pilots zipped around the tower in simulated dog fights. The Rhai fleet was acting as the enemy force for training purposes and were flying circles around the Volunteers. Ezra was so engrossed in his work he didn't notice Vincent enter, after a few moments he spun around in his chair and gave him a weak smile.

"Came to watch the show?"

"Something like that." Vincent said. "How is it going?"

"Well." He rubbed his tired eyes. "They are getting better. Training killed the dumb ones and the Battle of Lunar City took out the not so dumb ones. What we have left are the-" He paused for a moment thinking of a word and Vincent cut in.

"The good ones?"

"No." Ezra laughed. "I wouldn't go that far. I'd say we are left with a solid core that would be able to be good pilots in a few years."

"But we don't have a few years."

"That we don't." Ezra sighed. He reached over to a canteen and poured out two cups of Kaff. No steam rose from the drink and he had no idea how long it had been sitting in there, but Vincent took one of the cups gratefully. "The Warlord is asking a lot of the Fleet."

"She is asking a lot from all of us." Vincent agreed. Ezra simply nodded and sipped his drink. "Do you think you can do it?"

"You're asking me if we and our allies can secure the space over Baki Two long enough to deploy you onto the surface and then do our best to hold off the entire Anarch fleet, a fleet that we have largely no intelligence on." He took another drink. "On top of that hold the space over the moon so we can keep a resupply pipeline open to you so you don't all get killed in some godforsaken valley below us."

"Can you do it?" He asked again.

"I think we'll try." Ezra said finally. "That is all we can do."

"That has to be the least motivational thing I've ever heard you say." Vincent laughed and took a drink. The kaff was old and burnt and been in Ezra's canteen for so long the grounds had begun to congeal back together. He spit it out.

"You know the Warlord expects them to land on the moon to reinforce whatever garrison they have there pretty fast, right?"

"I assumed. Landing right on their door step ought to piss them off."

"You won't have time to dig in much before their counter attack hits. Not the first lines anyway. I'm hoping we will be able to give you orbital support the best we can, but the time will come when we will have to break off and fight their fleet. Thankfully the Titanians came through for us." Ezra slid a display to Vincent. It showed a what looked like a folding metal barrier. A user's manual showed two soldiers quickly throwing the barrier down, while one covered the other from some unknown threat. A tagline read "Deploys fast! No need to dig!" The entire page on the display looked like an ad of some kind, like Titan high command was attempting to sell him something. Maybe they were.

"And these will stop Anarch plasma weapons?" He laughed. "They look like they could barely hold themselves up."

"They say they will." He shrugged. "Pharos agrees apparently." Vincent thought back to the Martian rifle blowing up in a soldier's face.

"Well, that fills me with confidence." Their conversation was interrupted by the sound of an Elysian interceptor crashing to the ground, skidding at a high rate of speed across the spaceport and sending a towering plume of sparks into the air. It came to rest after crashing into a parked Rhai ship.

"That looked bad." Vincent gritted his teeth.

"Minor damage to the ship, the pilot is probably able to walk away." Ezra listed. "Compared to what I was seeing before Lunar City that guy is up for a promotion." He refilled his cup and leaned back into his seat. Outside of the tower ships danced clumsily through the air, spinning around one another pulling hairpin turns. One of the Rhai ships dipped its wings to the chasing Elysian, signifying that they had been beaten.

"Hey, we won that one." Vincent smiled.

"Yeah." Ezra nodded. "One out of ten ain't bad, is it?"

Ezra didn't have the years he wanted before the Warlord called for a full mobilization of the Clan. Only a week later the announcement was pushed out to all corners of the Elysian system. It was on a date agreed upon by Mars, Titan, and the Clan and kept close to the chest until the time came. Arai and Pharos' constant fear of Anarch infiltration into their security system only got worse as the date got closer.

Pharos no longer accepted plans, requests, or mail via his display. It would have to be hand written and sent through a courier which would have to be requested from his Cohort as they were the only ones allowed entry into his office. Arai's paranoia increased with several more layers of security popping up in the government quarter prior to the announcement. All government employees and representatives had their displays checked for any secure information.

Because of this, the order couldn't be sent out over public data networks. Despite the begging of Titanian and Martian governments, Arai couldn't be budged. So, one day before the order was given out, mysteriously, all nonmilitary network communications were cut off. The next day, thousands of couriers hired by every

Quarter within the city posted mobilization orders on every street corner. In other places loudspeakers mounted on shuttles swooped down low over the streets, blaring the announcement so loudly it shook windows. Soldiers were to drop what they were doing and immediately report to their units for further orders.

Thankfully, since the mobilization against Lunar City, the system had worked out its kinks for the most part. Gone were the scenes of confused mobs and screaming officers and instead Khaki uniformed Volunteers queued up at designated spots, many accompanied by their families. Each was equipped with the new Martian rifle and a satchel thrown over a shoulder.

Vincent was whisked back into the government quarter by a shuttle sent by the Warlord. While the rest of the planet and their allies attempted to get their forces together Arai sequestered the Gathering into a smaller antechamber, closed off and closely guarded. A yellow armored guard took Vincent's display as he entered and lowered himself to the floor behind his place at the table.

For the first time in a while, Vincent wasn't the only human at the table. Seated across from him was Erik and another older man in a grey uniform. They had dark skin, a shaved head, and a closely cropped greying beard. On the table in front of him was a peaked cap with an eagle shaped crest affixed to the front of it. The symbol of the Union of Titan.

"Consul Solaris." Erik beamed and held out a hand which Vincent took in his. "I believe you haven't met Field Marshal Vanya yet, have you?" The Titanian also held on his hand and they shook.

"I haven't." Vincent said. "You must be Denta's replacement."

"Replacement." Vanya said. His voice was a dull grumble and he reached an augmetic hand up to stroke his beard. "Something like that. I have heard much about you, Consul."

"Good things, I hope."

"I said *much*." Vanya repeated. Vincent sighed, another full of himself Titanian Field Marshal. Their pompous attitude must have been as uniform as the stick up their officer's asses.

"How is Denta anyway?" He asked, trying to change the subject.

"Retired." Vanya said quickly. The tone of which he answered led Vincent to believe that Denta was anything but retired.

"Right." He turned to Erik. "No representatives from Lunar City?"

"Not only that." Erik shook his head. "No answer at all."

"Wait, Shay is ghosting us?" Vincent pounded his fists on the table. Several of the Mawr and Rhai representatives gave him a sideways glance. Vanya laughed. Even his laugh was short and to the point.

"Of course, he did." He said. "You took out his enemies and now we are going off to fight the Anarchs on their own turf. He probably assumed, rightly I should point out, that we can't spare anyone to force him to comply. Now all he has to do is bank on the fact that we lose."

"Mother fucker!" Vincent screamed, punching the table again. At that Arai and Pharos entered the room, those in attendance rose to their feet. Vanya remained seated.

"I will assume from your outburst the Consul has learned of Lunar City." Arai said.

"I have." Arai sat down next to him.

"It is best we forget about it for now." He raised his eyebrows. Arai wasn't one to forgive someone for almost anything, let alone outright betrayal. "We have enough to worry about. Once we emerge from our next campaign victorious, we will deal with these traitors." Pharos cleared his throat, bringing the meeting back on track.

"This is likely the last time all of us will be in the same room until the conclusion of our campaign." Vincent thought it would be unlikely that all of them would survive, even if their plan actually worked. "So, considering our current network black out, this is the best way to pass along the last intelligence we were able to get regarding Baki Two."

"The last?" Erik asked. "We won't be able to get updates before we make planet fall?

"The Warlord and I have come to the conclusion that continued use of spy drones around the moon heightens the risk of the Anarchs being able to figure out our planned landing area."

"Makes sense." Vanya said. "Another proposition, if I may." Arai nodded and he continued. "If we are so worried about the Anarchs catching onto our plans, we should probably keep a full communications black out for as long as we can as we travel to Baki Two."

"Yes, that is a good idea." Arai agreed. "As the lead unit to make planet fall, I will initiate communications before doing so. All other units can consider this as a signal to deploy as well."

"The last updates." Pharos continued. "The Anarchs treat the moons of Baki as remote outposts. They have would could be considered a human firebase on each one. Scans show around fifty thousand warriors of various makes on each moon."

"Fifty thousand?" Erik pursed his lips. "And what is our collective strength?"

"According the last counts submitted by your subordinate commanders we will be fielding five million soldiers together. Humans being the most numerous, followed by Mawr, then Rhai. These numbers do not count our assembled fleets, which will number another two million." Erik laughed, leaning forward onto the table.

"Well, that doesn't seem like much of a fight." He said.

"We can assume that the Anarchs will not let us occupy Baki Two." Pharos said. "They will rapidly deploy reinforcements from Baki One and Baki Prime within seconds of us arriving.

Flight time between Baki Prime and Baki Two is two hours. The fleet will form a picket around Baki Two to engage the reinforcements as they arrive."

"So what is the problem?" Vanya asked. "Our combined fleets can surely hold them at bay."

"They will for a time." Pharos agreed. "But, the Anarch fleet will dwarf our own. It will only be a matter of time before they break through the picket and deploy their forces to the surface of Baki Two." A silence fell over the room.

"What kind of reinforcements as we talking about here?" Erik asked, his voice somber.

"Tens of millions." Pharos said. For the first time in his life Vincent saw the gathered Mawr gasp in disbelief. Vincent swallowed hard.

"So." He said, trying to move the meeting along and distract everyone from the prospect of fighting an unending wave of death machines. "Once we make planet fall, we have a few hours to dig in as much as possible."

"Yes." Arai said. "I am told the Titanian engineers are second to none when it comes to such things." Vanya nodded.

"I give you my word we will turn that valley into a fortress." Arai grinned, rising to her feet.

"Well then." She bowed to the table. "Until we meet again on the surface, may Paternazm guide you."

There was no parade when they left this time.

Vincent assumed the Lunar City occupation had taken the celebratory mood out of the air. Sitting around for a few weeks and hardly fighting. When they returned, they were still treated like conquering heroes, but it seemed pretty forced.Families were just happy to have their loved ones back. The idea of marching off to war against the Committee seemed realistic. It sounded winnable. They had fought the EDF on multiple occasions and just won their greatest victory on Mars against them.

The campaigns against them were daunting, but there wasn't a human alive that hadn't lived through or learned about wars against other humans while in school. There weren't many humans still alive that had stood toe to toe against the Anarchs and managed to survive. For most people they weren't just a race of aliens. They were monsters. They were devilish creatures that existed on the fringes of space and seemingly only emerged to enslave races or destroy entire planets.

The humans that survived the battle on Grawluck returned with horror stories. They told their friends and families about ten foot tall armored beasts that burned entire companies of soldiers alive with a single cannon blast. It didn't take long for those stories to make their rounds and become further exaggerated. Now, as the entire army of Volunteers was boarding their shuttles that would take them to orbit their families they left behind probably thought they were being sent off to fight an army of literal fire breathing demon creatures from beyond the void.

Vincent originally planned on leading the march towards the shuttles in order to raise the mood a bit but Fiona had kept him entangled in other matters in bed until the last minute. On their way out the door she had to make a pit stop to vomit. He wasn't sure if it was from a crippling hangover or nerves. By the time they got there, lines of somber civilians lined the streets to say farewell. They held flags and signs and more than a few children, husbands, and wives ran out to steal one last kiss from their family as they marched away.

"Man, talk about a downer." Fiona said. "It looks like we are going to a funeral."

"We might be." He said. "Marching towards our funeral, I mean." He offered Fiona a cigarette from a crinkled packet. It was an old pack of Lunar brand cigarettes and she turned it down.

"Damn." She laughed. "That grim shit sounds like something I would say."

"What can I say? You're rubbing off on me." The sad funeral march continued until all of the Volunteers had been transported from the surface to various ships in orbit. Once back aboard the *ESS Olympus* Vincent made a note to himself to thank Erik if he lived long enough to see him again. The rickety ship had gone through a total overhaul.

The damage done during the battle outside of Lunar City had been repaired. Mercifully, that meant they had restored running water and sewage treatment. Gone were the chemical treatment buckets that acted as emergency toilets and the accompanying gut-wrenching smell. The showers worked for everyone and there was even hot water in most of them. Though, the most welcome repair came to the power plant. When soldiers, overdressed in several layers of winter clothing, boarded the *Olympus* for the trip to Baki Two they were shocked to be greeted by the warm glow of a functioning heating system.

For the weeks of transit time, the somber mood hung heavy over the crew of the *Olympus*. The communications black out meant that nobody from the surrounding ships could exchange news or rumors. Personal displays had been confiscated, meaning sending messages to loved ones or even watching a movie was impossible. Soldiers lazed about, staring off into space chain smoking or playing cards to pass the time. The only momentary excitement that rippled through the ship was an outbreak of lice. By order of the ship's Chief Medical Officer everyone had to shave their heads in order to contain it.

After what seemed like entirely too long, Ezra called for Vincent to meet him on the bridge. As always, his command area was a mess of discarded rations and packets of instant kaff. Even him own aid had stopped cleaning up after him. His salt and pepper hair had already started coming back in forming a stubble that merged together with his unshaven face.

"Word from Arai?" Vincent asked. Ezra looked up from a report he was reading. It was hand written, as even military displays used for intra ship communication had been ordered silenced until ordered by the Warlord.

"No." He shook his head. "But we are getting very close. Another day or two at most I would guess." The bridge door opened and the rest of the Marshals entered. Each of them with a freshly shaved head. Felicity kept her uniform hat on, pulled down low to cover her what she had previously described as "her shame."

"Good god man." Aron laughed. "You look like you're living in a landfill."

"And you look like a human thumb in a uniform." Ezra grumbled, gesturing at Aron's bald head. The bridge crew stifled their laughter with their hands as Aron frowned.

"Gentlemen." Fiona held her hands out. "I think we can all agree you both look like shit." More laughter, Ezra eyed his subordinates until they stopped.

"So, I assume you called us here because we are getting close." Aron said, trying to bring everyone back on track.

"Yes." Ezra nodded. "I would recommend putting your forces on alert. All Fleet personnel have been put on standby outside of normal patrols."

"Every soldier should have already been issued everything they need for the first forty-eight hours of fighting." Fiona said. "Anything after that will have to been brought from orbit by my shuttles."

"The air is going to be hot within hours." Aron said. "Can you keep that line open?"

"Erik told me he is bringing every bit of surface-based air defense Mars has. If what he says is right it should take the weight off the Fleet for supply train defense."

"And if it doesn't?" Vincent asked. Fiona shrugged.

"I can't imagine we are going to be able to give you much cover once the Anarch Fleet shows itself." Ezra said.

"If Erik is wrong then I guess me and my shuttles get blasted from the air and you all die when you run out of ammo." She seemed to not care much about that possibility.

"Well, let's hope Erik pulls through then." Aron sighed. He reached into the pocket of his uniform and pulled out a scrap of people, unfolding it and holding it close to his face. "This no display rule is a pain in my ass by the way." He cleared his throat. "The Mawr are landing first, followed by the Titanians, then us. That Vanya character seems to think his engineers can put down defenses in less than an hour. Our goal is to land thirty minutes after they do."

"We'll launch the same time as the Mawr." Fiona said. "Get as many supplies on the ground as soon as possible before shit goes sideways."

"Good idea." Aron nodded. "and you?" He looked at Felicity. She found her own scrap of paper and glanced at it.

"I spoke to Commander Erik briefly before we left Elysian. As the valley will be split into different defensive lines, we have to understand there is a very good chance some of these lines were break. If the Anarchs manage to hold a sustained break-through and drive to our rear it'll all be over. So, the Commandos and Pathfinders will be held in reserve, here." She pointed to her paper, on which she had sketched a rough map of the valley. "We will stay in the rear and deployed to critically important areas as needed and withdrawn once the situation is stabilized." She glanced up at Vincent. "Assuming you agree, Consul."

"You're the Marshal." He said. "That sounds like a good plan."

"Speaking of the Consul, I assume you're going to stay with the fleet." Aron said. He wasn't asking. He also wasn't so bold as to try to order him to stay off of Baki Two. Vincent assumed he was suggesting the path that would make the most sense for him. He wasn't a military commander, he was a political leader. A political leader without much power anymore, after giving most of it to the Unions.

"I'm a soldier too." Vincent said. "I'll be on the ground with everyone else."

"Sir, in all due respect-" Aron began before Vincent cut him off.

"I'm not having this argument again." He scolded. "And besides how do you think the Volunteers would feel if they make planet fall and word gets out that I'm not there?"

"I don't want him on the front as much as you don't." Felicity sighed. "But he's right. I can't think of anything that would tank morale harder. I can task a squad of Commandos to guard you."

"I have Zinvor." He folded his arms. "I'll be fine."

"Speaking of which." Felicity addressed Fiona. "Are you sure you want to land, considering-" Fiona got in Felicity's face.

"Finish that sentence and I promise you won't live long enough to make planet fall." She snarled. Felicity's eyes went wide.

"Noted." She squeaked.

"Everything okay?" Vincent asked. The professional relationship between the two of them was always adversarial. It was almost entirely based in Fiona's own head and her intense hatred for anything prim, proper, and professional. Being a graduate of the Titanian military academy meant that was all Felicity stood for. Rarely did it devolve to outright death threats, though when dealing with Fiona that option was never truly off the table.

"Yeah." Fiona fired back. "Just peachy." She gave Felicity one more murderous glance before storming out of the bridge. Felicity bit her lip as she marched away. Vincent looked at her with a puzzled look.

"Don't ask." Felicity stammered and rushed out of the room.

"We can't have a single meeting without Fiona threatening to kill someone can we?" Ezra asked, jokingly.

"It comes with the territory." Vincent smiled.

The communication blackout ended abruptly one day in ship time later. Displays flickered back to life and links to the rest of the fleet were restored in a matter of seconds. The loudspeaker crackled to life as Arai addressed every ship in the Clan Fleet. The she spoke in the garbled language of her race. After a few second delay the words were repeated, translated into Earth Standard in an automated, static voice.

"Warrior of the Fidayi Clan. We stand at the cusp of history. Before us is the home of the monsters who took our home from us, scattered us to the stars, and drove us into hiding. We are hiding no more. Today, we step into eternity. Your names will ring throughout time and space as liberators of the entire galaxy. Take up your Ritens and join me in immortality!"

For the first time since they had left Elysian Vincent felt the come together as one. In one, rumbling voice a cheer cut through the barren hallways of the *Olympus*. Soldiers banged their helmets off the bulkheads, picked each other up, and fist pumped in celebratory glee. It didn't matter that none of them had Ritens, outside of Fiona and Vincent, it didn't even matter that the speech kind of sounded like a rallying cry for a suicide mission. Everyone was finally ready to strike back.

Fiona was strapping on her armor, dark red and covered in countless scuffs and gouges from battle. She checked the chambers of her Riten, spun the ammo wheel, and slid it into its holster before throwing on her gear harness that hung heavy with grenades and an ammo satchel.

"You know you're only supposed to fly in supplies, right?" Vincent asked.

"I'd rather have all of this and not need it then find myself in a situation where I do and I don't." She said. He was doing the same thing, checking over his armor and weapons one last time. His Martian rifle sat in the corner of the room and he hoped he wouldn't have to use the contraption. It would be his luck to blow out his last real eye with a misfiring cartridge.

"True." He said, shoving a few more grenades into his own ammo harness. He noticed she had left her flask and a pack of cigarettes sitting out and offered her them. Her eyes went wide and she fumbled trying to find words.

"Ezra put out a new rule, no smoking in the shuttles. So I might as well not take them." She finally said.

"Since when do you listen to Ezra?"

"Trying to set a good example and all, you know. I am a Marshal now." He eyed her with suspicion and set them back down.

"This might be the last time we see each other until this is all over." She said, her voice growing quiet.

"Yeah." He said.

"I hate this sappy shit, but I don't know what to say." Her eyes got watery. She was never one for emotions, but she was right. Normally, when they found themselves in the middle of a situation that might kill them, they were always right next to one another. Now, they both had their own roles to play, official duties to carry out. They weren't just Vincent and Fiona anymore, they were Marshal Olympus-Solaris and Consul Solaris. They had come a long way since they were both scared teenagers fighting for their lives on some hillside on Ryklar.

"I know." He smiled. "I love you too." She got closer to him and wrapped him in a hug.

"You better stick close to Zinvor." She poked him in the chest. "Don't do any heroic shit."

"When have I ever done anything heroic?" He said as tears began to fall from his good eye. "You better keep your ass in the rear with the gear." They were both full on crying now. Full throated sobs into each other's armor. Her closely shaven head pricked his face but he didn't care. She pulled away and kissed him. From the desperation of it he could tell it was the last one before she would have to leave.

"This isn't goodbye, goddamnit." She said. Her eyes here bloodshot from the tears. "I'll see you soon."

"Once we save the fucking universe." He smiled.

"Yeah." She laughed, wiping at her face. "Shit, I have to compose myself before I go out there and the boys see me looking like a giant goddamn baby."

"I love you." He said, kissing her one last time on the top of her head. "and I'll see you soon." She grabbed her rifle from the corner of the room and made for the door. He followed as far as he could, but only made it as far berthing until the crowds of departing soldiers made it impossible. The last he saw of her was elbowing soldiers in the side to get them to move while screaming death threats at them as she went.

He returned to his to find Tyr, dressed in their best flight suit. Medals and ribbons dangled from their thin chest.

"I didn't think you would get here in time." Vincent said.

"You have to forgive me." Tyr chirped. "There is much traffic between here and the Warlord's flagship."

"So, you brought it?" He asked, and Tyr nodded.

"It is here." They said, sliding forward a foot locker.

"Thank you, Tyr. That is all that I need."

"You won't need me to pilot you in the upcoming battle?"

"No. I'm going to land with the soldiers. Whatever duty you had to me is released. They are going to need every skilled pilot they can get holding the picket." Tyr stared at him in confusion for a second. Vincent added. "And I'll make sure I tell Marshal Vorbeck to promote you if we survive all this." At this Tyr bowed deeply and left the room. Vincent knew Zinvor was just outside the door, holding his post.

"Hey Zinvor, can you come in here?" The door slide open and he entered. He was still wearing his oddly fitting khaki uniform, one of the Martian rifles slung over his shoulder, so long in comparison to him it nearly dragged on the ground as he went.

"What did the skinny one do?" He grunted, talking about Tyr.

"Nothing." Vincent said, laughing to himself. "I got you something. A gift."

"Gift?" Zinvor mulled the word around in his mouth, clearly not coming up with a definition. Vincent rolled his eyes and slid over the foot locker that Tyr delivered.

"Open it." Zinvor bent down and unhooked the latches, folding the top over. It took him a few seconds but he stood back up, lost for words. In the foot locker in front of him was a set of khaki colored Mawr armor and a brand new Riten.

"I cannot accept this." He managed to get it. "I am not a Warrior any longer."

"I spoke to Arai." Vincent said. "She told me that when you died you were not only no longer a Tsarra, you were no longer *you*. At least legally in the eyes of the Clan."

"I'm not me?" He asked, not understanding.

"Yeah, for all intents and purposes Zinvor is dead. When you came back to life on the operating table you were, in Arai's words, reborn anew, free of all burdens and duties of your past life. That means, as you are now, you were never a Warrior, a Tsarra, or anything else for that matter. You aren't even technically a member of the Clan."

"Then what am I?" Vincent motioned down to the locker.

"The third Warrior of the Volunteer Army." He smiled. Vincent had never seen a Mawr cry, and he wasn't sure if they could. But if Zinvor was physically able to he would have. He knelt down and took up the armor in his hands, holding it close to his face before falling silently into a prayer that Vincent couldn't understand.

"You've always been a Warrior, Zinvor." He said. "Now you can just look the part again."

"We are such an understrength Cohort. Only three Warriors? A shame." Zinvor said, a smile creeping across his face. For the first time since they had known each other, he was pretty sure the Mawr was telling a joke.

"It's fine." He nodded. "Three is all we need."

The hallways to the berthings were crowded with humanity. Soldiers checked and rechecked their gear. Others stood silently, staring off ahead into nothing. The brief moment of zeal they had experienced after Arai's speech was over. Now, they were once again lost in the enormity of the task that lay ahead of them.

In front of each door a member of fleet staff stood with a box in between their hands. They spoke like they were reading from a mental script.

"Every soldier must take one rebreather. Place the rebreather into your nose and do not remove it once you make planet fall for any reason." As soon as the person had worked through their script, they would repeat themselves. Next to them was another fleet staffer, overexaggerating the act of placing the rebreather into their nose and then breathing deeply. It reminded Vincent of a bad infomercial.

The lines of soldiers shuffled forward, each taking a rebreather and stuffing it into their nose. Vincent reached in and grabbed one. He knew the device had been created by the Rhai, but there was so little to the thing, he was suspicious if it would work. It was hardly any larger than an intranasal cannula that they would use in the hospital. He put it in his nose, trying not to worry too much about it. If it didn't work it wouldn't matter for very long once they reached the surface.

Vincent made it to the front of a line and found a very confused Major staring down at a display, checking names off from a list. She noticed Vincent standing there and immediately straightened herself up, giving a salute.

"Consul, sir." She said, glancing down at how he was dressed. "You're making planet fall?"

"Of course." He said. "Was looking to hitch a ride." The Major beamed.

"I would be honored if you landed with my unit, Sir."

"You'll have to forgive me, which unit is this?"

"The eighty-ninth Anti-Tank Infantry Regiment, of course." She nodded. "Marshal Aron has given us the honor of sharing the forward positions with the Mawr." If Fiona knew he was headed to the front she would order her troops throw him in a footlocker and lock him aboard the *Olympus*.

"Sounds perfect." He nodded. "What was your name, Major?"

"Kolea." She said. "Juna Kolea."

"Nice to meet you." He smiled, putting out a hand. Kolea had the dark skin and accent of a Titanian. Her age, mid-twenties Vincent would guess, told him that she was probably one of the Titanian officers who switches either on Mars or at some point after. He assumed the Titanian Military Academy frowned upon shaking hands with your superior. After a few seconds of hesitation, she shook his hand with a nervous smile on her face.

"You too, Sir."

When it was his turn to step inside a shuttle, he was surprised at what he saw. He knew the mass production of Reapers had ceased a few months back in order to prepare for a coming invasion. Reapers were a catch all with dozens of different variants from interceptors to strike bombers they were meant to be a modular platform to fit the needs of the fleet and able to be changed to fit various situations. One of the things it wasn't supposed to be used for was invading an entire planet.

Instead, the old Earth Defense Force would pack entire companies into drop ships and fire them off towards the target planet by the hundreds or thousands from a Capital ship. Destroyers like the *Olympus* didn't have the ability to store and launch the drop ships. Not originally, anyway.

During its retrofitting on Mars engineers had installed an entirely new deck space. Hundreds of different flexible plastic tunnels had been grafted onto the belly of the *Olympus*, dangling underneath the massive ship like tentacles. At the end of each was a newly built, Martian designed shuttle. In order to reach the docked shuttle, Vincent had to climb down into the tube and pick his way down a wall mounted rung that carried him a dozen or so meters below him. A few rungs under him another soldier was climbing down and another under them.

The tube was pressurized and oxygenated. It wasn't translucent, instead it was a off grey color, and Vincent tried not to think about that on the other side of the who knows how thin plastic material was the endless void of space. Above him Zinvor grunted and growled his way down the ladder, each step just a few inches too far away from his feet or hands as he went.

After a few minutes of climbing and waiting for the soldiers below him to get out of his way, Vincent clambered into the ship below through a small hatch. The shuttle itself was clearly only designed for one goal: delivering hundreds of soldiers to a battlefield as quickly as possible. It was little more than a teardrop of metal bolted together into a hull, anything not needed for the immediate mission was stripped away for simplicities sake. A small cockpit was at the tip of the craft, manned by one person with a minimalistic control panel arrayed around them. Soldiers sat in the hull on two bench seats, each with a fabric four-point harness strapped to the wall behind them to be affixed around them and to the bench itself. The hull was so thin that the soldiers seated on the benches knees nearly touched and no room remained between them.

Vincent squeezed into a spot and sat down. Like everyone else he placed his rifle between his legs, the end of its barrel almost reaching the ceiling of the small shuttle. Major Kolea dropped through the hatch, sealing it behind her.

"Captain, last man on." She called out.

"Just in time, Major." Commented the pilot. "All packs on board." Packs was a colloquial term used in the military to refer to soldiers, packs of course meaning the packs they carried on their back.

"Prepare for launch. Flight time five minutes." The pilot droned in a monotone. A small hiss of air filled the hull and Vincent felt his body lift up gently from the seat. He would have kept going if he wasn't locked into his harness. He assumed the artificial gravity on board was tied to the Olympus and now that they were disconnected, they were at the mercy of space. The lone turbine began to rattle and whine as they pulled away from the mother ship. There were no windows in the shuttle, but Vincent imagined there being thousands of shuttles just like the one he was sitting filling the void, aiming themselves towards Baki Two.

"Hey Captain!" Vincent yelled over the growing din of engine noise.

"Yeah?" They answered, interested.

"Any sign of the Anarch fleet yet?"

"Not yet." They said. "If the Rhai timetables hold up our

landing window will last a few hours before shit hits the fan. Some scattered ground fire has been reported so far."

"Lose any shuttles?" At this, the pilot finally glanced back at who was talking to them.

"Don't worry, I've been flying since the First Martian war. Haven't been shot down yet, Consul. I'm not going to let these metal sons of bitches break my streak."

The five minutes of flight time went by in silence for the most part. Soldiers stared down at their feet, even the ability to fidget nervously had been taken from them due to the enclosed space.

"Entering orbit." The pilot said and as if on cue the shuttle began to rattle and shake as it burst through Baki Two's atmosphere. The soldier's heads all jerked upright, some of them tried to crane their necks to see into the cockpit hoping to sneak a peek as to where we were going. Vincent tried to do the same thing, but the pilot's windshield was obscured by rippling waves of fire.

It only took a few moments to break free of the grasp of the moon's atmosphere. The pilot leveled the shuttle out and they cranked the throttle, guiding it towards the valley they would be defending. Around him the soldiers breathed a sign of relief. Making it out of reentry was just one thing they could tick off of their list of things they would have to survive if they wanted to make it off of Baki Two alive.

Then the Anarch decided to greet them.

The hull filled with a dazzling blue light. Veterans of the Battle of Grawluck knew the eerie nightmare glow of Anarch plasma artillery. It would punch through any ship armor, melting the contents to their base elements, sear uniforms to skin, and skin from bone. Vincent had watched an entire company of infantry get charred into the dirt that was simultaneously flash fired into glass with a single impact.

The shuttle nosedived as the pilot took evasive action. The

light faded, but somewhere behind them something exploded, rocking the ship with the resulting shockwave. The dive continued and picked up speed. The shuttle shook more violently in their escape drill turned death spiral than it did during reentry. Vincent's stomach climbed into his throat and his body was forced down into his seat as if a million-pound weight had been placed directly onto his chest. The soldier next to him vomited, sending a cascade of greens and browns across the hull as the g forces sent chunks of undigested mess spattering across the occupants.

Blue light streaked by again and the pilot jammed the controls in a different direction. The shuttle lurched violently again, towards the front of the shuttle near the cockpit a soldier broke free from their harness. They rag dolled off of the walls and bounced off the still secured soldiers as the shuttle pilot jerked the controls again and again. By the time the evasive maneuvers ended, the soldier that had broken away from their harness laid unmoving across the laps of their comrades.

Mercifully the pilot brought the shuttle to a halt and a second later dropped the ramp that made up the rear of the hull. Sunlight flooded the shuttle followed by stinging dust. Soldiers rapidly untangled themselves from their harnesses, grabbed their weapons and quickly got out. A few stayed behind to strap the dead soldier back into a seat so they didn't get flung around when the shuttle returned to orbit.

Vincent stepped onto the surface of Baki Two and took in what he saw. As far as he could see on any side was the sheer cliff faces that made up the valley. The valley floor was alive with activity. Titanian and Rhai engineering crews were hard at work, planting explosives and blowing long strips out of the dense, rocky terrain. Actually digging emplacements was deemed unrealistic for their immediate defensive needs. So, they had resorted to using a kind of explosive that unspooled like a rope and setting off explosions every few seconds, scratching out improvised trenches. As soon as one line exploded, the next group of engineers would be laying the next.

The blowing dust forced Vincent to shield his good eye and he could hear the rebreather begin to hum as it filtered out the various compounds in the air that would kill him. Kolea was yelling at the soldiers, trying to rally them together and force them to their position. Her orders were drowned out by all of the moving parts, lost in the constant stream of shuttles making planet fall and watching thousands of soldiers find their way to their positions or the hundreds of tanks and APCs tearing across the valley floor.

Vincent met Kolea who was waving soldiers into their trench. The position stretched from one side of the valley to the other and was already populated by what seemed to be thousands of Mawr Warriors.

"How did you get picked to fill the frontline?" He asked. "Normally the Warriors aren't fans of sharing the glory of battle with us lowly humans."

"Necessity." Kolea said. "They wanted anti-armor abilities to complement the ground pounders I suppose. The Warlord is holding our armor in reserve."

"They're fast, can quickly move in to plug holes in the line. Makes sense." He said.

"True." She said. "It'll just make holding here a bit of a bastard" She turned from him and began to scream orders at the soldiers as they filed into the trench. They hurried into their position and started to deploy their weapon systems. It was the EDF standard, shaped like a box it acted as the sighting system for a rocket, which was loaded alongside of it. When fired it could be controlled by the shooter all the way to the point of impact using a small joystick and camera.

Dozens of the rocket systems were laid out along the top of

the trench. Well trained crews began to put them together and their assistants loaded their warheads. Another weapon was terrifyingly familiar to Vincent. A small shoulder launched tube that looked like it had been slapped together from spare plumbing parts and spot welds. The Martians had used the thing during the war, sometimes nearly blowing themselves up in the process. Instead of improving on the design, they seemed to have standardized it. The soldiers laid the launchers on the floor of the trench, alongside which they had ditched their ammo satchels and leaned their rifles.

"Now what?" Vincent asked.

"We wait." Kolea said. She dug in her pocket and found a cigarette. She lit it and took a hit. After a few seconds she discarded it. "Goddamn rebreathers." She spat. "They filter out the smoke." The two of them leaned against the trench wall, sliding down to sit on the floor. Soldiers around them fell into a watch routine while others snuck a few bites from ration packs.

"Have you ever fought the Anarchs before?" She asked.

"Yeah." He said. "A few times."

"I was still in academy for Grawluck." She stared down at her feet. "I missed it by a few weeks. Are they really as terrifying as everyone says they are?" Her voice dropped to a whisper so her soldiers couldn't hear her.

"I'd rather charge Victoria or the Mons again then sit in this trench and face them." He said.

"Shit." She sighed.

"But we don't need to think like that." He said, forcing a smile. "We either win here today or it's all over. We don't have time for fear." She nodded, cupping her hands around her mouth.

"You hear that boys?" She yelled. "The Consul says not one step back!" The soldiers punched a fist into the air and cheered.

. . .

It had turned out, Pharos was right. After a few hours the dark brown, dust choked sky of Baki Two began to flash with brilliant colors. The telltale signs of low orbit combat. Bright blues and red blinked and sparkled punctuated by the occasional bloom of orange. Every few seconds the smoking trail of wreckage punched through the moon's atmosphere, crashing to the ground like a meteor.

"Do we have any word on who is winning?" Vincent asked. Kolea motioned for her radio operator and a skinny Martian kid hurried over.

"Can you get the fleet on that thing?" She asked.

"Only in low orbit." The radio operator said. Vincent saw his nametag read *Tharsis*. Tharsis began to screw with his radio pack, fiddling with dials until the static that hissed through the speaker turned to panicked voices.

"Get that mother fucker off my ass!" Screamed a voice, heavily garbled in static and distortion it was hardly intelligible.

"Wing Commander is down." Said a different voice. "God-damn, they are everywhere!" The voice became more and more distorted until the only thing that came through was a guttural scream of a man before it was abruptly cut off. The soldiers who were listening to the voices on the radio eyes had gone wide, their pupils turning to pinpricks.

"Turn that shit off." Kolea ordered.

"Doesn't matter what we hear on that radio." Vincent said. "Marshal Vorbeck and everyone else up there isn't going to go down that easy." He wasn't sure if he was reassuring the soldiers around him or himself. He tried to push memories of the *Victory* crashing towards Ryklar from his mind.

A black streak cut through the swirling dust clouds overhead, followed by several others. They were the shimmering black, razor-sharp shape of Anarch ships. They dove down low, leveled off and fired off multiple bursts of blue plasma fire.

Soldiers through themselves to the trench floor as plasma bolts stitched across the valley floor. The chattering of small arms erupted from the trench lines behind them. The soldiers assigned the heavy belt fed machine gun in their line forced themselves to their feet and began firing blindly into the air as well. They had no hope of hitting the Anarch craft, they were so fast by the time they pulled the trigger the bullets would have been miles behind them.

As if defying physics the ships stopped on a dime, spun around, and took off in another direction. It all happened so quickly the human eye could hardly keep up. The valley wall exploded behind them as Erik's orbital defense weapons opened fire and missed. Smoke trails from missile batteries snaked into the sky and found purchase. One of the ships was hit and spun wildly out of control before crashing into the valley wall.

More ships appeared from the sky. They opened fire as soon as they entered the moon's orbit and the first burst slammed directly into the frontline. Blue light erupted from further down the line, followed by secondary explosions as ammo dumps nearby the impact zone detonated. This time the ships didn't have time to do another pass. The Martian defense systems had finally found their marks.

The sky filled with dark plumes of flak and the spiraling trails of rocket and missile engines. Together they formed a dense net of death in the sky for the Anarch ships. They were riddled with holes and exploded into cartwheeling balls of fire. The next wave of Anarch ships didn't even make it far enough to fire a burst at the defenders before they were smacked out of the sky. After that, they stopped coming.

Vincent breathed a sigh of relief. He didn't know how much carnage the Anarch ships were able to wreak onto the lines behind them but it could have been a lot worse if Erik's gunners didn't get their defense systems working as fast as they did. At least one thing was going as planned. Though, the number of ships that were able to dive bomb them before they were chased off made him start to worry about what was happening above them.

He didn't have much time to worry though.

The horizon began to glow blue, hazy behind the billowing clouds of dust.

"Get down!" Vincent screamed. "Incoming!" Everyone through themselves back down, landing awkwardly on top of one another. Zinvor came crashing down on Vincent's back.

The sky changed colors as the slow-moving cloud of plasma artillery descended onto them. The ground shook as it impacted. Geysers of blue fire exploded into the air, sending spouts of dirt and debris into the air, intermingled with the mangled remains of its victims. There hadn't been enough time for the engineers to dig artillery proof bunkers like they normally would have. At least not in the front. Instead they could only cower into the small confines of their position and hope the artillery didn't find them.

The muffled boom of the responding Martian and Rhai artillery fired in response. The Martians firing their standard explosive shots and the Rhai with their own plasma rounds. The constant drumfire of incoming and outgoing artillery pounded Vincent's earth and rattled his brain. He put his hands over his head to try to dull it but it made no difference. The shaking grew worse, as if the entire moon had been taken up by a celestial god and throttled in its hands. It was so loud he could hardly think.

A flash of blue landed only feet away, nearly wiping them out. Another round exploded amongst the Mawr to their right, churning them to a consistency of preserved canned meat in a second. As the bombardment wore on their shots only got more accurate. Blasts landed on either side of the trench with regularity and the only thing they could do is hope their own artillery was doing the same thing.

Vincent did his best to remain glued to the wall of

the trench, shifting back and forth to either side as the deadly rain continued. Soldiers attempted to do the same but the cramp space made it difficult and it became a race to the other side after each impact. Finally, one of the soldiers broke under the pressure. They ripped off their ammo harness, climbed over the trench wall, and took off running. Some had attempted to grab them before they made it over the top, but they didn't want to expose themselves to the fire and gave up after a few moments.

In their mania they didn't even know which way they were running. Instead of fleeing further back into the valley they ran towards the valley's opening. Towards the enemy.

"Anyone else stands up I swear I'll fucking shoot you myself!" Kolea yelled. "Stay down goddamnit!" As if to underline her warning a round impacted directly behind where she was sitting, backlighting her with a magnificent blue glow. Her eyes were furious, but filled with panic. It had become the default expression on all of their faces after what seemed like hours of shelling. Just when it felt like the Anarchs would be fine with sitting back and shelling the valley until they had turned it all to glass, the bombardment stopped.

The soldiers exchanged confused looks. The deafening thunder of the plasma had been replaced by the distant sound of their own artillery. Slowly, they came to their senses.

"Get to your positions!" Kolea yelled and began pushing soldiers to their feet. She reached over and grabbed the radio and repeated her orders into it. "Stand to!" She said into the receiver.

Vincent tried to stand up and felt his legs wobble underneath him. He steadied himself on the trench wall and for the first time was able to survey the damage done by the Anarch artillery. For as far as he could see the dirt had been flash burned into glass, only to be shattered by a follow up blast. The entire valley floor shimmered, covered in jagged broken glass.

Litter teams were already hard at work. They loaded up the wounded who had not been completely obliterated by a direct hit. Skin had been charred black and bones melted away. If they were able, they screamed as they were moved. Litter teams jogged back towards the rear where the medical tents had been set up. Mawr Cohorts heaved their dead out of their trench behind them. If the wounded were able to move, they slowly made their way to the rear as well. If they were, they were left to die in the open.

"You think this is it?" Vincent asked. Kolea adjusted her rebreather and wiped dust from her forehead.

"What else could it be?" She said, staring off at the mouth of the valley.

"They lost the artillery duel?" He said shrugging. "Commander Erik was an artillery expert back in the day. Maybe our side won."

"He ever duel the Anarchs before?" She asked. He hadn't. During the fighting on Grawluck he was stationed on Mars, probably already plotting the coming revolution. "And besides, those air attacks tell me if they didn't make planet fall yet, they are about to."

He chewed the inside of his mouth, joining her eyes at the valley's opening. She was right, they were coming, it was just a matter of time.

"Hey, Consul." She said, her voice lowered. "Can I ask a question?"

"I'm in your unit, Major." He said. "ask away." Her eyes darted around and she got closer so nobody would overhear her.

"Do you think we can pull this off?" She whispered. "Face off against millions of these fuckers?" He thought for moment. Should he try to pull off the triumphant leader shtick? Or should he just be honest?

"To be honest." He sighed. "I don't know." He saw her features drop. It was obvious she was looking for him to lift her up. "But." He continued. "I didn't know if we would beat the Black Coats. I didn't know if we would take the Mons. I sure as hell didn't think we were going to take Victoria." He laughed. "Nothing we've done so far should have been possible, but here we are. What I do know is the same people we had during all of those battles are right here with us now. So, fuck it." He shrugged. "Anything is possible."

"Well." She said. "whatever happens next, we'll give 'em hell, sir." She smiled, grabbing another cigarette from her pack. "Fuck it." She said, lighting it.

Not a minute passed when a soldier called out.

"Ma'am!" A voice cried. "I think I see something." The soldier was peering through the optics of their rocket launcher, swiveling the camera around. Kolea ran over and shoved them out of the way, taking their place. She pulled the black eye cups up to her face and scanned. After a moment she leaned back, turning the optics to Vincent. He did the same thing. The cups were warm with the sweat of the last several users, dusty had caked to the black rubber forming a gritty sandpaper feeling against his face.

The optics were switched to their thermal setting. He couldn't see what the soldier did, so he moved it back and forth. The opening of the valley was a dense red, the color fading to orange and then yellow the further up he looked. He pulled his face away.

"I don't see anything." He said.

"Look again." Kolea nodded. He pressed his face back to the cups and squinted. The valley opening was still a solid red. Then he saw it.

The wall of red was *moving*. It flickered to the left and right and then got larger. It was moving towards them.

"Oh shit." He gasped.

"Get on the radio!" Kolea ordered. "Tell everyone what we are seeing. Get word to the batteries. I want this entire goddamn valley carpeted with artillery, orbital strikes, anything they got." She turned towards Vincent. "You speak Mawr, right sir?" He nodded. "I need you to get on our radio and let them know. I don't know what they can see but I don't want them to be surprised."

The radio operator handed Vincent the radio, fiddling with the dials and then nodding to let him know it was turned to the nearby Mawr Cohort.

"Cohort Leader, this is Warrior Solaris." He said. The office of the Consul meant nothing to the Mawr, but they would pay attention to his status as a Warrior.

"Yes." Grunted a voice. "This is Cohort Leader Axar, First Riten of the Warlord Herself!" Vincent ran through the catalogue of the various Cohort Leaders he had meant over the years and he didn't remember an Axar. Though, his status as *First Riten* meant he was somebody important.

"We have positive identification of the enemy entering the valley. They're closing in fast. We have ordered strikes onto the area, so stay low."

"Let them come." Growled the voice. "Glory to the Warlord."

"Glory to the Warlord." Vincent repeated. He handed the radio back to the operator and they went to work calling the artillery batteries. Seconds later, the air filled with the angry screams of thousands of artillery shells. They crashed into the ground and obscured the entire valley with dirt and dust. The ground under their feet shook, but Vincent breathed a sigh of relief that they weren't on the receiving end this time.

The trench was alive with activity. Soldiers were hustling around, spreading out boxes of ammo for rifles, machine guns, and the rocket launchers. If they weren't checking and rechecking their weapons they were hunched over, only their eyes showing above the parapet, rifle clutched tightly in their hands. Vincent took his place on the line, leaning his rifle against the wall next to him. Every half second it seemed another artillery round impacted somewhere, sending spouts of destruction into the air. He had no idea how many were dying in the blasts, but he knew it wasn't going to be enough.

The ground in front of his face lit up. Small arms began to smack into the lip of the trench. The area around his head filled with the angry snapping and buzzing sounds of a beehive. The machine guns rattled to life down the line. They couldn't see anything through the dusty haze but if they were close enough to shoot at them, they were close enough to be shot at.

"First rank!" Kolea called. Vincent grabbed his rifle, pulling the bolt back to double check a round was seated into it correctly.

"I can't see shit through the smoke!" Vincent yelled.

"Present!" Kolea ordered, ignoring his comments. In front of the trench the artillery had churned the valley into a swirling storm of dust and smoke. Incoming rounds smacked wildly into the ground, whoever was coming at them probably couldn't see them either. He rested the heavy rifle on the parapet, wrapping his finger around the trigger.

"Fire!" He pulled the trigger and the rifle bucked hard against his shoulder and the acrid stench of burning powder curled up into his face. All around him soldiers were grabbing their rifles and kneeling behind the protective wall of the trench. He quickly did the same thing.

"Second rank!" Came the order. A soldier behind Vincent leaned over him, placing their weapon in the same place he had and waited for the order to fire. Before they could, their head snapped back and they crumpled to the ground. Their face had been pulped by an enemy round. They twitched and gurgled through their ruined features. He fumbled with the reloading process, his shaking hands made feeding a new bullet into the breach a chore. He forced the bolt forward and stood up, just in enough time to fire another round with the second line.

An artillery shell landed a short ways from the front trench, sending everyone diving for cover.

"Any closer and they are going to drop one on top of our damn heads!" Vincent cried.

"Call them off!" Kolea demanded. "The damn fumes from their guns must have melted their brains. Can we get any air support? Maybe they won't kill us." The radio operator was sitting on the floor of the trench, screaming into his handset.

"No Ma'am." They shook their head. "Command says air support is off the table." Vincent motioned at the radio.

"Is that Marshal Victoria?" The radio operator nodded and he grabbed the hand set from them.

"Aron?" He asked.

"Consul?" Asked the voice on the other side. "Is that you? Where are you?"

"I'm with Major Kolea here at the front. What is going on with our air support?" Aron groaned, clearly wanting to tell him to get the hell out away from the frontline. At this point he had to know that Vincent wouldn't listen and falling back was hardly an option for anyone at the front by that point.

"The Anarch fleet is giving them hell up there. They are doing their best to just hold them off so they don't cut their losses and glass the whole valley. Trust Ezra, Consul. He can pull it off. But until then we are alone down here."

"Thanks, Aron. Oh, one last thing."

"Hm?"

"Don't tell Fiona where I am." Vincent heard soldiers around him fight back laughter and he gave them a knowing smile.

"Yeah, yeah." Aron said. "Good luck out there. I'd tell you not to do anything stupid, but you are already out with Kolea. Command out." The radio hissed and went silent as he closed the channel.

"No air support for a while." He told Kolea. "But we can assume they made planet fall."

"Oh no shit." Kolea frowned. "Wonder what gave you that idea." She flinched as another round thumped off of the parapet next to her head.

Wind howled through the valley and slowly the curtain of dust began to lift. The rattle of machine guns replaced the drumming of artillery. Their crews worked fluidly so they could fire without break. A gunner fired short bursts, moving the gun side to side. As the gun ate through the belt of ammo another crewmember replaced it with another, making sure they didn't have to stop. The result was a nonstop staccato, doing unseen damage to the oncoming enemy.

Then, finally they did see the attackers. They emerged from

the smoke clad in armor and carrying an array of arms. They weren't Anarchs, they were Mawr and Rhai. They ran forward, firing from the hip, sweeping automatic and plasma weapons across the trench. Before they could make it very far a storm of fire cut into them, dropping the first wave in a cloud of gore.

As quickly as they fell, another wave was at their heels. They ran, jumped, and climbed over the dead in front of them, coming forward as if nothing happened.

"Fire at will!" Kolea called out. Vincent raised is rifle and fired. The booming shot hit an oncoming Mawr, blowing its arm off at the shoulder. He reloaded and fired again, this time evaporating a Rhai above the waist. No matter how many they took down, they kept coming. The soldier to his left was hit in the throat and fell, sputtering blood. Another shot glanced off Vincent's arm sending searing pain down to his hand. His armor held, protecting him from any real damage.

His arm hurt enough that he dropped his rifle and unholstered his Riten, switching it to his off hand. He thumbed the hammer back and plugged two rounds into a Mawr, dropping them onto their face. As he moved over to fire at another attacker one appeared to his right. A Rhai with a plasma rifle pointed right at him, having him dead to rights. Before the Rhai could fire, their head vanished, reduced to little more than a fine pink mist. Zinvor nodded towards him, retracting the bolt of his rifle and loading in another round.

A grenade landed in front of Vincent's face and he dropped down behind the trench wall. It detonated with a dull thump, raining dirt and glass down onto him.

"Zinvor!" He yelled over the fighting. "Why the hell would Mawr and Rhai soldiers still be fighting with the Anarchs?"

"Alliance auxiliaries." Zinvor said, dropping another attacker with his rifle. "They are being used to charge our lines, break them with their bodies before the Anarchs come to exploit it."

"Wait, so they are just a shield for the Anarchs?"

"Yes." He nodded, unholstering his Riten and putting a well-placed shot between the eyes of a Rhai. "They were probably promised liberation in exchange for taking our line."

"At this rate they are going to bog us down and the Anarchs will overrun us." Vincent said, slamming his bolt forward and firing again. A Mawr twisted and fell into the dirt.

"That seems likely." Zinvor nodded, blasting another in the chest. A grenade landed on the ground next to him and he lazily bent down and flung it back over the trench. Another explosion sent blood and dust flying through the air.

"They are within grenade range!" Yelled a nearby Sergeant. Soldiers began throwing grenades over the wall and they detonated altogether. Each time an explosion or burst of gunfire cut a gap in the attacking wave's line they were replaced. The incoming fire picked up as they got closer, their sprinting bursts of automatic gunfire became more accurate.

Their newly acquired rifle's ability to punch through Anarch armor had yet to be seen but the decrease in rate of fire had begun to screw them over. As the Alliance troops got closer their Martian rifles couldn't keep up with the autocannons they faced. Vincent fired, taking another enemy off of its feet. As he went to reload a Mawr was running up onto him, the barrel of its autocannon pointed directly at him, only inches away.

He reached out and backhanded the barrel of the gun away from him and the Mawr let out a uncontrolled burst down the trench. Vincent grabbed for his Riten and the Mawr went to do the same thing. He was just seconds quicker, firing a shot just as the barrel cleared its holster. The Mawr was struck in the stomach, doubling it over. He fired again, hitting it in the top of the head.

With his free hand he reached down and grabbed the dead Mawr's autocannon. He holstered his Riten, took up the captured weapon and raked a long burst to his left and right.

The autocannon rocked him with each shot but the enemy was so thick in front of him he could hardly miss. His new gun chugged through its magazine quickly. By the time it ran dry Vincent was surrounded by the dead. He bent back down to free a magazine from the dead Mawr's ammunition harness when he was jerked back into the trench by Zinvor. He landed hard on his back.

"Sorry, Fiona told me to not let you die. You seem to be attempting to do the opposite of that." He said. Before Vincent could respond three Rhai dropped into the trench. Zinvor upturned his rifle like a club and savaged two of them before they could react. The third turn and shot, grazing Zinvor on the face. The Warrior was on the last Rhai in a second, mashing their head to a pulp with his blood covered rifle. He turned to face Vincent, blood leaking from the glancing blow.

"I require your assistance holding our position, Consul. Unfortunately, I do not think I can do it myself." He pushed himself up to a sitting position just in time for another Mawr to jump down in front of him. Zinvor spun around and smacked it in the face with his rifle, knocking it off balance. Vincent wrapped the Mawr's short legs up with his arms and drove his shoulder into its back, tackling him to the ground. He mounted his down foe and began punching it repeatedly in the face. The Mawr drew a knife and slashed Vincent across the face, from his forehead down to his chin. He howled in pain, blood stinging his eye, blinding it.

Before the Mawr could attack again its head vanished in a plume of gore, coating Vincent. He wiped the mess from his eyes and saw Zinvor reloading his smoking Riten. He took the chance to do the same thing himself, also taking time to steal the dead Mawr's knife.

"Are you okay?" Zinvor asked, looking at his newly mangled face.

"Yeah." He blinked away blood. "It hurts like a bastard and I'm a bit uglier but I'll live."

"Duck." Zinvor said suddenly. When Vincent hesitated one of his big hands simply slapped him aside as Zinvor raised his rifle in one fluid motion, blowing an enemy off of its feet. A plasma bolt slammed off of Zinvor's chest, flooring him. Vincent leveled his Riten and shot the attacker, hitting the Rhai in the throat. He scrambled back to his feet and ran over to Zinvor who was slowly sitting back up. A small back scorch mark showed at the center of his chest.

"You good?" He asked. Zinvor rubbed his hand on the mark.

"I am always good." He said. More enemies were landing in the trench every second. The floor of their position was now full of khaki uniformed dead or dying. The wounded were still trying to reload their rifles as the enemy came on. Vincent began burning through his Riten's ammo wheel, killing several of the attackers. Zinvor shot the rest of them, advancing on them as they tried to climb back out of the trench.

"Get up!" Vincent yelled at the downed soldiers. "If you can still fight you need a weapon in your hands!" Another group of enemies jumped down into the trench and a Warrior let rip with a long burst from a belt fed machine gun. The burst cut through a group of wounded soldiers before they were shot down. Another thunderclap of rifle shots finished off the rest of them. At such close range the Martian rifles exploded whatever they hit, coating the trench in viscera.

Zinvor peered over the trench, reloading. He dropped back down as the dirt exploded around his head.

"Get ready!" He roared. "They are upon us again!" Vincent grabbed a handful of Riten cartridges from a pouch on his harness and thumbed them into the ammo wheel. In his offhand he found the knife he stole from the down Mawr. At this range, he thought, the rifle would just be a hinderance. As the next wave made it to the top of the trench they were met with a storm of gunfire. Not from Vincent and the others, but from the other side of the trench.

The deep throated chug of heavy caliber weapons and the crash of cannons filled the air. The occupants of the trench stayed low, occasionally the twisted remains of an attacker would collapse on to them.

"They're breaking!" Zinvor called out, peaking out. "Cowards!" He mocked. The defenders rose back up. Zinvor was right, they weren't conducting an orderly withdrawal. It was a rout. Vincent had never seen a Mawr Warrior flee from combat before. They ran as quickly away as they attacked, though this time they made no effort not to trample their comrades to escape. None of them made it very far before more gunfire from the trench's saviors cut them down.

Behind them sat the idling form of hundreds of Martian constructed tanks. Martian Stars and Elysian phoenix's were painted across their front armor. Smoke rose from their engines and guns and a single soldier climbed down from the lead tank. An older Martian wearing a dark red flight suit approached.

"There is our armor support!" Complained Kolea. Vincent had lost track of her during the chaos of battle but was glad to see she survived. Her arm was in a sling and her face was obscured by black soot.

"You will have to forgive me." Said the Martian soldier, he saw now the man had the silver eagles of a Colonel on his epaulettes. "We were held in reserve for the Anarchs. We didn't think they had any Alliance auxiliaries left after the savagery on Grawluck."

"Are the Commandos with you?" Vincent asked, pulling himself out of the trench. The Colonel saluted him.

"Ah, Consul Solaris. I did not know I would see you up here. I have a feeling Commander Erik is jealous that you were able to separate yourself from Command and fight with your comrades.

But your Commandos are with the Titanian Pathfinders, held in reserve by central command."

"There is a central command now?" Vincent asked.

"This may shock you but if you get enough people, er" he thought for a moment. "Or not people, together to command an army they just constantly bicker and fight. So, the Warlord, Commander Erik, and that Titanian are all in joint command, the odd number means votes don't take very long at least. Though I reckon the Warlord and the Titanian hate one another something fierce."

"I'll Consider myself lucky that I'm in this trench." Vincent laughed.

"I'll consider you lucky for several reason." The Colonel smiled. "When those little bastards attack again, we will be here." He slapped the front of his tank. "With the armor of Mars at your back we cannot possibly lose."

"I have a feeling we are going to need it." Vincent said. "I don't think the Alliance axillaries are coming back." Kolea nodded.

"The next phase of this battle will be the decisive one." She motioned to the killing fields they had created in front of the trench. The ground was covered with the blasted and mangled remains of what had to be hundreds of thousands of Mawr and Rhai. The artillery had killed most of them before they could get close, the machine guns, rifles, and tanks did the rest. "I don't think the next wave is going to retreat when we smack them around."

"I hope not." The Colonel beamed. "I came to give these metal beasts a dose of their own medicine, not watch them run away."

"I've been fighting them for years." Vincent said. "I assure you, I've never seen them run."

"Ma'am!" Came a voice from the trench. A soldier had gotten

behind one of the sets of launcher optics and was scanning the valley once again. "I see something!" Kolea cursed.

"Not even enough time to breathe." She turned towards the Colonel. "Good luck, Sir." The man nodded and they crawled back into their positions. Around them soldiers were doing their best to clear the trenches of the dead. Enemy were rolled out front to add to the defensive works while friendly casualties were being lugged back to the rear on stretchers. Ammunition points were being restocked and anti-tank crews busied themselves fixing their positions that had been knocked over or otherwise discarded during the last fight. "Get on the radio, have them start dropping artillery at the head of the valley again. That should buy us enough time."

"Are you going to be okay with that." Kolea asked Vincent. "That looks ugly as hell." He forced a smile.

"This little thing?" He shrugged. "After getting an eye blown out this is hardly worth noting. What about your arm?"

"Turns out those Mawr are strong as hell, Medic says it's probably broken." She sighed. "Turns out they're not stronger than getting shot at close range."

The drumbeat of artillery began to fall once again, crashing down at the mouth of the valley.

"What in the.." Kolea gasped. "Look!" She pointed out to where the artillery was coming down. It was exploding dozens of feet above the ground, blue energy rippled under it. Like a shield. The tanks behind them joined in on the firing, again blue energy flashed and the shells exploded midair.

"Batteries. Fire at will." Kolea commanded. The antitank crews fired, sending hundreds of missiles flying off across the valley. Again, they exploded far from their unseen target. The glowing blue light shimmered and slowly moved forward.

"What the hell is it?" Vincent asked to nobody in particular. Then, he saw the blue light was acting as a shield and something moved behind it. Hundreds of dulled chrome shape walking on spindly legs, several stories tall. Before he could tell anyone, the blue light ruptured, crackling outwards towards the trench like bolts of lightning. It cut through the far right of the trench, bathing the Mawr positions in an eerie glow as they were evaporated. Another flash of lightning sent a bolt into the line of tanks. Dozens exploded, cartwheeling through the air and sending their turrets flying like the cork out of a bottle.

This was too much for some people. Several soldiers, staring down what looked like something straight out of their nightmares, ran for it. They grabbed their rifles and vaulted over the other side of the trench, running as quickly as they could towards the second line. Some of their Sergeants tried to keep them in line. But another burst of blue lightning sent the wavering running regardless.

"Goddamnit." Kolea gritted her teeth.

"The worst part is." Vincent flinched as another bolt crackled. "I can hardly blame them."

"You going to do a runner on me too, Consul?" She sneered.

"Me?" He shook his head. "I'm too stupid to run."

"Look!" Zinvor pointed. The walkers spat lightning again, tearing a horrible gash through the line somewhere far off to the left. "Each time it fires, the shield has to lower. It is redirecting the plasma into a weapon." It flashed again and Vincent saw it. The shimmering blue energy wall twisted and warped before forming itself into projectiles before returning and protecting the walkers.

"Kolea!" Vincent yelled. "Do you see it?" A bolt cracked through the air, only a few dozen feet above their heads, and cut through a few more tanks behind them.

"Yeah!" She nodded. She turned to the radio operator and shouted more orders at him which he dutifully relayed. A bolt flashes again at the same time an artillery shell impacted, blowing the legs off of the unprotected walker. Another one fired and a missile launcher found purchase, toppling its target. Cheers went up through the line as they watched the otherworldly machines get brought down. The walkers lashed out at the tanks and missile gunners. Vincent felt the heat of the lightning as it flashed through the line only a dozen feet away.

Ammunition for the launchers exploded, sending shrapnel and gore flying in every direction as they scythed through the gunners. The soldiers hit directly by the lightning were burned black, their twisted forms burning into place. Vincent fell to the ground, blinking the heat from his eyes. His augmetic eye struggled to regulate itself and he felt his lungs burning. As he caught his breath a flaming tank turret crashed into the trench, crushing several people.

The walkers inched closer. They kept their shields up as plasma cannon rounds began to burst out of it. Vincent squinted, his eyes still adjusting and saw that between the legs of the lumbering giants, marching shoulder to shoulder, was thousands upon thousands of Anarch soldiers. Tank rounds, machine guns, and missiles exploded harmlessly in front of them. Their fusillade ripped through the trench. Vincent's face was seared by a near miss and he collapsed backwards.

Zinvor spun awkwardly and fell, groaning in pain. He held up an arm that was burned off from below his elbow. No blood came from the wound as the superheated plasma cauterized his arm as it was obliterated. He gritted his teeth and pushed himself up to a sitting position. He looked around and said.

"Consul Solaris." He held up the stump where his arm used to be. "I am afraid I have dishonored you. My Riten was in my hand and I seem to have lost it."

"You know." Vincent winced, his face still feeling like it was on fire. "I think I'll let it slide." He reached in his first aid pack and found a burn dressing, placing it over the right side of his face. The trench around him was littered with the burned remains of soldiers and half melted weapons.

"I don't think we can hold here." He said. "Where is Kolea?" Zinvor motioned further down the trench.

"I think that's her." She was laying on the trench floor, surrounded by soldiers. Her entire left arm and most of that side of her chest had been blown away. Her death must have been quick, her eyes were still frozen and her mouth open as if she was hit in the middle of yelling a command at someone.

"Fuck." The sporadic gunfire around him told him their position was already untenable. He unholstered his Riten and handed to Zinvor who refused to take it.

"I cannot take your Riten, it is yours. I must not share my shame."

"Deal with your shame later, I need you to have a gun. We have to get the hell out of here. If we're lucky we can make it to the second line."

"We are running?" He asked, taking the Riten in his good hand.

"No, we are pulling back. See if you can get that radio to work and let the Warriors on the flanks know." Zinvor nodded and ran at a crouch towards the radio. It was still being held by the dead hands of its former operator, now missing everything above the middle of his chest. As Zinvor worked on the radio lightning flashed again and again, sending arcing bolts of blue down either side of the trench, where the Warriors would have been. The center, where they were, was all but destroyed. Even the mechanical brains of the walkers knew they couldn't put up much of a fight anymore.

Behind them lay a field of shattered glass, bodies, and the burning husks of tanks. Plasma bolts and cannon fire was tearing into it and now the fight was already moving beyond them. The second line was only a few hundred feet away but at that moment it might as well have been several miles. There was no way they would make it by foot. Out of the armor graveyard he saw tank slowly pulling away.

Its turret had been scored by a hit of something large, hobbling it. Its cannon drooped at a strange angle and smoke curled up in thick clouds from its engine.

"Zinvor!" Vincent yelled, he was locked in an argument with the Cohort Leaders on either of their flanks. He knew suggesting them to withdraw to the second line wasn't going to go over well in the best of circumstances but it looked like it was going worse than he thought. Zinvor was holding the receiver away from his face to dull the volume of the screaming from the other side.

"I found us a ride, we have to go!" Zinvor put down the radio, angry Cohort Leader still yelling, and joined him. Vincent helped him out of the trench and they jogged towards the struggling tank. The commander's hatch popped open and a face appeared. A young woman with a smoke blackened face peered out.

"Holy shit!" She exclaimed. "Consul, is that you?"

"Yeah!" He said. "We need a ride back to the rear!"

"You might want to keep looking." She said. "I don't know if we will make it that far."

"I'll take the risk." He jumped onto the front of the tank and clambered up to the turret. A plasma bolt hissed over his head, so close he could feel his bare scalp burning.

"Quick, get inside." She kicked open the loader's hatch, to the next of hers. He got inside, turning to Zinvor, helping him down into the bowels of the tank. The inside of the tank smelled like they had climbed into an engine itself. Burning oil and sweat mixed with the sweet smell of hydraulic fluids. The turret walls were coated in black soot. The tank's cannon was twisted and broken, its breach burned. Normally, the turret crew would have at least three people, with the driver being alone, piloting the vehicle from the front. But, the woman was alone.

"Where is everyone?" He asked. She motioned towards the breach.

"Took one of those Anarch shots straight to the gun. Barrel acted like a funnel right into the turret." Her voice trembled.

"But you made it?"

"I was on the turret. Getting another case of ammo when it happened." She sniffed. "When I got back, well." She nodded at the walls. "That was all that was left of them." Vincent pushed off the turret wall that he was leaning against, a trace of black soot had stuck to his armor and he quickly brushed it off. "Now it's just me in here and Garo driving. Well, trying to drive anyway. Engines been shot to shit. At this rate it is only a matter of time before one of those fucking monsters kills us too."

"Listen." Vincent said, putting a hand on her shoulder. She flinched. "You're doing fine. We've lost a lot of people today, but it isn't over. Not yet, anyway. Can you get us to the rear?" She nodded, climbing back into the Commander's seat.

"Yeah. Let's go."

The tank trundled into the Command Headquarters which had since been gripped by chaos and panic. Wounded soldiers walked, crawled, or were carried to the nearby medical station. The number of wounded and overwhelmed the doctors. Piles of the dead and the too far gone were left outside, the blowing dust slowly concealing them. The stench from the medical areas overwhelmed the headquarters and the rebreathers did nothing to filter it out.

Vincent climbed off the tank and strode towards the headquarters. The engineers had dug several feet underground, leaving only a small door at the surface which was concealed with a tent flap. The entrance was guarded by Warriors of Arai's Cohort and they moved aside to let him in. He went down uneven wooden stairs had been shoved into the dirt, very close to one another in order to serve the Mawr. The stairs led to a large bunker that had been converted into a planning room. Displays hung from the dirt walls and several maps were being updated in real time.

The gathered Warlord and Marshals were standing around a table in a heated argument when he entered. They slowly turned and saw him and Aron walked over and gave him a hug.

"I thought for sure you were dead." He said, smiling. Vincent winced, the abuse he had put himself through was starting to catch up to him. He ached all over and it felt like there was a jackhammer in his skull.

"That bad huh?" He asked.

"You're kidding." Vaynom laughed. "You don't know?"

"We lost the first line." Arai said. "The second line doesn't have much of a hope of holding for much longer either."

"We deployed the Pathfinders and Commandos to plug the gaps for now. But they won't hold long." Aron said.

"And those things." Vincent said. "Can eat right through our armor."

"Yes." Arai nodded. "None of my armor Cohorts have reported back to me. I assume they are lost."

"Warlord, how much more time does Pharos need?" He asked directly. Arai glanced around at the group. He knew he shouldn't have said it, but after watching the massacre at the front he had to know.

"I don't know." She said for the first time he could remember, she sounded demoralized. "But, regardless of that, we need to reinforce our third line. After that they will be upon us and there is nothing more we will be able to do."

"We have to stop those walkers or nothing we do will matter." Aron said. "We can't even shoot the goddamn Anarchs with those on the field."

"An orbital bombardment." Vincent suggested.

"This close to us?" Vaynom scoffed. "We would die too."

"We evacuate the second line and hunker down. I know from experience the Titanian fleet gunners are accurate. We will just have to hope they don't fuck it up."

"Can the fleet even pull that off right now?" Aron asked. "From the sounds of it, it is pretty grim up there."

"Can we talk to them?" asked Vincent. "Ezra won't bullshit

us." Arai nodded and a Rhai appeared, holding a bulk orbital radio. He grabbed the receiver and heard a mess of garbled static.

"Ezra, can you hear me?"

"Vincent?" Answered a voice. "I heard you were dead."

"Yeah, me too." He laughed. "How are you doing up there?"

"We're holding." He said. "Giving 'em hell, sir. How about you?"

"We need to ask you for a favor."

"I don't like the way that sounds."

"You shouldn't. They deployed some new weapon and it is tearing straight through us. We don't have anything that can stop them, but you do."

"Wait." Ezra said. "You want us to bombard the moon? We'll kill you. And that is if we can even get into position. We are hanging on by the skin of our teeth up here."

"If you don't we won't last another few hours if we're lucky."

"Okay." He said after a moment. "Get low, and evacuate your forward positions. Have someone send me the exact location you want these rounds dropped on. You don't have long, they are going to blast us out of the sky as soon as they figure out what we are trying to do."

"Oh, one more thing." He said, his voice lowering. "Have you seen Fiona?"

"Yeah." He said, Vincent could hear him laugh. "She's okay. The only reason your guns down there still have ammo is because of her."

"Good. Thank you, Ezra." He handed the receiver back to the Rhai. "Order a full evacuation. Ezra is coming in hot and won't have any time to linger." Arai nodded and Command staff went to work immediately.

The evacuation only added to the chaos. Soldiers fighting in the second line dropped what they were doing and ran as fast as they could towards the last line. The lucky ones jumped onto tanks and APCs as they fled, the unlucky were made to catch up. Everything that couldn't easily be carried in hand was abandoned, this included the wounded that couldn't carry themselves to safety.

Soldiers crowded into the final line. While the first line had been a rush job, the engineers were able to spend much more time with the last. The trenches were much deeper and solidly built with metal reinforcements along the walls to prevent cave ins. They even had dug outs to duck into when they came under shell fire. Or, if a fleet of warships was about to drop tons of kinetic munitions down right in of them.

Vincent sat in the Command bunker, which was now filled to capacity. Soldiers piled in anywhere and everywhere they fit. Nobody spoke. No commands needed to be passed down. They were all waiting for the sky to explode.

"Command, this is Fleet." Came Ezra's voice. It was more distorted than normal and he sounded strained. "We are coming in fast and will be on station in thirty seconds. Taking heavy fire, no time to stay on station longer than it takes for us to fire. Can you confirm the target?" Arai squeezed by a few Mawr who had sat down on the floor, pulling out a display. She relayed the information to Ezra with a few taps on the screen.

"Alright." He said. "Get low everyone."

The time it took from the firing of the munitions to impact couldn't have been long but to Vincent it felt like an eternity. Time froze as he waited, wincing, hoping that the gunners aboard the ship didn't screw up their calculations. But if they did, he would hardly notice. They would all be gone in the blink of an eye. Just like Victoria was.

The sky rumbled and a sonic boom cut through the bunker. The occupants didn't have enough time to react before the ground under them shook violently. The displays on the walls flickered and died and the hum of a nearby generator sputtered and died. A second impact sent the few who remained standing falling awkwardly onto the people around them. Cracks spidered across the bunker's ceiling and it sagged heavily onto its bracers.

"Shots complete." Ezra said, his voice hardly audible. "Good luck down there."

The silence inside was broken as soldiers, suddenly grappling with their continued survival, were ordered back out into the line by their Officers. Vincent followed them out, not wanting to be in the bunker when its ceiling finally came down. Lines of tired soldiers of all races jogged back towards the last line of defense. The tanks were racing off in front of them as the artillery continued to thunder in the distance.

The battlefield was cloaked in a black mushroom cloud. It ended just before the start of the final line and stretched up into the clouds, beyond what Vincent could see. He saw what the force of an orbital bombardment could do to a city, he only hoped it would be enough to slow down the Anarchs, if only for a second.

The smoke slowly rose from the valley floor. A cheer began rippling through the lines of marching soldiers. The shimmering blue light was gone. The valley was littered with the twisted remnants of broken and burning machines. The orange blood of Anarch soldiers highlighted where they died in the greatest numbers. Just beyond them, lines of Anarchs continued to march towards them in lock step. Artillery crashed down on their heads, blowing them apart and sending the great armored demons flying into the air, in pieces. Tanks began launching cannon shells into their ranks, obliterating them in great numbers with every pull of the trigger.

"We might actually pull this off." Remarked Vincent. The infantry line was reforming and their Martian rifles fired volley after volley into the Anarchs. Every fusillade felled rank after rank of the armored soldiers. If the Anarch knew any better, if they could know any better, they would have broken off their attack. But for an enemy that couldn't think or feel such grievous causalities simply didn't matter. They would keep coming.

The Anarchs didn't have to stop and aim or set up bases of fire to advance like anyone else would have. They were living weapons platforms that would aim flawlessly on the move. Plasma cannons flared from arm mounts and spinning multi barreled chain guns whined, sending unbroken torrents of fire at the defenders. The momentary cheers of victory were silenced as bunkers exploded and tanks were set on fire. Soldiers that didn't get behind cover fast enough were reduced to ragged hunks of meat.

"They're not slowing down." Aron commented.

"How much time do we have, you think?" Vincent asked.

"At this rate?" We'll be dead within the hour." Aron seem nonplused at the idea of his impending doom, his eyes staring off at the scene unfolding below them on the line. Vincent left him, going back into the command bunker where Arai was busy tending to the various displays. She was crossing off positions as she went. She had lost contact with them and was writing them off as dead. Standing next to her was Felicity.

Felicity's uniform was scorched and battle worn. Her dark features were smudged with dirt, soot and blood. She looked exhausted and was drinking deeply from a canteen. When she saw him she quickly saluted and he returned it.

"I thought you were dead!" She exclaimed.

"People keep saying that."

"I just made some kaff." She said. "Grab some and help us figure out how to stabilize this line."

"We don't enough time." He blurted out. Arai looked up from her work, her gaze distant and tired. She glanced around at the numerous aids of all races that were in the bunker and her look told him 'stop now'. He didn't care anymore.

"It doesn't matter if they know or not. We don't slow them

nobody will be alive to find out what Pharos is cooking up anyway." Her gaze was murderous, but she relented.

"I'm open to suggestions." She said, her hands gesturing to the maps, displays, and notes around her. Vaynom and Aron reentered the bunker.

"We need to commit our last reserves." Vaynom said, he wasn't asking or suggesting. There was a resignation in his voice.

"We would have nothing left." Felicity scolded.

"She is right. This is drastic." Arai said.

"Our backs are against the wall." Vaynom said, approaching the map. "That last line falls we will have nothing to fight from. I see what these monsters are capable of, in the open we stand no chance. If we are going to hold, we do it there." He jabbed a finger at Arai's display.

"I'm with Vaynom." Aron nodded. "Look, I don't know what your plan is and it's not my position to ask. But if you need time, the only thing we can do is commit everything we have left."

"What are our reserves?" Vincent asked.

"I have my personal Cohort." Arai said.

"We don't have much." Felicity admitted. "The Commandos and Pathfinders are mostly in the medical tent. But I'll see what I can slap together."

"A few battalions of infantry at the end of their enlistment periods." Vaynom said. "Not exactly spring chickens." The Titanian enlistment period was for a minimum of twenty years, assuming a committee of Officers deemed the twenty years of service "honorable" at the end of it.

"We consider these Veterans." Arai commented.

"Then you haven't met a trooper with a chronic case of short timer syndrome." Vaynom laughed.

"We have soldiers who were assigned to planet fall that haven't gone to training yet." Aron said. "We have been using them for labor."

"We deployed soldiers who didn't get any training yet?" Vincent asked, astonished.

"You can only scrape the bottom of the barrel so many times, Consul." Aron shrugged. "We can train them on the new rifles in a few minutes, at least enough so they know which direction to point the thing."

"I'll send a few of the *Veterans* over to help." Vaynom grinned at Arai. "What about Commander Erik?"

"He is commanding the artillery, the Martian reserves have already been deployed. Mars is fully committed." Said Aron.

"I'll send for my Cohort." Arai said, making for the door.

"Can you find me another rifle?" Vincent asked. "I seem to have lost mine."

"Among other things." Arai nodded at his empty holster. Vincent gestured at Zinvor who had his Vincent stuffed awkwardly in his beltline. Arai laughed and walked off.

"You intend on going back to the front?" Vaynom asked. "You barely made it out last time. Leave this to their commanders."

"If you were one of these guys getting called up you would know shit is going sideways, right?" He said. "Deploying all these guys just to have them run isn't going to get us anywhere. They need to know one of us is right alongside them."

"I assume you'll ignore me if I tell you this is a bad idea." Aron sighed.

"You assume right. And if the line doesn't hold staying back here will only buy me another hour anyway."

"You shouldn't." Felicity said, clearly anxious. "What about Fiona?"

"The only reason she would be mad is because she is missing out." He smirked. Felicity glanced around the room and Aron averted her gaze.

"You can't be this dense." She groaned. Vincent looked at her quizzically, not understanding what she was getting at.

"Fiona, the chain smoking, drinking, asshole." She started. "You didn't notice her quit smoking or drinking? Or the vomiting?" She rolled her eyes. "What do they teach you people on Earth? I swear."

"She quit drinking?" He asked. "I thought that was why she was puking." Felicity rubbed her temples.

"She is going to kill me for telling for telling you this, but we are probably going to die anyway, so I don't care. But she is pregnant you damn idiot." Vincent's jaw dropped and he felt his heart begin to pound behind his eyes. Words caught themselves in the back of his throat as he fought for something to say.

"What." He finally managed.

"You're going to be a dad." Felicity said, smiling. "But if you go running out there you're never going to meet your kid." He paused and took a deep breath.

"How many of these soldiers have loved ones back home? Pregnant wives or kids? Do they get that option?" He didn't wait for her to answer. Zinvor reappeared handing him a new rifle and he took it, throwing the sling across his shoulder. "If anything, it makes me want to go fight more. Because if we fail here nobody's children have a future, do they Felicity?"

"No, I suppose they don't." She said, her voice faltering. Behind them the heavy metal sound of a bolt slamming forward pulled them away.

"Congratulations." Aron smiled, holding a rifle in his hands.

"You're going too?" Felicity asked, clearly exasperated. Aron hefted a satchel of rifle ammunition across his shoulders.

"We have a future to win, don't we?"

Vincent stood in front of the gathered reserves. Felicity's Commandos looked like they had been dragged through hell. The fresh soldiers of Titan and the mostly untrained labor standing next to them in their clean uniforms made it look like a before and after photo. Behind them was the dark yellow armored forms of Arai's Cohort, their ribbons and award fluttering in the wind. A few scattered Rhai soldiers filled in the gaps standing alongside a few wounded Martians who had snuck away from the supervision of the medics.

"It's time." Arai said. She had never grabbed a rifle, instead she was only holding her Riten in her hand.

"Yeah." Felicity nodded, her voice trembling slightly.

"In anything happens." Vincent said. "Make sure Fiona doesn't teach our kid how to carjack someone or something, alright?" He felt his eye begin to tear up. Aron and Felicity began to laugh, he couldn't help but join them.

"Shut up." She said, wiping a tear from her face. Arai lifted her Riten into the air.

"Comrades!" Her voice boomed. She wasn't speaking Mawr, but rather she stuck to Earth Standard. "My weapon remains in my hand until I holster it in victory or it slips from my dead hand!" The Warriors began to stomp their feet, rising their Ritens above their heads.

"Join me!" She said, her voice getting even louder. "In victory or death!" The Warriors erupted in a guttural roar. The humans joined them, holding their rifles and shaking them. Vincent found himself getting caught up in the mood. He screamed as loud as he could, his rifle above his head and slamming his fist against his armored chest.

Arai took off at a run, a slow lumber to those with Human sized legs. Everyone followed her as they jogged towards the line. In front of them the Anarch army had inched closer and closer. They were only a short distance from the defenders now. The valley was covered in the broken forms of their fallen, orange blood soaking into the dry soil but still they marched forward.

The line held its cohesion together in the face of the never-ending onslaught. At once, soldiers rose up and fired volleys on command, quickly followed up by the soldiers behind them. Together, they created a constant drumroll of punishing fire. Every time they fired another rank of Anarchs would explode and collapse. The ones behind them would advance, taking their place on the moving firing line.

Vincent sprinted into the line the same time one of the thousands of Anarch guns found him. Chain gun rounds stitched into the dirt around him and he dove for cover into the trench. The soldiers behind him had been pulped, their remains spilling into the position behind him. The Anarch fire turned towards the advancing reserves, blasting into their ranks. The survivors tripped over themselves, falling into the line as they rushed for cover.

Vincent rolled to face forward, brought his rifle up, and fired. It kicked wildly and in front of them, only a short distance away, and an Anarch's midsection exploded in gore. He dropped to a knee, reloading as another soldier fired over his shoulder. All around him the fire rate was picking up as the thousands of reserves began to join in.

He rose and fired again, blowing the leg off an oncoming soldier. The Anarch stumbled, attempting to take a step with the appendage that was no longer attached and toppled over. As it fell it fired a burst from a chest mounted auto cannon and Vincent was jerked off his feet, slamming into the rear of the trench.

His heart pounded in his head and his chest throbbed with pain. It felt like he had been hit with a bat and had the wind knocked out of him. He leaned forward, attempting to get up when he was seized with pain and fell back down. He couldn't catch his breath. Every time he tried to breathe in it was like someone stabbed into his lungs. Vincent checked his rebreather to make sure it was still in place and it was.

He glanced down where the pain was coming from. The armor covering his chest had been shattered and blown away. Every time he breathed in bright red blood bubbled out in thick pulses. He reached over to his first aid kit, tore open a bandage, and stuffed it into the wound. He gritted his teeth as a jolt of pain shot through his entire body. He grabbed his rifle and pulled himself back to his feet, using the gun as a cane.

Vincent propped the gun against the trench wall and reloaded it. His arms felt suddenly weak. He supported the gun with his knee to make up for it. He fought with the bolt, his fingers fine motor skills starting to fade. After a few seconds of struggle, he managed to get another round loaded in and kicked the bolt forward. He raised and fired again, dropping an Anarch with shot that vaporized its head.

The force of the shot knocked Vincent onto his back, the rifle clattering to the ground next to him. He coughed and specks of blood spattered onto his hand. The bandage had soaked through completely, and blood flowed freely out of the wound, pooling around him and soaking into the dirt. Each breath made him wince in pain.

Under him, the ground began to shake. Stronger than ever before. The soldiers still on their feet and firing braced themselves on anything they could, others were knocked to the ground by the violent earthquake. The sky, choked with dust and smoke, suddenly cleared. A brilliant, shimmering blue light rippled overhead. The roaring of what sounded like a nearby ship engine's turbine overtook the deafening sounds of the battlefield. The smell of burning ozone curled its way through Vincent's rebreather and he gagged. The light overhead flickered and faded with it went the sounds of the engine, the clouds of dust swirled back into place.

This had to be it. He thought to himself. The projector had fired. Pharos' plan had worked.

Vincent rolled over onto his stomach, pushing himself to his knees. It took every ounce of his strength. His eyes lingered on the pool of blood he left behind but he pulled himself away from the scene. He got to his feet, slowly and almost fell right back down, his unsteady legs nearly failing him. He through his arms over the top of the trench, propping himself up. The scene in front of him made him forget about the pain in his chest.

The Anarchs had stopped mid step. Freezing in place like a wall of armor. Their guns had fallen silent and it was as if someone had flipped an off switch. They were dead on their feet. Soldiers stood, confused, exchanging puzzled looks with one another. Someone fired off a rifle, blowing out the chest of a nearby Anarch. They dropped and still nothing around them moved. Without their hivemind on Baki Prime, nothing was passing them orders to attack.

It was done. It was over. They had won.

His legs finally gave up and he crumbled back to the dirt. He didn't feel any jolt of pain this time. Breathing was getting harder for him. Blood began freely flowing from his mouth. He noticed he couldn't taste the copper tinge of his own blood anymore.

A medic knelt down next to him, giving him a quick once over. The medic pulled out a marker and drew something on Vincent's head. He couldn't see what he had written there. But he knew what it was: An X. It told any other passing medic that he was too far gone.

His head was swimming, he felt like he was floating. His aches and pains melted away. He didn't feel the ragged hole in his chest nor the stabbing in his lungs when he tried to breathe in anymore. His augmetic implant flickered and went out and soon all he could see was the darkness.

EPILOGUE

It was a hot day in Elysian. The sun had only just peaked above the skyline and the temperature was rising fast enough that Fiona sat down her cup of kaff, not wanting it anymore. She was never a morning person. She had warned her assistants and soldiers from the Office of the Commissariat to never wake her up with work unless they were at war again. Something that thankfully hadn't happened in eighteen years.

This morning was something special though.

It was for that reason that she had sent her aid to prepare her dress uniform. A sharply pressed number with so many medals and ribbons pinned to it that she had long since forgotten their reason or purpose. She had to squeeze into it, the years of comfort and peace made the buttons strain a bit as she fingered them together up to her neck. She thought for a moment about sending her aid to let it out so it fit more comfortable but settled instead to never wear it again after today.

She strapped her gun belt around her waist. The Riten was lighter in its holster without the ammo. But, in the years since the war had ended the weapon had become ceremonial. A nod to a time that everyone hoped would never come again. She hoped she would never need to unholster it again as long as she lived.

"Almost ready, Marshal?" Asked a voice. It was Zinvor. He wore his ceremonial armor a Riten on his hip. It was Vincent's, dull blue and ornate. When he died the rest of the Marshals and the new Consul demanded the Riten be buried with him, like an Officer with their sword. But Mawr tradition the weapon be passed on and as Vincent had given the gun to Zinvor before he died it was only suitable, he kept it.

"I suppose it is almost that time, hm?"

"Yes, ma'am." He nodded. "The shuttle leaves very shortly." She got up, walking across the small apartment, and peaked her head into a room.

"Are you almost ready?" She asked. "You're going to be late to your own flight."

"Yes, Mom." Came a voice. A few seconds later she appeared, a plain green duffle bag thrown over her shoulder. Anastasia Olympus-Solaris sat down her bag, its weight thumping off the tile floor. She wore a loose fitting dull red uniform, a single star pin over her heart. She looked like Fiona when she was her age. Rail thin, like a marathon runner. She had the pale skin of a Martian but the brown hair and eyes of her father. She kept her hair short like Fiona did, just a bit longer than a standard issue Volunteer buzzcut. A small blue tattoo peaked out from the corner of her left eye.

"Ugh." Anna sighed. "Why is the packing list so long? I could barely fit it all in the bag they sent me."

"Well, you're going to be at the Academy for a long time, dear." Fiona smiled. "You're going to need all of those clothes."

"I can carry the bag if you would like." Zinvor said. Fiona held up a hand.

"Our little princess is going to have to toughen up to compete with those Martian cadets." She said. "Better to start carrying your weight now." Anna frowned, hauling the bag up to her shoulder.

Zinvor opened the door and they went out, getting into an aero car that was waiting for them. The car took them up into the crowded sky, the driver swerving in and out of the cars around them. The Human Quarter was laid out all around them. The tram lines and walkways had expanded to connect every corner of the city planet. They wrapped around the towers of housing, green houses, and markets that had shot up into the sky over the years.

"I wanted to go to the Academy here, like my friends." Anna frowned, looking out of the window.

"Weren't you the one always complaining that no matter what you did, everyone would always know you as *The Consul's Daughter?*" Fiona laughed. "I know you got into the military academy here, but imagine every single one of your professors being someone who worked for your Dad."

"And they've never heard of Dad on Mars?"

"Oh, honey. There isn't anywhere in Human space you're going to be able to go where nobody has heard of Vincent Solaris. On Mars they just won't care so much. As long as you ignore the statue of him on the Mons." Anna rolled her eyes.

"So, what is Mars like?" Anna asked.

"The Mars you're going to is much different than the Mars I grew up on." Fiona said. "The place has made one hell of a turn around. Kind of like here, honestly."

"Is the school better?"

"You want to be an Artillery officer, don't you?" She nudged the girl's shoulder. "No better place to learn."

The aero car dipped back towards the surface, the spaceport stretching for a few miles in every direction. Thousands of terminals stretched out to long, tear dropped shaped shuttles. These craft would take travelers into orbit where they would dock inside of much larger ships that would take thousands of people across space to their destination. The driver piloted the car alongside dozens of others that were parked alongside a terminal labeled *Mars - Olympus City.*

The spaceport was normally crowded but today was especially bad. Millions of people and not people traveled to and from Elysian every day. Since the end of the war the distances between Mars, Titan, and Elysian had gotten much shorter. Lunar City had so far refused all communication with them. Even the smuggling routes had been closed down.

"The one day we run late." Fiona sighed as the car doors opened. When they got out, she saw the extra press of people in the parking area weren't normal people, they were soldiers.

Volunteers in their dress uniforms stood on watch, polished rifles held against their shoulders. They were the Consul's Honor Guard. Out of the rigid standing soldiers stepped the Human Consul, Felicity Haagen. She was wearing a plain khaki tunic and matching pants, a single Clan standard Riten and sword pin over her heart. Fiona noticed she still wore the boots of a soldier and they were shined to a mirror finish.

"I thought you would be at work." Fiona said. "You always are."

"You think I would miss sending the Consul's daughter going off to academy? And Ezra told me to send his regards. I think he is regretting becoming the Ambassador to Titan." She laughed, turning her gazed to Anna. "You know I made sure you got a slot at the Titanian academy? Did you Mom tell you that?"

"She got into every school she applied for, she didn't need favors." Fiona smiled and added "Unlike her mom and dad." Felicity laughed.

"I know." Felicity nodded. "Nobody ever gives a Solaris anything without a fight." She grinned.

"Five minutes!" Came an electronic voice over a loud speaker. "Five-minute warning for Mar – Olympus City."

"That's you, kid." Fiona said. She tried to fight it, but she could feel her eyes welling up with tears. "Time to go." Anna hefted up her duffle bag again, leaning into it to balance out the things weight. Fiona leaned forward and kissed her daughter on the forehead.

"Mom!" Anna complained, wiping her sleeve across her forehead. "I'm going to military academy, not summer camp!" Fiona laughed, dropping down to a knee to get a good look at her.

"I know, you'll have to forgive me, kid. I'm still your Mom." She choked back the tears that were coming. "But let me give you some advice." The look on Anna's face was one of annoyance, but Fiona kept going.

"When you graduate from that school, they are going to pin lieutenant's bars on your shoulder. But that doesn't make you a leader. It doesn't earn you any respect from whatever soldiers you're going to have, god forbid if we ever go back to war." She poked her daughter in the chest. "You have to go out there and earn it with your words and actions. That's why I named you after bravest person I've ever met in my life."

"Last call, Mars – Olympus City." Said the loudspeaker. "Last Call."

"Mom." Anna said, she was crying now. "I have to go."

"I know, Annie." Fiona sniffed.

"You know I hate it when you call me that." Anna said.

Anna kissed Fiona and hugged Felicity one last time. The two old soldiers turned and watched Anna walk into the terminal, disappearing into the crowd.

They came to start a new life. Now they have to fight for it.

GET BLOOD & STEEL NOW!

Go to war or go to jail.

GET CONTACT FRONT NOW!

"Aliens, agents, and espionage abound in this Cold War-era alternate history adventure... A wild ride!"—Dennis E. Taylor, bestselling author of We Are Legion (We Are Bob)

GET THE LUNA MISSILE CRISIS NOW!

THE COMPLETE SERIES
RECLAMATION
SALVATION
OCCUPATION
RISE
NATHAN FORD HYSTAD
3
2
1